THREE LEFT TURNS
TO NOWHERE

Praise for the Authors

The Unwanted by Jeffrey Ricker

"Ricker's prose transports readers into the world of bullies and redemption, love and loss, and prophecies and being the chosen one. Readers are also treated to Jamie's snarky comments throughout the book—which left this reviewer laughing out loud."—*Ruth Compton, American Library Association's Rainbow Round Table*

The Dubious Gift of Dragon Blood by J. Marshall Freeman

"From swoon-worthy romances to epic dragon fights, this has a little bit of everything for readers to enjoy."—*School Library Journal*

"The recurring emphasis on personal agency and consent is a pleasant surprise, especially as it is applied to both intimate relationships and the chosen-one trope."—*Kirkus Reviews*

Exit Plans for Teenage Freaks by 'Nathan Burgoine

"Burgoine (*Of Echoes Born*, 2018, etc.) has created a gay teen protagonist who is a bit goofy at times but who is comfortable in his own skin…Overall, a feel-good, contemporary read with strong LGBTQIAP rep and an unusual fantasy subplot." —*Kirkus Reviews*

Visit us at www.boldstrokesbooks.com

THREE LEFT TURNS TO NOWHERE

'Hope' all is 'well'!
xo
'Nathan

by
Jeffrey Ricker, J. Marshall Freeman, and 'Nathan Burgoine

2022

ISBN 13: 978-1-63679-050-3

THIS TRADE PAPERBACK ORIGINAL IS PUBLISHED BY
BOLD STROKES BOOKS, INC.
P.O. BOX 249
VALLEY FALLS, NY 12185

FIRST EDITION: FEBRUARY 2022

CREDITS

EDITORS: JERRY L. WHEELER AND STACIA SEAMAN
PRODUCTION DESIGN: STACIA SEAMAN
COVER DESIGN BY INKSPIRAL DESIGN

THREE LEFT TURNS TO NOWHERE

Roadside Assistance

Jeffrey Ricker

His mother's going to ask the question again.

Lyn can tell by the way she sets his travel mug on the bathroom vanity next to him. Fortunately, it's hard to talk with a mouthful of toothpaste, so he just grunts his thanks and keeps brushing.

She retreats to the doorway with her own mug and leans against the doorframe.

"I promise this is the last time I'll ask."

Bend, spit. When he straightens back up, he turns on the faucet to rinse his toothbrush. "You said that the last time, you know."

"Okay, but this time I really mean it."

Lyn drops his toothbrush into the holder, swirls some water from his tumbler, and spits again. When he picks up his coffee mug, his mother frowns.

"What?" he asks.

"I feel like I'm enabling your poor dental future."

He doesn't reply until he's taken a long sip of coffee. "Look at it this way. You're also enabling my continued wakefulness at work today."

"Off at noon?"

"Yeah."

"Want me to make lunch?"

He shakes his head. "It's Friday. I'm getting lunch at the diner and hanging out with Josh." She knows this, and he knows she knows this, so why she's suggesting an alternative is anybody's guess.

He leans back against the vanity. "You were going to ask your question?"

She tilts her head. "Do I have to say it out loud?"

He tilts his head right back at her. It's as close as they ever get to arguing. "Maybe just to make it official."

"What's your plan after this summer?"

She asks the question as if it's something she's reciting. It's not the first time she's asked him this. Probably not the last, either. The asking doesn't bother him so much as the feeling that she finds his answer somehow disappointing. If only that didn't matter so much to him.

Despite his best attempts to be light-footed, his steel-toed boots still clomp when he goes downstairs. His mother doesn't follow right away. She's already preloaded the toaster with two slices of bread and taken the butter out of the fridge. He hits the lever on the toaster with one hand and pulls a travel mug out of the cabinet with the other. He pours the rest of his cup in the travel mug and tops it up with the last of the pot. He's about to turn off the coffeemaker, but stops to look over his shoulder toward the stairs. No sign of her yet. She always makes another pot once he's left the house.

He gets as far as taking the filters down from the cabinet.

"Not on your life, mister."

He jumps a little and turns to see her at the foot of the stairs.

"How do you *do* that?"

"It's a gift. That, and no steel-toed boots."

She takes the box of filters from him and gently nudges him out of the way. Normally, they'd laugh about the casual gesture. So why does it bug him more than he can put into words?

"You know," he says as she begins measuring beans into the grinder, "I *can* make coffee."

She pauses long enough to throw back her head for one loud "ha!" He starts to reply, but the burr of the grinder cuts him off. She holds up a finger for him to wait. Shaking his head, he screws the cap on his travel mug and turns toward the toaster just as it pops. He snatches the two slices and smears butter on one before sandwiching them together and heading for the front door.

"Hey." When he turns back to the kitchen, his mother leans in his direction and taps her cheek. It's so hard to stay mad at her for more than a minute. And anyway, it's just coffee.

After pecking her on the cheek, he says, "I guess I inherited my coffee-making skills from Dad."

She rolls her eyes. "Worst coffee ever." It's a familiar, comfortable routine between the two of them, and it has the added benefit of putting more distance between them and her earlier question. "He made good tea, though. Maybe you got that from him."

"Not that we'll ever know." Tea, him? No.

"I haven't forgotten about my question, by the way."

He gives her his best puzzled puppy head tilt. "You had a question?"

She doesn't say anything, just tilts her chin down at him in a "really?" sort of way, with one eyebrow raised. "Your summer plans?"

"I think they're pretty much the same as they've always been. I'm going to work at the garage and hang out with my friends until the auto repair program starts in August."

She nods, but she's facing away from him now, her attention on the coffeemaker as she fills the water reservoir. "And then?"

"After the program? I'll go full-time at the garage." He waits for her to answer, but she says nothing. He's tempted to just head for the front door and walk down the street to the garage—it's all of two minutes to the bottom of the hill—but he lingers a bit longer. "So I'm guessing you have some thoughts on that."

She shrugs, still not turning around to look at him. She turns on the coffeemaker and braces her hands against the counter on either side of it. There's a slight bow to her head, which he almost misses because he's latched on to something about her stance, the slope of her shoulders and the tilt of her head that telegraphs…disappointment. Is she disappointed in him?

"Mom?" He's always known how to get her attention with the right tone of voice, although he tries not to hit that note too often for fear overuse would dull its effectiveness.

In any case, it works. She turns toward him and leans back against the counter.

"Do you think I'm making the wrong decision?" he asks.

She shakes her head. "Oh, honey. No." Pushing away from the counter, she steps closer and rests her hand in the crook of his shoulder. "But you've been focused on this choice for a long time. Are you sure you don't want to explore other options first to make sure this is really the one?"

"It feels right, Mom."

"And it will still feel right after you do some exploring. You're too young to—"

"I'm eighteen." An adult, technically. He can vote and drink and buy a car if he wanted. Which he doesn't. Not yet, at least. The garage is close enough to walk.

Now she puts both hands on his shoulders, which means she's going to say something profound. "And you are one of the most mature and responsible people I know. And yes, that includes most of my colleagues-slash-your-teachers. Have some fun before you grow up, honey."

"I have fun."

"You should hang out with your friends more."

"I'm having lunch with Joshua at the diner today."

"You mean you're eating lunch while he's *working* at the diner."

"It still counts." Doesn't it? He stops short of saying that out loud.

"Well, at least order something other than a tuna melt and pasta salad."

"I gotta go, or I'm gonna be late."

She kisses him on the cheek. "Tell Sloan hi for me."

By the time he's out the front door and halfway down the hill, he's fully inside his own head and wondering why she was so insistent this time. Is it so bad he wants to stay in town and do this? Sure, most of his friends are going off to uni, a couple even heading to Europe, a handful of others joining the forces or the RCMP. He's not the only person from his class who's—

He stops in the middle of the street. Is he the *only* person from his class who's staying in Hopewell?

It shouldn't—*doesn't* matter what other people choose or what they think of his choices. All his life, she's encouraged him to think for himself, so having her make this sudden about-turn…Maybe that's why he feels so dizzy all of a sudden. He looks down at the pavement, his gaze following tiny cracks in the blacktop until the dizziness subsides and it feels safe to lift his head.

Naturally, that's also when he sees the man again.

Or ghost. Whatever he calls it, he's never seen his face, but the outfit is always the same: blue jeans, tan work boots, heavy-duty plaid work shirt even in the middle of summer, and a trucker hat. His hands are always in his pockets, his head bent slightly downward as he walks up the step of the diner and goes inside. Even though he mimics the action of grabbing the handle and pulling the door open, it remains closed and he walks through it.

The last time he saw the ghost was…Christmas? It doesn't seem like it was that long ago, but snow was on the ground. The ghost left no footprints.

He continues walking toward the garage after the ghost vanishes. The apparition isn't a fright so much as a reminder of the town's weirdness, one that he can't discount or dismiss as easily as his mother's comments about how Hopewell has a certain kind of magic. Even the eternally practical and no-nonsense Sloan can't resist saying Hopewell used its magic to bring Dina into town and into her life. Whenever she says it, he resists rolling his eyes. He wants to keep his job, after all. Even so, people in town tend to lean on that a lot of the time to explain everything. Sometimes, a coincidence is just a coincidence. Things happen without any explanation other than blind luck. People meet or don't meet, fall in love or don't, live or die. Even seeing a ghost on a semi-regular basis doesn't make that any less true.

He's still deep inside his own head when he opens the shop door. He nearly takes a keyring to the face, but grabs it just before it makes contact with his nose.

"Catch," says Sloan. She's standing behind the counter, sleeves rolled up, a dark stripe already painting one forearm. No matter how early he arrives, she's always there before him.

"Thanks." He pockets the keys. "The warning's more helpful if it comes before the throw."

"Yeah, but it's not as fun. Anyway, don't get comfortable. I need you to head out to Highway 11. Another breakdown."

"Again? How many is that so far this month?"

"Three. Still short of the record, though."

Seven, in February last year. Three on February 14 alone. That was a good Valentine's Day for the garage, at least. He'd spent it with Joshua and Logan at the diner, when they were celebrating their second Valentine's Day together. He was supposed to be picking up takeout but wound up sitting in their booth and wondering aloud if he was ever going to meet someone.

He shakes his head, trying and failing to dislodge that particularly embarrassing memory.

"What?" Sloan asks. She turns to the coffee carafe and refills her cup.

"Nothing, just thinking."

"Better multitask and do your thinking behind the wheel. They just called, but they sounded pretty—"

"Desperate?"

"Impatient."

He sighs. "Great."

"I'm sure you'll win them over."

"Please tell me this isn't happening," Ed says.

Just to underline the point, he thuds his forehead into the back of the driver's seat, then does it again. Curtis turns around, concern evident on his face along with a light sheen of sweat. Before he can say anything, though, Siobhan levels a glare at him from the passenger seat, crosses her arms, and leans against the door.

"Why are we not moving?" she says.

Curtis doesn't miss a beat. He turns to Siobhan and flips his hands wide. "It's not my fault!"

They've been at this off and on ever since they'd picked Ed up. After he'd thrown his bag in the trunk and slid into the back seat, Siobhan had turned to Curtis and said, "This hunk of junk is never going to get us to Toronto."

"Don't count her out just yet," Curtis said before turning the key in the ignition.

Now, though? Nothing. Suddenly the dashboard lit up like the cockpit of the *Millennium Falcon* and the engine died. Curtis steered toward the side of the highway.

That's something Ed still can't wrap his head around. They call a two-lane road a *highway* up here?

Siobhan doesn't say anything in response to Curtis's protest. She pulls her bag from the footwell into her lap. She extracts her phone and her wallet, from which she takes a card. Curtis settles his forehead on the steering wheel.

"Please tell me you're calling a tow," he says.

"I'm calling a tow."

"Thank you." He doesn't sound like Han Solo anymore. He turns toward the back seat again. "Sorry, man. Hopefully, it's something easy to fix. And inexpensive would be nice, too." He glances up toward the roof, but his next words are aimed higher. "You hear that, universe? Make it easy and cheap."

Ed snorts. "So many comments I could make in response to that."

Siobhan doesn't laugh, but she does make a little huffing noise and purses her lips, which Ed recognizes as a sign she's amused, and it's about as close as she gets to laughing out loud.

Curtis narrows his eyes in what is hopefully mock offense. "Very funny, fuzzball."

"So I'm Chewbacca in this scenario, is that it?" Ed says.

"Please," Siobhan says. "You're clearly the Threepio."

The neurotic, fussy butler android? The grumpy walking carpet would be preferable. Everyone wants to hug Chewbacca. The only one who wants to hug C-3PO is…Does anyone? R2-D2, maybe. And he doesn't have arms.

"Earth to Threepio," Siobhan says. He jumps a little in his seat. Did she ask a question?

"Sorry." He blinks a couple times, gives his head a shake. Get it together, Ed.

Mercifully, the tow truck rumbles up behind them before he can embarrass himself further. He gets out after Curtis and Siobhan and lets the cool air settle over him. He tugs his hoodie closer around him but doesn't zip it up. Back in St. Louis, at this time of year, it would already be in the eighties with humidity to match. But here? He won't even break a sweat today. His hair won't flop the way it did back home no matter how much product he put in it. This is awesome.

Home. In his head, home is St. Louis, and he can't imagine *not* thinking of it that way. Any place he's ever really known is back there, all the people, too: Stacey, Dorlita, Kyle, Samar…Kyle.

Well, Kyle won't be there much longer, either. College awaits after senior year. And for him, Northwestern, as long as he doesn't tank senior year, which he has to get used to calling grade twelve. The first time he told Curtis and Siobhan he was going to be a senior in the fall, Curtis laughed and asked if he liked prune cobbler and wore bifocals. Siobhan hit Curtis in the arm and told him not to be ageist before explaining to Ed that they call it grade twelve up here. Just one more thing he has to get used to, along with fewer *z*'s—*zeds*, they call them *zeds*—and all the extra *u*'s.

A car door clanks shut, and he raises his head. Over the roof of the car, Siobhan's watching him with a concerned expression. Stuffing his hands in his pockets, he smiles and hopes it's convincing.

The first thing Ed notices about the tow truck driver is that he's not much older than them. The second thing is that he's cute in a blond, country boy sort of way, the kind that reminds him of Jeff County boys who, if you looked at them like you might think they're cute, would haul off and punch you without asking another question. This guy doesn't give off that kind of energy, but heck, this could be banjo country just as much as Jeff County.

"Morning," Blond Guy says. "Seem to be having some trouble?"

"No, we always stand by the side of the road in the middle of nowhere," Ed says, then immediately cringes. Siobhan cuts her eyes in his direction for a moment. Best not to antagonize the Hoosier in bumpkin country.

Fortunately, the guy just smiles and approaches the hood of the car. "Lucky for you you're not in the middle of nowhere." He pops the hood without even fumbling for the latch, like he knows exactly where to find it. Curtis, standing by the driver's side door, shuffles closer and leans in, too.

"So what happened?" Blond Guy asks.

"Dashboard lit up like a pinball machine and then everything went dead."

"Like my soul," Siobhan adds under her breath. Blond Guy hears it and laughs. He leans over and peers into the engine compartment.

"Any idea what's wrong?" Curtis asks, sounding a little too hopeful, like maybe something came loose and just needs to be tightened down.

No such luck, though. Blond Guy straightens up and shakes his head. "Nothing that jumps out at me."

"Guess that rules out mynocks, then," Curtis says, and Ed cringes before he can stop himself. Do they have to out themselves as nerds so easily?

"What?" Siobhan asks, meeting his gaze over the car roof. Caught out again. He's got to work at schooling his expression. Dad's forever telling him anyone can see what's on his mind just by looking at his face.

He tries to laugh it off. These are his only two friends going into senior year. *Grade twelve, you nitwit. Call it grade twelve.* He can't afford to alienate them.

"Didn't know how high we wanted to fly our geek flag," Ed says.

Siobhan crosses her arms. "You mean how high *you* wanted to fly it."

"Sorry." He really is, and he hopes he's rearranged his expression into something convincing. Siobhan side-eyes him before turning back to Blond Guy, flinging her braid over one shoulder in the process. He could not be more dismissed.

This trip was a mistake. He's gonna lose his only two friends in the whole country by the end of it, and now with the car trouble, they're probably not even going to make it to the con on time.

"Fly your geek flag as high as you like," Blond Guy says, letting the hood clang shut, "but there are no mynocks chewing on anything in here."

Curtis laughs, and Ed stops contemplating his shoes long enough to glance up in hope. One of them! Maybe. At least he recognizes obscure *Empire* references. Siobhan catches his eye again. No smile, but a cocked eyebrow as if to say, *See?*

"So what's the problem, then?" Curtis asks.

"Could be the alternator, maybe," Blond Guy says. "We'll know more once we get it back to the shop."

"How long do you think that'll take?" Siobhan asks. At least she was the one to ask instead of him. He can just imagine the death glare she would have given him.

Blond Guy rocks back and forth on his heels, hands in pockets, staring at the hood and frowning. He's cute when he frowns, which just makes it even more annoying when he shrugs again. "Hard to tell right now. Electrical stuff can be a real headache. We'll have a better idea when we get it—"

"Back to the shop."

Wait, did he say that part out loud? He must have, since everyone's staring at him now. Blond Guy gives him the once over, up and down. "Nice shirt."

Ed reflexively runs a hand across his shirt, smoothing out any imaginary creases. It's the *Doctor Who* shirt with Matt Smith in profile, his silhouette filled with stars, and in the middle of it floats the

TARDIS, with Amy Pond floating outside, holding on to the Doctor's hand reaching through the open doors. It's his second favourite Who shirt. He's saving his most favourite for tomorrow, when he finally gets to meet the man himself.

If he gets to meet him. But at least Blond Guy recognizes him, which has bumped him up in Ed's estimation.

"Thanks," Ed says.

"Tennant was better."

Blond Guy walks toward the truck like he doesn't even realize the bomb he just dropped. Siobhan clearly does, given her open-mouthed stare at Blond Guy's retreating back. Curtis circles around to Ed's side of the car.

"Remember, people are allowed to like different things," he says, putting a hand on Ed's forearm.

"People are allowed to be so obviously wrong, you mean." He adds a little volume to *so obviously wrong*, but if Blond Guy hears it, he doesn't react.

Ed fumes quietly while Blond Guy hitches up Curtis's car, which takes less time than he figured it would. His friends say nothing, focused instead on watching Curtis's baby get its nose hauled off the ground as the truck's lift whines.

"Okay," Blond Guy says, hands on hips, "there's four of us but only room for three people in the truck. Obviously, I'm the one driving, so you three will have to decide who's walking."

They look at each other. Ed imagines all the various calculations going on in their heads, but he also already knows how the math's going to shake out.

"It's my car, so I have to go," Curtis says.

"And I'm his girlfriend."

They both turn to Ed, their expressions apologetic and braced for an explosion at the same time. What's he even supposed to say to that? He stares at the car, half suspended behind the tow truck. "I could ride in the—"

Blond Guy shakes his head. "So many safety violations. I'd lose my job before you can say liability."

He flaps his hands uselessly. "Fine."

Before they pull away, Blond Guy leans out the driver's window. From this vantage point, he's at least a foot above Ed. Shorty must *love* this angle. "Just turn left up at the next road," he points in the direction the truck faces, "and it'll lead you straight into town. Garage is on the right side of the street. You can't miss it. About a kilometer or so."

Ed blinks. "Or so?"

No answer.

"I hate you all."

Blond Guy doesn't respond, instead tilting his head and giving a half-smile. He'd kick the truck if he thought it would accomplish anything. He'd probably just wind up breaking his foot, the way his luck's gone.

The tires kick up dust as the truck pulls away. He lifts his arm to shield his eyes from the grit. Out of the passenger side of the truck, Siobhan waves at him. Maybe she thought his raised arm was a wave, too. If it were Blond Guy, he'd be *so* tempted to flip him off, but not Siobhan. He waits until the truck turns the corner out of sight before he kicks the dirt, which stirs up more grit and does nothing to relieve his frustration. Why did he let that guy get on his nerves? Where the hell has his chill gone? He did have some before. It wasn't just his imagination, was it? Back home, he would never have—

Home. The thought stills his feet for a second before he shakes his head and keeps going. The thought lingers, though. He needs to stop calling St. Louis home, even though every friend he's ever made is back there, every place he knows so well he could get in the car and go there on autopilot is back there. Kyle is back there.

Well, not for long. Kyle graduated last month and is off to Cornell in the fall. They'd already decided long-distance was going to be too hard, even before Ed found out about his dad's transfer.

He pulls his phone out of his pocket by reflex, but doesn't unlock it until he's turned the corner where the tow truck went. Dad would tell him not to walk and use his phone at the same time, but the road's a straight shot and there's no traffic anyway, so whatever.

No notifications. He slides his thumb over the unlock button and pauses, considers texting someone, maybe Curtis or Siobhan. He'd love to know what they're talking about with Blond Guy.

Or maybe he wouldn't.

❖

"So," Lyn says, "your friend seems a little…"

"High strung?" Siobhan asks. She introduced herself and Curtis shortly after they drove off and left Ed to follow on foot.

"I guess you could put it like that." *Piece of work* is what Mom would say. She's used that phrase plenty of times to describe students in her class who were a bit much. Some of them were his friends. He didn't disagree with her.

"I think he's just upset this weekend might fall through," Curtis says. "He's really been looking forward to it."

Siobhan laughs. "Understatement."

"Where are you all headed?"

"Toronto."

He considers a moment, then adds up the clues. "Going to SciCon?"

They're silent for a second or two. If he takes his eyes off the road, will one of them be raising an eyebrow, Spock-style?

"What gave it away?" Curtis asks.

Again, Siobhan laughs. "Hon, your car has a bumper sticker that says, 'My Other Car Is The Millennium Falcon.'"

"Okay, fair."

"And your friend is upset because—"

"Ed."

Lyn frowns. "Pardon?"

"He has a name." Siobhan shifts in her seat and feels a little bit taller next to him, loyalty practically radiating off her. "His name's Ed."

Lyn smiles. Hopefully, Ed knows how lucky he is. "So why is Ed so upset your trip might fall through?"

"Because Matt Smith is going to be there."

"As in *Doctor Who* Matt Smith?"

Siobhan crosses her arms. "As in the Matt Smith you dissed by saying David Tennant was a better Doctor."

"Oh." Well, he certainly put his foot in that one. It explains the T-shirt, at least. It was a nice T-shirt, too. "He must think I'm a real dick."

"I can't be sure since he's not here for me to ask him."

That sounds like an accusation. "Seriously, there's barely room for three in here." He gestures at the cab around them and adds, maybe a little too forcefully, "Either of you were more than welcome to walk with him. It really is only a kilometer to the garage."

After that, the only noise for a while is the thrum of the tires and the throaty exhaust of the engine in low gear. The silence, though, only lasts so long.

Curtis says, "Then you meant what you said about riding in the car when it's hitched—"

Lyn's laugh is loud and abrupt. It's not like him at all, and he nearly chokes on air trying to stifle it. "Oh, a thousand percent, yeah. Sloan would literally kill me if I let someone do that."

Siobhan snorts. "Let's hope not."

"Pardon?"

"I don't know about you, but I wouldn't want to work for a homicidal maniac."

Wait, what? Now he does take his eyes off the road, just for a second. Siobhan's leveled a steady gaze at him, somewhere between a stare and a glare. On the other side of her, closest to the passenger door, Curtis puckers his lips and shakes his head.

Siobhan doesn't wait for him to ask. "If he would literally kill you—"

"She. Sloan's a she."

Siobhan doesn't miss a beat. "If *she* would literally kill you, your boss is a homicidal maniac."

He returns his attention to the road. There's never much traffic, but it doesn't pay to get sloppy in the company truck. Still, he spares another sidelong glance at her. Is he the only one who thinks this is weird? As far as conversations in the tow truck with strangers go, it sure seems that way. Usually, they're focused on the condition of their car or how long it's going to take or is he really old enough to drive this thing, no really show me your license. Well, that only happened once, but still.

"Oh…kay. I can tell you for sure that my boss is not literally a homicidal maniac. Or even a figurative one."

"Good to know," Curtis says.

"So, tell us about *you*, Lyn." Siobhan's voice, suddenly bright and jarring, makes him grip the wheel as if it might wrench out of his hands. Definitely weird.

"Uh, what would you like to know?"

She angles in her seat toward him. "Is this where you grew up?"

"Yeah."

"Never left?"

"Nope."

"Going to uni?"

"Trade school."

"Got a girlfriend?"

"Excuse me?"

Out of the corner of his eye, Lyn sees Curtis lean forward. "Should I be worried, babe?"

"No, *babe.*" So, clearly she hates being called babe. Not that he blames her. Her attention turns back to him. "Girlfriend?"

"No."

"Boyfriend?"

He hesitates, but he's never really had any gaydar to speak of. Most of the queer folk in town are people he already knows. Everyone else is either cool with it or doesn't cause any problems where he's concerned, so he didn't have to develop a sixth sense about who he can and can't talk to about that stuff.

He does the math and shrugs on the inside. Not like he's going to see any of them again after their car is fixed and they're on their way.

"No, unfortunately, no boyfriend." The admission stings more than he thought it would. He's only ever really talked about it with Joshua and Logan, which was bad enough. Not like they could do anything about it, anyway. No one can make more eligible gay guys miraculously appear in a place as small as Hopewell.

"Must be tough in a small town," Curtis says.

He relaxes his grip on the wheel and leans one arm against the windowsill. "Maybe not in the way you think. Hopewell's a pretty accepting place. There's a GSA at the high school, the mayor's bisexual—no, wait. She's pan, I think." He shakes his head. "Wait, bi? Anyway, she's married to my boss."

"Sounds pretty nice," Siobhan says, and he thinks she really means it. "But…"

She's inviting him to continue. "The dating pool is less of a pool and more of a puddle."

"That's rough." She pauses. The drone of the wheels fills the silence. "Thought about moving?"

He shakes his head emphatically. "No."

Siobhan almost flinches in her seat, but seems like she catches herself. He's surprised by his own vehemence. Civic pride? Not quite, although he's not got the words for how he feels about this place.

"How come?" she asks. Her question practically begs him to take offense, but the way she asks it doesn't imply any criticism. Mom would probably say he needs to go somewhere else first to find the words to explain how he feels about Hopewell, but her logic still seems flawed.

"This is just…it's *home*."

Mercifully, they get to the garage before she can ask another follow-up question. He tells them to go inside to the service desk and help themselves to some coffee. He doesn't dawdle, but he doesn't rush through lowering the car to the service bay floor and unhooking it from the tow truck. He needs a moment before Siobhan has the chance to resume her interrogation.

"'82 Ford LTD?"

He flinches, but manages to keep from yelping. When he turns around, Sloan is almost right behind him. At least he didn't have the hood open and his head buried in the engine compartment. One of these days, he swears, she's gonna give him a concussion.

"Why so jumpy?" she asks, but she's really not paying attention to him. She slides a hand across the LTD's hood, coming to stand in front of it with her hands on her hips, her gaze flicking between each of the double headlights. She whistles. "What a beauty. What's the mileage on her?"

He'd like to be mad at her for scaring him, but he can't. Sloan has eyes for exactly two things: classic cars and Dina. He lets out a sharp exhale, gathering himself before he leans through the open driver's window and peers at the dashboard. "Thirty-eight thousand and change."

"That's all?" Sloan takes his place at the window and peers inside. She lets out another low whistle. "This thing has been babied. What seems to be the trouble with her?"

He rocks back on his heels, hands in pockets. "Maybe the alternator? I need to test it to make sure."

"You check the belt?"

She's still leaning in through the driver's window. He waits for her to extract herself before he gives her the *do you think I'm completely stupid?* look. She raises her hands in mock-surrender. "Okay, okay. I was just asking."

"It's not the belt."

Sloan frowns and considers the car again, crossing her arms. "We don't have one in stock for this model. Maybe check with Hodges."

"If it turns out to be the alternator."

She reaches back in and turns the key in the LTD's ignition. There's a click and nothing else. "If it's not the battery, it's probably the alternator. And yes, I know you know that." She glances out through the bay door toward the glassed-in service desk, where Siobhan and Curtis wait. Curtis takes a sip from his paper cup, grimaces, and shakes his head. They each stare down into their cups as if to ask *what the hell is this stuff?* Sludge, is what he'd tell them.

"Hope they're not in a hurry," Sloan says.

"Everybody on 11 is in a hurry to be someplace other than here," he says.

She smiles and shakes her head. "Don't know what they're missing."

"Right."

She leans against the side of the car. "Why don't you let them down easy, and I'll see if I can't figure out what's wrong with this thing here?"

He turns his head slightly to the side. "You sure you're not just going to fondle the car?"

She smiles sheepishly and spreads her arms wide. "What can I say? She's—"

"A beaut, right. And yes, I'll go ruin their weekend."

"How long do you think it'll take?" Siobhan asks when he tells them he needs to run a couple diagnostics. She seems worried.

"Tests won't take too long," he says. "Should be able to get them done in the next hour or so."

Curtis's face tenses, as if he's almost afraid to ask his question. "If it's the alternator, about how much will it cost?"

"Usually runs around four hundred installed," he says. Curtis sucks in a breath through his teeth. Yeah, he wouldn't want that bill, either.

"Let's hope it's not the alternator, then."

Lyn hesitates before following up, long enough that Siobhan says, "What?"

"I don't mean any offense, but you can afford it, right?" After the expression that crosses her face and the way she opens her mouth to answer, Lyn hurriedly adds, "It's just that I have a bad habit, or at least Sloan thinks I do, of doing a lot of work for friends at, well, a steep discount."

Before Curtis can say a word, Siobhan answers emphatically, "We can afford it."

"It's my car, babe—"

"I know, *babe.*" She glares at him, tight lipped, before returning her attention to Lyn. "And anyway, I guess it's a good thing for you we're complete strangers and won't see each other again after today. You expect to keep your job if you give away the business?"

"Yeah," he admits, "it's probably not the smartest thing I could do."

"Maybe you could tell us someplace around here where we could get some coffee or something that's…" She gestures with her paper cup. "Not this."

He laughs. Although Sloan drinks garage coffee all day, he only resorts to it if he's really desperate. "If you feel like a walk, there's the gas station on the way into town. Their coffee is pretty decent. There's the café," he points out the window toward Main Street, then off toward the opposite corner, "or the diner. Their coffee is fantastic, and if you're hungry, they're good for breakfast. The grilled cheese is always a winner."

"Grilled cheese?" Curtis asks. "For breakfast?"

"You'd be surprised. I'll call when I have news one way or the other."

"Tell Ed where to find us when he shows up," Siobhan adds before they head out the door.

They're only about halfway across the street when Siobhan stops and turns to Curtis. Her face gets stony, and she says something Lyn imagines would be icy if he could hear it. Curtis gesticulates a little wildly with his left hand, the one that's not holding the cup of sludgy coffee. The glass muffles the concussion of their argument, but he's pretty sure they're not arguing about the quality of the coffee or whether to get the grilled cheese for breakfast. He shakes his head. Not his problem, anyway. He turns back toward the service bay and the LTD, which *is* his problem, for now at least. Unless Sloan decides she can't keep her hands off it.

❖

Can't miss it, Blond Guy said, so of course he misses the garage. Walks right past it with his head down, staring at the blank accusing glass of his phone as he debates for the thousandth time whether to text Kyle. Which he eventually decides against. When he puts his phone back in his pocket without thumbing it on, he lifts his head to find himself along a stretch of road with few buildings, mostly houses, and no sign of a garage or anything looking remotely like a business. A stiff wind sweeps up the road, staggering him a little. He pulls his phone back out to check the map. There's a text on the lock screen, from Siobhan:

WHERE R U?

Where indeed. He has no idea. According to the clock on the phone, he's been walking for nearly an hour. How long does it take to walk a kilometer? Is a kilometer longer or shorter than a mile? He should know this, right?

He texts back:

sorry, got lost

Her response is almost instant.

IT'S A STRAIGHT LINE

yes, thank you, I know I'm an idiot

He watches the little dots bounce at the end of his message. She must be writing a novel, the way they bounce for so long with nothing coming through. But when she does eventually hit send, all he gets is:

just get here soon ok

Whatever she wrote will always remain a mystery, probably. At least she's not shouting at him anymore. He types k and hits send without hesitating, and closes the text app.

He stops. Yes, he really *is* an idiot. This whole time, he's still been walking in the wrong direction. He turns around and heads back the way he came. Hopefully, it's still a straight line, but he can't remember if he took any turns to end up where he is now. That's what happens when he's thinking so hard he gets lost. In that respect, maybe he should thank Siobhan. He won't, but maybe he should.

And maybe he should text Kyle, too, but he doesn't do that either.

And it *wasn't* a straight line, not by any stretch. He had to make at least three turns to wind up where he did before turning around. What the actual hell? Even with his head down, how could he miss that?

He couldn't. The thought makes his shoulders rise up to his ears, and he shivers. What the hell is going on in this place?

By the time he reaches the garage—how did he even miss it when he walked by?—he's warm and starting to sweat a little despite the coolness in the air and the persistent wind that sent him stumbling off the side of the road a couple times. Instead of going through the glassed-in area with the counter and the cash register, he heads through one of the open garage doors. It smells faintly of motor oil and is cleaner than he expected it to be.

The bay on the open door side of the garage is empty. The LTD sits on the other side with the hood open. Blond Guy—he assumes it's Blond Guy, there's no one else around—is leaning over the open engine compartment. He's not very tall, so he has to lean pretty far, and dang it if he doesn't wear a pair of jeans well.

Ed shakes his head. Focus. Where are Curtis and Siobhan? Probably something else he should have texted her to ask. But he might as well ask Blond Guy, assuming they told him before they went wherever they are.

"Did Curtis and Siobhan say—"

He practically feels the bonk in the back of his own head when Blond Guy bolts upright, hitting his head against the open hood. Whatever he had in his hand clangs to the ground. Ed winces.

Blond Guy rubs the back of his head gingerly. "Give a guy a little warning first, will ya?"

"Sorry. Did my friends tell you where they were going?"

Blond Guy lowers his head and curls his lip. "Yes, I'm just fine, thank you for asking. It hurts, but I don't think it's bleeding."

Ed flinches and takes a step back. Not blood. The sight of blood makes him either faint or barf. Or barf then faint. At least he's never fainted and then barfed.

"You're not bleeding, are you?"

Blond Guy tilts his head and gives him an exasperated look. How many of those has he been getting lately?

"Did I not just say I don't think it's bleeding?"

"Well, you were also being sarcastic, so for all I know maybe you *are* bleeding and just saying that to be funny. Which it isn't, by the way. Funny, I mean." God God *God,* stop babbling, Sinclair. "Sorry, I'm usually not this dumb."

Blond Guy lowers his head and touches the crown again as if just to make sure, muttering, "You sure about that?"

"Excuse me?"

Blond Guy looks up, a panicked expression on his face. Ed glares at him. *Yes, blondie, you said the quiet part out loud. Fine, whatever.*

Ed slices the air with one hand, silencing him. "Look, don't say anything, just point. Which way did they go?"

Crumpling a shop rag in one hand, Blond Guy points behind Ed. "Diner."

"Fine. I'll go there. Why don't you just fix the car, and then I can get on my way and live my life, and you can do whatever passes for life in this place."

Finally, the last word. He *never* gets the last word, not lately. So why does he feel like crap as he marches out of the garage and aims himself like an arrow toward the diner.

Halfway across the street, he stops. His messenger bag's in the back of the car, along with his wallet. And he could really use some coffee. Enough to go back, though, and face Blond Guy's ire? Coffee is eternal. So, yes. He turns and heads back to the garage.

Blond Guy, mercifully, is not bent over the open engine compartment this time—although that would give him another chance to check out his practically perfect ass—*focus*, Sinclair. He does cock an eyebrow when he sees Ed, though. If that's all the shade he has to deal with, well, lucky him.

"Forgot my bag," he says. "It's in the back seat."

Blond Guy ducks his head toward the LTD. "It's open."

Quick as he can, he opens the passenger door, reaches into the back seat, snags his bag by the strap, and shuts the door with a clunk that echoes loudly. He flinches.

"Thanks," he remembers to say before he leaves as quickly as possible without looking as if he's leaving as quickly as possible. Which he probably failed at, but at least he doesn't look back.

The parking lot slopes steeply up the hill in front of the diner, which is a low, glass-fronted building with blue neon accents along the roofline. As he trudges up to the front door, he feels shittier and shittier until he's staring down at his feet. He should apologize. He's totally going to do that.

He should probably find out what Blond Guy's name is first.

He doesn't notice the name of the diner until he has a grip on the door handle: the Softshoe Diner. When he opens the door, a wave of fried food scents greedily compete for his attention, along with the smell of coffee and the cloying sugary syrup. Or maybe that's grease. There's even a jukebox against the wall between the restroom doors. It's a modern digital one, but it's playing oldies at the moment, one of the many Duran Duran songs his mom listens to over and over and over in the car until he begs her to please stop.

He scans the row of booths along the windows, where one guy is sitting with his back to the door, before spotting Curtis and Siobhan sitting at the counter talking to a tall, lanky guy standing on the other side. A cute, tall, lanky guy. Siobhan says something that makes him laugh, revealing toothpaste commercial teeth.

Diner Guy catches Ed's eye and says something he can't hear, and Siobhan and Curtis both swivel around. For a heartbreaking moment, Siobhan's smile dims before she lights it back up and waves him over. He perches on the stool next to her as Diner Guy, whose name tag says Joshua, pours him a mug of coffee.

"Your friends here tell me you're a member of coffee nation, so you've come to the right place." He slides the container of sugar packets over. "Need any cream?"

He shakes his head. "Black, like my soul."

Joshua throws his head back and laughs a little too much, but it probably endears him to customers, right? "I'll get you a menu," he says.

"Before you ask," Siobhan says once Joshua's out of earshot, "he has a boyfriend."

Ed gives her a *spare me* look. "Do I come off that desperate?"

"You don't need to be desperate to appreciate that."

She tilts her head toward Joshua, who has his back turned to them.

Ed sighs. "Nice butts must be a thing around here."

"What," Curtis says, "you had time to check out the can scene while you were getting lost?"

Before Ed can answer, Joshua comes back with a single laminated sheet where breakfast takes up one side...along with grilled cheese sandwiches.

"Grilled cheese, for breakfast? Seriously?" He sets the menu down and looks over at Siobhan's plate, which still has a corner of a sandwich sitting on it. She picks it up and looks as if she's considering handing it over to him, then takes a bite.

"Trust me," she says once she's swallowed. "This place'll change your mind."

"Besides," Curtis says, pointing at the clock over the kitchen window, "it's already past eleven."

"Ugh, where has this morning gone?"

"We were wondering the same thing," Siobhan says.

He points at a tiny bowl on her plate. "What's that?"

"That is garlic butter dipping sauce," she says, "but liquid crack would be a more accurate description."

"Come on. What makes their grilled cheese so good?" What makes any grilled cheese that good, for that matter? When was the last time he ate a grilled cheese, anyhow? Probably sometime when he was sick. Even more than chicken soup, grilled cheese and tomato soup was Mom's go-to combo whenever a cold struck.

Curtis ponders his own empty plate. "Might be magic, I dunno."

Josh comes back with a pen and an order pad. "What'll it be? The grilled cheese or the grilled cheese?"

"Kind of required on your first visit, right?" Mentally, he adds *first and last*, but he keeps that part to himself. "Which one do you recommend?"

"Start with the basic. You can always go three-cheese or bacon next time."

He sets the menu down. "Sounds like good advice to me."

Joshua makes a note on his pad. "And sauces? Comes with two."

"Get the ketchup," Curtis says.

"And the garlic butter," Siobhan adds.

He considers his choices for maybe one whole second. "I'll have all six."

Joshua glances up and raises a single eyebrow. Is he impressed? Ed can't tell. "That's extra, just so you know."

He nods. "This morning's been kind of extra, anyway."

Joshua steps away to pass the ticket through the kitchen window. Ed turns to his friends and schools his face into what he hopes is a serious expression.

"Look, I'm really sorry. I don't know why I got so bent out of shape."

"It's okay," Curtis says, almost at the same time Siobhan says, "I do."

"Oh?" Ed raises his mug to his lips slowly, as if it might scald him. More likely, Siobhan's going to say something that'll make him splutter and spill it all over himself. Fortunately, she's focused on dipping the tiny remaining corner of her sandwich in the bowl of liquid crack and polishing it off, which gives him time to get a sip in. Surprisingly decent coffee.

"Well, you can't take it out on the LTD or Matt Smith. All that frustration needs somewhere to go."

"I think I worked off most of it by walking too far and getting lost." He takes a longer sip of his coffee and considers raising his grade from surprisingly decent to pretty good. Instinct makes him reach for the sugar packets, but he draws back. It doesn't need it. "I still have no idea how I managed to get lost on a road that goes in a straight line."

Siobhan picks up her now empty ramekin of liquid crack. She's clearly thinking of swiping her finger around the inside to get whatever's left. "Maybe it was the town."

"Pardon?"

Curtis leans both elbows against the counter and shakes his head. "Still not buying it."

"What are you talking about?" Ed asks.

Joshua has returned with the coffeepot to refill his mug. "Aw, you guys were right. He *is* cute when he's flustered and confused."

"What is this, dunk on Ed day and no one told me?"

"Every day is dunk on Ed day," Siobhan says.

"Except when it's crap on Curtis day," Curtis adds.

That earns him a look of surprise from Siobhan. "When is it crap on Curtis day?" When he doesn't answer right away, she splutters, "I don't crap on you."

Curtis lowers his head and stares at her over his glasses.

Ed turns back to Joshua. "What are they talking about, maybe it was the town that made me get lost?"

Joshua sets down the coffeepot and leans against the counter. "Hopewell has a reputation for being…offbeat."

"And Austin has a reputation for being weird. I still don't get it."

"He's saying the town is kind of cursed," Siobhan says.

"Not cursed." The sharpness in Joshua's tone makes Ed sit up straight. Siobhan, too. And *she* looks like she's getting ready to give him a dose. At least Joshua's observant enough to notice, and he takes it down a notch. "More like enchanted. People say the town has a way of looking out for people and nudging them in the right direction."

He can't be serious. Can he? Ed wonders. The skepticism must show on his face because Joshua holds up a hand and shakes his head. "I'm not saying I believe that, but I'm not *not* saying I believe that, either."

Siobhan leans against the counter. "What *are* you saying, then?"

"That enough strangely coincidental things happen around here to make you wonder. The mayor says she would never have stopped in Hopewell if it hadn't been for her car breaking down, which means she never would have met Sloan and they never would have gotten married, and she never would have run for mayor."

Siobhan tilts her head and purses her lips. "That's a lot of coincidence to hang the word 'enchanted' on."

"Maybe this town is just prone to causing car trouble in passersby," Ed says. "Maybe the garage owner's got some kind of scam running."

Joshua half laughs, half scoffs. "Sloan? The straightest arrow ever? Hardly." He pauses, frowns, and turns toward Siobhan and Curtis. "You haven't told him about the tree, have you?"

Uh-oh. "Tree?"

Siobhan has gone stone-faced, and Curtis is suddenly very interested in the remaining grilled cheese crusts scattered across his plate.

"There's a tree down on Highway 11," Joshua says. "Big one.

Even if your car *could* go, you wouldn't be getting past that any time soon. They've called Hydro—"

"Hydro?" Ed interrupts. "What does water have to do with it?"

"Hydroelectric," Siobhan says, as if it's the dumbest question in the world. "The power company?"

Joshua points at her. "What she said. Anyway, it'll take them a while to get here and clear it."

If there had been a plate in front of him, Ed would have slammed his head into it. As it is, he thuds his forehead gently against the laminated granite-look counter. "My life sucks."

The weight of an arm settles gently across his shoulders, and Siobhan says, "At least you have us to keep you company, and we don't suck, do we?"

"No." He lifts his head, stifling the prickling feeling at the corners of his eyes with a couple rapid blinks. *Please, nobody notice that.* It's a convention, a stupid nerdy gathering, not something worth crying over.

Joshua gives him a sad smile. "Welcome to well north."

A bell dings in the back, and Joshua heads toward the kitchen. Ed straightens up and pats his hands flat against the countertop. *Enough with the feeling sorry for yourself, Sinclair.* "Okay, if we're stuck here, what do we do to make the time pass?"

"Joshua has told us about some places we should check out."

"There's a comic book shop," Curtis adds.

"All right if I tag along?" he asks.

Siobhan rolls her eyes. "Duh, of course. We may not be at the con, but we're still on this trip together."

"Actually…" Joshua is suddenly back. The only thing Ed's seen move with more stealth is their cat. And his smile is kind of Cheshire-like. "I was wondering if I could borrow Ed here for a little bit. Do you mind?"

Siobhan gives Joshua the suspicious squish look, where she pulls her head back until her chin nearly disappears. "Say what now?"

"Nothing sinister or evil, I promise."

"Oh, darn," Ed says, but suspicious Siobhan is still suspicious.

"Text us later, and we'll figure out a place to meet up," she says.

After Curtis and Siobhan pay and leave, Joshua returns to the kitchen, and for a moment Ed has the place to himself, except for the guy in the booth, who has for some reason moved to the other side of the table now, so he's facing the door. Maybe he's waiting for someone. Maybe he has a life. Ed vaguely remembers what having one of those is like.

He gets his phone out of his pocket more from habit than anything else. No texts. Figures. He sent one to Samar a couple days ago, to tell her how excited he was about SciCon and did she want him to get Matt Smith's autograph for her, too. She'd probably say no, since she's more Trekkie than Whovian, but he still wanted to offer. And it gave him an excuse to get in touch without coming out and saying straight up that he misses her. He misses everyone.

His message is the last one in their thread. Radio silence from back home. Should he send another one? No, too desperate sounding. Besides, if he's really honest with himself, the one he wants to talk to is Kyle, but what good would that do? It's like a bruise he can't help but poke to see if it still hurts. It does.

He returns his phone to his pocket and looks up in time to see Joshua emerge from the kitchen with two to-go containers, which he stacks on the counter in front of him.

"I was hoping you'd do me a favor and run Lyn's lunch across the street to him. I know it doesn't look like it right now, but I'm going to get slammed with the lunch crowd in about five minutes."

Lyn. So that's Blond Guy's name. He glances over his shoulder. The garage is within sight down the hill and across the street.

"It's not that far," Ed says.

Joshua gives him a pointed look. "True. But apparently Lyn is trying to fix something for a demanding customer and can't take the time to come across the street."

A demanding customer. Okay, he deserves that. The fact that there are two containers is not lost on him, either. "I guess I don't get to eat my own lunch first?"

Like flipping a switch, Joshua's sunny smile returns, which seems like his natural state. The pointed looks probably take a lot of effort for him. "Your grilled cheese will still be hot by the time you make it across the street. And it's going to be a nice day, so maybe you can eat outside. Lyn can probably suggest a spot or two."

I bet he could. "Nice day?" Nice if you like gale force winds. But when he turns around, the view outside is placid and serene, the trees bordering the parking lot only rustling in a gentle breeze. "Huh, I guess it is."

"See? It all works out. Oh, I almost forgot." Joshua grabs a paper to-go cup and fills it with coffee. "That's on the house for making a delivery run for me."

He slings his bag over one shoulder and slides off the stool. "Guess this'll be my good deed for the day."

Joshua tilts his head. "You only allow yourself one per day?"

Joshua holds the door open for him as he balances the to-go cartons in one hand and braces them with the other, which also holds his coffee. If the breeze turns into a gust, he's hosed. Luck seems finally to be going his way, though.

He's halfway down the hill when his phone's text message alert chirps. Not just any text message—it's Samar. It's only been a couple days since he texted her, but in his head it's been weeks, months.

Of course there's no place to set any of his things down. On the ground? Food? Ha, no. He sets the coffee cup on top of the to-go containers and rests his chin against the lid to hold the entire Jenga tower in place, and with his now free hand he retrieves his phone. He puts it on the to-go containers next to his coffee so he can unlock it and read the text. He starts walking again, looking down at the screen and waiting for the text app to open.

Which is when everything goes flying. The coffee, the to-go containers, his phone, and him.

He lands on his ass and yelps more at the sudden impact than at any sense of pain. His right palm stings where he's braced himself against the asphalt to keep from falling back on his head. At least his hand's not bleeding when he looks at it, holding it in front of his face as if trying to block out the sun. By some miracle, he's not wearing either his coffee or his grilled cheese and six sauces.

Probably because most of it has landed on Lyn, who has managed not to fall back on his ass and now towers over Ed, who starts to laugh because, this guy? Not likely to tower over anyone except maybe ten-year-olds. His shirt is painted with coffee, something clumpy has landed in his hair and down the side of his face—is that tuna? Pasta?—and the exploded containers of dipping sauce are at his feet, their contents striping his shoes and the legs of his jeans.

Oh, this is…not good. His friend Daniel would call it suboptimal.

Lyn's mouth hangs open in fly-catching astonishment, one arm held stiffly away from his side, his other hand clutching a phone, and… this is the part where Dad would start laughing so hard he'd probably hyperventilate, which would at least prevent him from saying that's what they both get for texting instead of watching where they were going.

"What." That's all Lyn gets out before falling silent again.

"You're supposed to be in the garage," Ed says.

Lyn finds his voice again. "I was on my way to pick up lunch." He looks down at himself. "Which I now seem to be wearing." He plucks at his soggy shirt. "Along with some coffee."

Coffee, piping hot coffee. Ed lurches to his feet. "Oh shit, you're not scalded, are you?" He reaches forward to check Lyn for burns, but Lyn takes a couple steps back, which, okay, is understandable, but also kind of hurts. More than he expects. "I'm so sorry. Really. I was bringing you your lunch. Joshua—"

Lyn waves his phone. "Yeah, I was reading the text when—"

His phone, where's his phone? He looks around frantically, sees it half concealed under an overturned to-go container and scrambles over to it. Picking it up with all the delicacy of an unexploded bomb, he flips it over, expecting a spiderweb of cracks across the glass. But it's in one piece, unbroken. The corner is scuffed, but when he presses the home button, it lights up.

"Oh, thank the maker," he says.

"No, don't worry about me," Lyn says. "I'm fine."

Okay, that's *so* not fair. The first thing he did once the shock wore off was ask if Lyn was scalded. He is *not* that self-centered. And as soon as he opens his mouth to say that, he shuts up again. No, Sinclair, this is not a situation you can talk your way out of.

He gets up and wipes the screen of his phone as gently as possible with the hem of his T-shirt. This time, he approaches Lyn at a more cautious velocity. "I really, *really* am sorry. You sure you're okay?"

Lyn looks down at himself again. "I—" He stops and sighs, his shoulders sagging, and in that moment he just looks so defeated, it tugs at Ed in a way both sudden and unexpected. He glances over his shoulder toward the diner.

"They can probably help get you cleaned up in—"

"I think I'm just going to go home and change."

"You sure?"

Lyn turns and gestures vaguely behind him. "It's just up the hill."

"Okay. But I'll go get your lunch replaced and bring it to you. You heading back to the garage after changing?"

"You really don't have to—"

"No, I really *do* have to."

"Okay. Thanks."

He waits a moment before heading back up the hill to the diner. Even from a distance, the slope of Lyn's shoulders radiates something close to despair. Ed looks down at the asphalt around him and starts picking up the debris from their collision.

As he approaches the diner, the door opens and Joshua leans out, his expression somewhere between concern and *maybe* a little amusement.

"I guess you saw all of that back there," Ed says.

Joshua nods. "Oh, yes. Are you okay? That looked like a hard landing."

"I'm…fine. Can you make him a replacement lunch? I'll pay for it."

Joshua takes the pile of garbage from him and heads behind the counter. "Already put in the order for both of you. And it's on the house." Once he's dumped the containers in the trash, he points at a stool. "Now, sit. I'll get you something to wipe off your hands."

While Joshua heads back to the kitchen, Ed sets his phone on the counter and unlocks it. He stares at the green text message app icon, at the red notification alert overlaying it, and his finger hovers, but he doesn't tap it. Instead, he lets the display go to sleep and leans against the counter.

Enchanted, Joshua said. Or cursed, as Siobhan put it. At the moment, he's leaning toward cursed.

His phone chirps. Another text message. Surprisingly, not from Samar asking, **Did you get my text?** with its implied *Why haven't you responded yet?* subtext, because even if it's taken her a week to respond to his, God forbid he take more than five minutes to respond to hers. No, this one is from Dad.

Hey slugger, everything okay?

It never fails, even from a couple hundred miles away, Dad always seems to know when something's up.

Ran into some car trouble. We got a tow, but we're sort of stranded in a town called Hopewell.

I noticed. You haven't moved more than a kilometer or two for the past two hours.

The find-my-phone app strikes again. And even though they'd never use it to snoop on him, sometimes it'd be nice to go off radar for even a little bit.

Yeah, it's a pretty small town.

Is it serious? You want us to come get you all?

He pauses before replying. How cool would that be? They come swooping in to the rescue, pay for the repairs, and ferry them all back home. But maybe they can still get to SciCon, despite the car and the tree and, well, everything. When will he ever get a chance to be this close to Matt Smith again?

We're okay. Hoping they can fix it and we can still get to the con.

OK. If you change your mind, let us know. Hey, did you know the town's mayor is a lesbian? That's cool, right?

As soon as he said the name Hopewell, his dad probably started checking Wikipedia. He can't help smiling. Somehow, Dad always knows the right thing to say. Except when he says the absolutely wrong thing, but with Dad it's either extreme. He really did luck out in the parent lottery.

That's pretty freaking awesome, actually.

"I guess either the coffee's working or you got good news."

Joshua's returned with a new set of to-go boxes, which he sets on the counter in front of him.

"Not so much good news as a good reminder, maybe." He taps out a quick *gotta go, talk later* and thumbs the screen off. He feels somehow lighter now as he pulls the containers toward him. "Hopefully Lyn won't lock the door to the garage when he sees me coming with these."

Joshua waves a hand. "You're fine. He doesn't hold grudges. If he did, he'd probably hold it against me."

"Why's that?"

"Long story, never mind." Joshua puts his hands flat against the counter and leans forward, which does fantastic things for his upper arms, but Ed's not about to tell him that. "Just use both hands this time and try to be a little nice to my friend, okay?"

Joshua smiles while he says it, but it stings anyway. Just then his phone chirps again. Another text from his dad pops up on the lock screen:

Try and make the most of it while you're there. (Maybe you can meet the mayor!) You change your mind though, let us know.

Perfect timing. Which could really be annoying coming from anyone other than his dad. He meets Joshua's smile with his own, but with the wattage toned down slightly. He slides off the stool and stands.

"I'll be nice to your friend."

"Good." He taps the topmost container. "I can't guarantee these'll be on the house if I have to beg the cook to replace them again."

He pauses mid-reach for the containers. "You begged?"

Joshua's smile falters for like the briefest microsecond—as opposed to the longest microsecond. There is a difference, which Ed would explain if anyone asked.

"I'm nice like that," Joshua says.

"Good to know. And thank you."

Joshua holds the door open for him as he exits, the to-go containers held firmly with both hands, one on top and one underneath. He takes shorter steps than usual as he walks down the hill toward the garage, not just to keep from tripping or dropping the containers, but also because his resolve is trickling away to nearly nothing. And if he brings Blond Guy—Lyn, he needs to remember the name—his lunch and he's like, *see ya*, then okay, fine.

What's bothering him is that whole "the town is enchanted" thing. In fact, it bothers him that it bothers him. Isn't this the sort of thing he'd love to be real? And yet it sounds so kooky.

"What would the Doctor do?" He stops a moment. Did he just say that out loud? He did. He's asked himself that on more than one occasion, although usually in silence. The Doctor always runs toward the danger, toward the mysterious or the weird or the I-wonder-what-that-is, and he does it with eager, almost childlike excitement.

Of course, he also nearly gets his friends killed before it's all said and done, but this isn't nearly that risky. Probably. Hopefully.

But anyway. He'd approach it in the spirit of scientific inquiry, and that means coming up with a hypothesis that can be tested, or at least can be judged based on observable data. And if the data doesn't support the hypothesis, then come up with a new hypothesis to test.

The other thing the Doctor would do: she'd bring her friends along.

"Okay then." Great, is he turning into the sort of person who talks to himself now? Well, so be it. He sets off again toward the garage, stopping at the side of the road before crossing.

"Ed!"

Behind him, a banging noise makes him turn. The door of the diner has slammed open, and Joshua is jogging down the parking lot toward him, another to-go container in his hands, which he places on Ed's stack.

"You mind giving this to Sloan while you're at it?"

"Sure."

Like he'd really say no? Even so, Joshua smiles and reaches out pats him on the cheek before Ed can flinch.

"Thanks, doll. You're a peach."

Joshua doesn't wait for a response before turning and sprinting back up the hill. Lunch rush must really be a thing. As if in response to his guess, three cars are pulling into the lot when he turns back toward the road.

Make the most of it, Dad said. Well, all right then. He'll see if he can find proof, or at least evidence, of whether this place really is as magical as Joshua claims it is.

Assuming he doesn't trip over his own feet on the way.

Shortly after he closes the front door, Mom calls from somewhere upstairs, "I thought you were having lunch with Josh and Logan."

He pauses with one foot on the stairs, cringing. Serves him right for not getting around to oiling the hinges on the door like she'd asked. No point in being quiet about it now. He lumbers up the stairs.

"What happened?" She's standing at the top by the time he's halfway up. "Food fight?"

"Ha. I had a run-in with something. I'm just gonna change." When he reaches the top, he veers as close to the banister and away from her as possible. It doesn't keep her from putting a hand on his arm and squinting at him.

"Hon, there's tuna in your hair."

Suddenly, all he can smell is fish, and even though it is, or *was* his lunch, the thought makes him suddenly queasy. "Maybe I'll take a quick shower."

She follows him down the hall. "I'm still wondering what happened?"

In the doorway to the bathroom, he raises a finger. "Hold that thought."

He doesn't realize he forgot to bring a change of clothes into the bathroom until he turns off the water and reaches for a towel. Worse, he can still smell tuna. Hopefully, the smell's just in his head, and not on it.

"I'm still waiting to hear what happened," his mother says when he opens the door, startling him enough that he nearly loses hold of the towel around his waist.

"*Mom*. Seriously, could we *not* just right at this moment?"

He catches her frown before turning toward his room. He doesn't bother checking if she's following, because of course she is. At the door, he turns to ask her to please *please* give him some privacy, but she's already backed off. She holds up her hands.

"I'll wait outside. But leave the door open a crack so you can tell me what happened."

She's being weird, but he does as she says before he starts pulling clothes out of drawers. Instead of putting any of them on right away, though, he sits on the edge of his bed. He just wants a second to... Why does he feel out of breath all of a sudden? He leans forward and rests his arms against his thighs. A drop of water plunges past his nose to the floor.

"Hon," his mother calls from the other side of the door, "what's got you so flustered?"

Good question. Also a good word for it, flustered, and having that lets him shrug it off enough to get up and start getting dressed.

"Just a difficult customer, I guess."

"Who's being difficult?" Her voice is instantly defensive. It makes him feel safe, but it also makes him cringe. Thankfully, she never deployed it at school in his defense. "Let me guess, is it Martin? Is he still trying to keep that rusty old Renault on the road?"

Mr. Martin, the music teacher, who dresses in stuff that was *maybe* in style back in the '90s. "No, I think it finally died for good. This is an out-of-towner. Some cranky American kid and his friends who broke down on Highway 11 on their way to SciCon in Toronto."

It's quiet a moment before his mother answers. He can guess what's going through her head. "So a cranky American threw tuna salad at you?"

"No, and it's a tuna melt, not tuna salad. He was bringing me my lunch from the diner and we…ran into each other."

"I thought you were having lunch with Joshua and Logan."

"I was before I had to start working on a cranky American's car." He shakes his head. "No, wait, it belongs to one of the other ones."

"The others aren't cranky?"

"Aren't Americans."

"So he was bringing you your lunch, but he was cranky?"

"Mom."

"So what does he look like, this cranky American?"

"I don't know."

"What, you didn't look at him while he was being cranky at you?"

He pauses with his T-shirt ready to pull over his head. "Does it matter?"

"Hey, humor your mother." He can practically hear the shrug in her voice.

"Fine. Tall. Um, kind of skinny. Dark hair, flops over one side. Seems like the kind of person who gestures a lot when he talks, you know?"

She goes *hmm* noncommittally. "Wearing jeans and a hoodie?"

"Yeah. You can come in now, by the way," he says once the T-shirt's on. "Did you become psychic and forget to tell me?"

"No." She pushes the door open but doesn't walk into the room. She points down the hall. "But it looks like he's bringing you your lunch again."

He leans out the door. The hall ends in a window overlooking the front porch. From there, they can see down the hill, over the back of Sloan's garage and across the street to the diner's parking lot. And there's the cranky American, carrying three to-go containers as he walks toward the garage.

"For someone who doesn't know what he looks like," she says, "you just gave me some fairly specific details about his appearance."

"What's your point?"

"My point? Nothing, really."

Right. Why does he feel like he's just been busted?

"It's just some guy passing through who had car trouble." He sits on the edge of his bed again, scooting over when he remembers the damp spot, and puts on his shoes.

"It's funny," she says while he's tying the laces, "how many people wind up having car trouble along that stretch of Highway 11."

"I'm sure Sloan finds it funny in a laughing-all-the-way-to-the-bank kind of way. Good for business."

"Good for more than business. She and Dina never would have met if Dina's car hadn't stalled on her way to Toronto." She comes and sits next to him on the bed. "And they did *not* hit it off at all when they first met. More like they were liable to hit each other."

"Mayor Dina hit someone? That doesn't sound like her."

"They seriously rubbed each other the wrong way." A pause. "Until I guess they figured out the right way."

Ew, phrasing. "Mom, please. I have to work with Sloan, and that's really not the image I want in my head."

"What? Oh." She laughs. "You're so squeamish. You know, when your dad and I met, we didn't exactly hit it off right away, either. I think the first thing I told him was to get his Elmer Fudd ass out of my way."

He snorts before he can stop himself. "True love."

"We didn't know it at the time, but yes."

He gets up and swipes his keys and wallet from the dresser into his pockets as fast as he can. "I'm honestly not sure what the point is that I'm supposed to take from all this."

She tilts her head and smiles enigmatically. "Just that you'd better get a move on if you want to eat your tuna melt while it's still warm."

By some miracle, Ed manages to get across the street without dropping the to-go containers, tripping over his feet, or chickening out.

Or getting run over, although heavy traffic doesn't seem to be an issue in Hopewell, as far as he can tell.

Lyn's nowhere to be seen, but the woman who owns the place comes out of the service bay when he arrives. She looks about his dad's age, maybe older. She's got a wrench in one hand, a shop rag in the other, and a cranky expression, but she also has the kind of face that was probably born cranky. She smiles when she sees him, although she doesn't wear the expression easily.

"So," she says, "do you want the good news or the bad news about your car?"

He looks behind him, as if Curtis and Siobhan might be coming up behind him, which, duh, obviously not. "I'm just a passenger. The car belongs to my friend, Curtis, so maybe you should wait to talk to him?"

She smirks. "It's not like confidentiality's involved here. I'm a mechanic, not a doctor."

"Say that in reverse and add 'dammit, Jim' in front of it, and it'd be perfect."

"Ha." She points a rag at him. "Which you want first, good or bad news?"

Get it over with. "Bad news."

She gestures for him to follow her into the customer service area. "It's the alternator. Good news is I've got a supplier who has one on hand for this make."

When she twists the rag in one hand and doesn't say anything right away, he prods her. "I'm guessing there's more bad news."

She nods. "My supplier's on the other side of the tree that's down across Highway 11. So it'll be a while before he can get the part to us."

"How long is 'a while'?"

She bows her head as if the answer is somewhere on the floor. "Maybe this evening, but more likely tomorrow morning."

From good to bad, moving right along to worse before finally settling on worst. They're never going to make it. He puts the lunch containers on the counter before his sagging shoulders make him drop them.

"Well, what can you do?"

"What I can do is keep calling around and see if I can find another alternator on this side of that tree. No promises, though." He can tell from her tone that this is unlikely. She points the wrench at the stack of to-go containers. "Please tell me one of those is mine. I'm starving."

He slides the top one off the stack and hands it to her. "At your service."

She smiles. "Personal delivery. They should give you a job."

"Is Lyn around? This one's his."

"Not yet. If you see him before I do, tell him he might as well take the rest of the afternoon off. Not much else we can do here."

He takes the other two containers, which are still warm, and goes outside where there's a wooden bench in front of the shop. He sits and puts them on the seat beside him. The breeze has died down, and the sun is bright overhead. He takes off his hoodie and ties it around his waist. He closes his eyes and lets the sunshine warm his face. A sense of exhaustion slides over him in a way that's not unpleasant, kind of like settling under a blanket.

"Are you okay?"

Instant unsettling. Lyn's voice nearly jolts him off the bench, but he manages to catch himself. The sun has become dazzlingly bright while his eyes were closed, and he has to blink several times to clear his vision. Lyn stands two or three yards away, eyeing him in a way that could mean wariness or just curiosity.

"Yeah, fine." He sits up straight and tugs at the hem of his shirt.

"I didn't wake you up, did I?"

"No, I was just—the sun felt nice. After how windy it was this morning, I mean." Something about Lyn's appearance seems off. He leans closer. "Is your hair wet?"

Lyn raises a hand, as well as his eyebrows, and touches the shiny patch of hair that's gone darker than blond with dampness. "Yeah, I took a shower. Didn't want to risk having tuna still in my hair and end up smelling like my lunch all day."

"That reminds me." Ed picks up one of the to-go containers and holds it out. "That guy at the diner made you another lunch to replace the one I got all over you. He said this one was on the house."

"That sounds like him." Lyn hesitates. "You know, maybe you want to set it back down on the bench and I'll pick it up. That way neither of us ends up wearing it."

It's right on the tip of his tongue to say something indignant, but he stops just shy of letting it leap into the air. Joshua had told him to be nice. Okay then, this is him being nice. He can do this. He sets the container back on the bench.

"Yeah, you've probably got a point there."

Maybe there's a hint of a smile as Lyn picks up his lunch. He peeks under the lid, probably making sure their lunches aren't mixed up, and closes it once he seems satisfied.

"So," Ed says, "we got off on the wrong foot, and I was hoping you might let me rewind a little and…"

For a brief, mind-paralyzing instant, the words evaporate before he can say them, and the inside of his mouth goes dry. Why's he getting flustered now? Maybe because Lyn's looking at him as if he's an unexploded bomb about to go off. Finally, he just sticks out his hand.

"Hi, I'm Ed."

Lyn's expression says *I have no idea what your deal is*, but not in an unfriendly way. He shakes Ed's hand.

"Lynden. Everyone calls me Lyn."

"Nice to meet you, Lyn."

They stand there in silence, each holding his to-go box. Could this *be* any more awkward? Think, Sinclair. What would the Doctor do?

Information. He'd start making inquiries. He scans around them, the quiet street, the short, scrubby trees that seem to be barely hanging on to the ground. He thought Canada was land of towering forests. Maybe that's in a different province.

"So, Hopewell," he says. "Nice town. You like it here?"

Lyn turns his head so he's watching him, not out of the corner of his eye, but from a different angle, as if appraising him. But why would he—oh, right. His earlier comment comes racing back: *whatever passes for life in this place.* Not his best moment.

Lyn doesn't mention that, though it's probably exactly what he's thinking. "Yeah, I do," he says. "I mean, granted, it's the only home I've ever known, but I've been happy here."

Ed nods, turning in a slow circle and taking in the surroundings again: hill, flat, hill, more flat. Judging from the road he got "lost" down earlier, the whole town is mostly flat. He's got to bring that up if he's going to find out more about whether this town is enchanted, but how to do it without making Lyn think he's not all there?

"Are you okay?" Lyn asks. Ed stops turning, and dizziness tugs at him. Maybe too late on not making Lyn think he's a little strange.

"Yeah, fine," he says, shaking his head. "Just, there's something about this place I can't put my finger on."

Lyn does that head tilt again, but slightly different this time. He may have a limited range of expressiveness, but he makes the most of it.

"You've been talking to Joshua, haven't you?"

"The guy in the diner, right?"

Lyn nods, so obviously not buying any of his vagueing it up. "He's as bad as my mom. Folks have this idea about Hopewell that it's"— he hesitates, and seems to be hunting for the right word—"that it's magical. But it's not like that. People here are just nicer than normal, overall. Maybe that's magical enough."

"Sounds like you're enchanted with it."

Lyn smiles—not one of his previous lopsided grins that might be mistaken for a smirk on someone less good-natured. When he looks past Ed toward the garage, his smile fades, and Ed has to resist turning around to see what Lyn's looking at.

"I hate to run, but your friend's car isn't going to fix itself, and—"

"It's the alternator."

"'Scuse me?"

"The woman in there—what's her name?"

"Sloan. The owner."

"Right. Well, she said it was the alternator, but it might be tomorrow before a replacement gets here. On the bright side, she said you should take the afternoon off."

"Oh." Lyn stares at his to-go box, flicking the unclosed lid with his thumb. Probably trying to figure out how to ditch the weird out-of-towner so he can eat his lunch in peace. Maybe best just to leave him be and go find Siobhan and Curtis.

"Did you get the grilled cheese?" Lyn asks.

"Yeah."

Lyn plunks himself down on the bench and nods toward the seat beside him. "In that case, better eat it while it's still hot. They're not that good cold."

So far, so good. Ed's being nice, and Lyn is not telling him to please go away. He sits and opens his lunch. Buttery, savory goodness wafts up and practically licks his face. Maybe there's something to this sandwich's reputation after all.

"I guess you like dipping sauces, huh?" Lyn asks. He leans a little toward Ed and his lunch. Two halves of a grilled cheese, diagonally sliced and perfectly golden, sit in the box surrounded by six lidded plastic containers.

"I figured if I'm only going to be here once, I should try them all, yeah?"

"Makes sense."

Ed pries the lid off each container and stacks them in the upturned lid of the box. The different aromas compete for his attention: garlic, honey mustard, something smoky, one that might be buffalo sauce, a green one that's maybe pesto, and an unassuming-looking ketchup.

"Wow."

"They really go all out on the grilled cheese. The one with bacon's really good, too."

Ed picks up half of the sandwich. The edge is so golden and crispy, it practically glistens. But which sauce to dip it in first?

"Start with the ketchup," Lyn says. "They make it themselves, and it's probably the best ketchup you'll ever taste."

"That's a tall order."

"Trust me."

Lyn turns his focus back to his own lunch, and Ed is about to do the same to keep from staring at the guy's profile. The shape of his chin catches the sunlight as he bows, almost prayer-like, over his lunch. Maybe he *is* praying. He doesn't know Lyn's life. But the sunlight catches a dusting of fuzz on Lyn's cheek and makes it look as if he has a halo.

Oh great, he *is* staring. He turns away, dips at random, and takes his first bite.

"Oh my God." He closes his eyes. Heaven, this sandwich is heavenly. A plain old grilled cheese, this good? And that ketchup is really ketchup and not some divine nectar?

When he opens his eyes, Lyn's watching him with obvious—no, not amusement. Pleasure. He seems genuinely happy.

"See? I told you."

He dips the other corner of the sandwich back into the ketchup, this time getting a big dollop of it. He waits until he's finished that bite before answering Lyn.

"Calling this a grilled cheese seems like, I don't know, an understatement or something."

"What would you call it instead?"

He dips the sandwich in the smoky sauce, which turns out to be barbecue—a weird choice but it works—before he answers. "Life changing."

Score one in favor of Hopewell's reputation for being magical. He polishes off the last bite and reaches immediately for the other half of his sandwich before pausing. Lyn has been watching him eat this whole time.

"What? Do I have ketchup on my face? I have ketchup on my face, don't I?"

He fumbles for his napkin until Lyn, laughing, puts his hand on his arm.

"You don't have ketchup on your face."

For an instant, they freeze. It's also over in an instant, Lyn withdrawing his hand to give him a napkin from his own stack. "But here, just in case."

"Thanks." Ed wipes his mouth to have something to do and to keep from rubbing his forearm and obsessing about why it feels like it's been burned. Lyn rubs his hand against the leg of his jeans, as if he doesn't know what to do with it now.

"You want to talk about enchanted," Lyn says, pointing at the remaining half of Ed's grilled cheese, "that's probably closest to the most magical thing in town. If you can figure out how the cook does it, you'll be the first."

"What, seriously?"

Lyn nods. "Won't tell anyone what the secret is, not even Joshua, not even the other cooks. He's got things in unmarked bottles and jars and just says X amount of this and this much of that. Won't let anyone see what he puts in them, either."

Now this is intriguing. "What could it be?"

Lyn shrugs. "If I knew the answer to that, he'd probably hunt me down. His grilled cheese is legendary around here."

"And yet I can't help but notice you're eating a tuna melt."

"Something wrong with a tuna melt?"

"Nothing, nothing." Except that it's kind of gross, especially when it gets in your hair. "It's just not really legendary around here, I'm guessing." Or anywhere, probably.

Lyn looks down with the expression of someone considering all the ways his sandwich did him wrong before dismissing them. "I like what I like. Besides, you can't eat grilled cheese every day."

Ed shakes his head and picks up the other half of his sandwich. "I'd be willing to try."

❖

Lyn laughs as Ed dunks his grilled cheese into another sauce. A ponderous expression settles over Ed's face as he chews, but it passes like a breeze and he smiles. Apparently, the combo agrees with him, and he dunks in that sauce again before moving on to the next one.

The way the intense, skinny guy gets into his grilled cheese is cute.

Okay, fine, *he's* cute. But Ed's also just passing through and is going to be gone as soon as his friend's car is fixed. So, there's that. But he definitely didn't imagine the reaction when he put his hand on Ed's arm—which, granted, unsolicited physical contact. But whether the reaction was positive or negative, who could say?

He averts his gaze to keep from staring at Ed while he's eating, and he sees the ghost again across the street.

Only this time, the apparition is leaving the diner, not going in.

Lyn blinks hard. He's never seen it from the front, and never twice in one day. Heck, twice in the same week only ever happened that one time during finals when he was convinced he was going to flunk chemistry. From a distance, the figure's half-transparent face is not very clear. Lyn leans forward and squints, trying to get a better look, but the ballcap the ghost's wearing doesn't make it any easier.

"You okay?"

Ed's finished the last of his sandwich. Three of the sauce containers are empty, too, and he holds a fourth in one hand, as if he might be considering licking it out. Lyn settles back against the bench and puts down his sandwich.

"Yeah, just thought I saw a bird over there."

"A bird." Ed's expression goes from concerned to deadpan. Definitely not buying it. But that gives Lyn an idea. He points in the general direction of the diner's roof.

"Pretty sure it was a hawk or something, and it was sitting on the roof right above the door."

Ed follows Lyn's cue and squints toward the diner. The parking lot is filling up now, the lunch crowd appearing like clockwork. The grilled cheeses are probably flipping fast at this point. The half-invisible figure is walking toward the street, passing through parked cars like water. If Ed could see the ghost, he'd be looking more or less right at it from this distance. But he shakes his head.

"Must've flown away," Ed says. He puts the sauce container down and closes the lid of his to-go container, looking almost regretful. Lyn points him toward the compost container down by the side of the road, which gives him time to wolf down the last of his tuna melt and pasta salad before getting up and heading in the same direction. Ed looks left, then right, like maybe he's planning to cross the road. Mostly, though, he just looks lost.

On the other side of the street, the ghost heads toward the intersection with Main Street. This behavior is all new, as if reality has bent around a corner and gone someplace it was never meant to. His rational mind feels like it's in free fall, as if he's just coming off the top hill of a roller coaster.

"Seriously," Ed says, "you're kind of freaking me out a little here. What's wrong?"

The ghost turns right. The urge to follow is overwhelming. Mom would probably say it's the town giving him a sign, but that's just cr—

He's seeing a ghost. What's not crazy about that already?

"Sorry." He smiles at Ed. "My head's not screwed on straight today."

Ed tucks his hands in his pockets. "Okay, so, since you've got the rest of the afternoon off, want to help me kill time until the power-Hydro-whatever people clear that tree?"

"You sure you don't want to catch up with your friends and hang out with them?"

Ed shakes his head. "We've been cooped up in the same car since like five this morning, so they could probably use some alone time.

And anyway, I want to see if there's anything to this whole 'this town is enchanted' thing." He spins around, as if looking for a likely direction to start in, before facing Lyn again. "You're the local expert. Where should I start?"

"Well, let's see. We could go—"

His plan is to turn toward Main Street and point casually in the direction the ghost went and suggest they go that way. Ed doesn't need to know they're following an apparition.

From the corner of Main Street, the ghost is staring directly at him.

He can't help it. He yelps and stumbles backward, nearly colliding with the compost bin. He braces one hand against the bin and the other against his heart, which feels like it wants to bust out of his chest and run for home.

"*Hey.*" Suddenly, Ed is in front of him, gripping his shoulders firmly. Ed looks him right in the eye, which would be weird at any other time—and is kind of weird now—but his expression is kind and his voice is gentle when he says, "Breathe. Take a deep breath. You're fine, everything's fine."

Everything's not fine, but Ed takes a deep breath himself, nodding for him to do the same. And it does make him feel a little better. He's facing the diner across the road, and he really doesn't want to look over toward Main Street again in case the ghost is still looking at him or, worse, coming toward him.

He glances out of the corner of his eye. It's not watching him anymore, but it's still there.

Ed follows his glance. "What is it? You look like you've seen a ghost."

Lyn laughs. His voice sounds borderline hysterical. And if he's scaring himself, he's probably scaring Ed, too. But he's not slowly backing away. His hands are still on Lyn's arms, and Lyn doesn't mind.

"I'm okay," he says.

"You sure?"

He nods. Ed gives his arms a little pat and lets go, but he's still standing pretty darn close. No one stands this close to him. Is it an American thing, or just an Ed thing?

"So, what just happened?"

Lyn doesn't answer right away. If anyone's going to think he's losing his grip on reality, it's probably better if it's the out-of-town guy who'll be gone before the end of the day, right?

"Okay, first you have to promise not to think I'm crazy."

❖

Ed doesn't think Lyn's crazy.

"Right," he says, "so first of all, the term *crazy* is super judgmental, but let's put that aside for now. Second, it's not very descriptive because it doesn't get to what your real question is, which is, do I believe that you're seeing this ghost."

Ed starts pacing, staring down at his feet as he catalogs everything they know so far. The more he moves, the more each of the individual pieces of this puzzle seem to settle and remain still, so he can examine their contours and see how they fit together. Right now, though, nothing lines up.

He stops and faces Lyn. "Today is the first time you've seen the figure twice in one day, right?"

Lyn nods.

Ed goes back to pacing, picks up another puzzle piece, and flips it around in his head. He stops again. "And today is the first time you've seen it anywhere but going into the diner?"

Again, Lyn nods.

"And it's also the first time it's seemed to interact with you."

No point in waiting for Lyn's response. He knows the answer is yes. He's not convinced the figure *was* interacting with Lyn, but he's not discounting the possibility. But the why…What's he missing?

Okay, enough pacing. He stops in front of Lyn, who seems…well, haunted *is* the only word that fits. Lyn's gaze calm but clouded with uncertainty, he looks at Ed as if he might have answers. All he has are more questions.

"And no one else has seen this figure, right?"

"As far as I know," he says. It's the first thing he's said since he unloaded all of the details.

And then, lightning.

"Today," Ed says. "It's something about *today*. What's different about today?"

Lyn frowns. "Apart from meeting you, nothing."

"Can't be that. There must be something we're overlooking because of its sheer mundaneness." Ugh, so frustrating. He turns toward the intersection with Main Street, peering as if he can will himself to see the apparition. The corner remains stubbornly empty.

"My mom and I had a low-key argument this morning about what I'm going to do with my summer and the rest of my life, basically," Lyn says, "but we've been having that at least once a week since midterms, so it's not really new or different."

"Could be enough, though. This apparition shows up each time you're stressed about something, so maybe it's trying to offer you an answer to whatever's got you stressed."

Lyn finally smiles a little. "You're really Sherlocking the shit out of this, aren't you?"

Guilty as charged. "Time Lording the shit out of it was more what I was aiming for, but fair enough. It beats running away from it, right?" That gives him another idea. "Maybe in this case, we should run toward it."

"You mean try and chase it off?"

He shakes his head. "What if we follow it? See where it goes, or maybe where it leads us. If the only thing about today that stands out is your argument with your mom about the direction your life is headed—"

"That and you and your friends showing up."

"And that, but we're inconsequential in the grand scheme of your life." He waves his hand down the road. "Maybe it's trying to offer you a direction."

Lyn stares down the road, hands tucked in his pockets, shoulders riding up toward his ears. "Okay."

"Yeah?"

"We don't have anything else to do, or anything to lose. Let's do it."

"Yes! Excellent." Ed claps his hands together and immediately feels foolish for doing so. To keep from making any other ridiculous gestures, he clutches the strap of his messenger bag with both hands. He must look like he's expecting to be mugged as they head down the road toward Main Street. The sidewalk's on the other side of the road, so he walks in the grass while Lyn stays as close as he can to the edge of the blacktop.

So much of this day has gone unexpectedly, from the breakdown on the edge of town to the bizarre way he walked right past the auto shop, and now this quiet, cute guy who sees ghosts. Or *a* ghost, at least. It's almost enough to make him forget that he's probably going to miss seeing his favourite Doctor ever. Almost.

"So, this is the only apparition like this that you've seen, is that right?" he asks.

That gets a humorless laugh from Lyn. "One is more than enough, thank you."

"But that means it's not some generalized sensitivity you have to these phenomena."

Lyn frowns. "Generalized sensitivity?"

"Work with me here. If you had the ability to see ghosts in general, you'd see more than this one. Make sense?"

"We're back to calling them ghosts, then?"

Ed looks over. Lyn's frown has turned upward into a smirk. "Fine, call them ghosts. Or rather, call this a ghost, since you only see one." It's easier to say than *apparition* and maybe more descriptive than *figure.* "And since you don't see any others, that would seem to indicate a specific connection between you and it. Him. Whatever. You don't recognize him, though, right?"

"I've never been able to see his face before today, so it never occurred to me it might be someone I know."

"It never occurred to you to tell anyone else about it before today either, did it?"

Lyn stops abruptly, forcing Ed to stop, too. "And how would that be a good idea?"

"What do you mean?"

"I mean telling someone about him." Lyn points toward the intersection, clearly pointing at someone specific, and it's unnerving Ed can't see who. "Who am I going to tell who wouldn't think that I'm going craz—"

Ed throws up his hands. "Would you *please* stop using that word? Why are you losing your chill over this?"

"I am *not* losing my chill."

❖

He is *so* losing his chill. Lyn can practically see the chill seeping out of his shoes and collecting in a puddle at his feet, and yet he can't stop. He didn't expect his day to include one meltdown, much less two, but here he is.

"Who could I tell who wouldn't think I'm hallucinating and maybe in need of psychiatric attention? People don't go around seeing people that aren't there."

"You told me, though."

"That's because you're not going to be here after tomorrow. I won't have to see you day after day and know you're thinking *he's not right in the head.*"

How is all this rudeness coming out of him all of a sudden? He hears himself saying the words and even when he knows he's about to say them, stopping himself is impossible.

Ed crosses his arms. "So I'm a convenient stranger, is that it? You really know how to make someone feel wanted."

"*That's not what I meant.*"

Lyn realizes he's the one who's pacing now, going out into the middle of the street. Thankfully, there's no traffic. He comes to rest in front of Ed, out of breath, as if he's just spent the last minute or so fighting with a lug nut. He expects Ed to say something snarky, but Ed remains silent, arms crossed. The funny thing is, he doesn't even look mad. His expression is calm, not stern or stoic or pinched, like it's usually been today. Has Ed soaked up all the chill that's spilled out of him?

"Feel better?" Ed asks softly.

Surprisingly, he does. "Yeah."

"Good. Let's keep going before we lose track of him."

"No worries about that," Lyn says as they set off again. "It's almost like he's waiting for us."

"Really. What's he doing?"

"He's just standing there." At least he's not looking directly at Lyn anymore. The figure's facing the right side of the intersection. Lyn points. "He's looking that way."

"Probably the way he wants us to go."

Sure enough, the ghost has moved on before they reach the intersection. When they turn the corner, he's standing in front of the resale shop.

"You think he wants us to go in?" Lyn asks.

"Is it a good store?"

He's never thought about it before. "I guess so."

"Then let's go in."

Walking into One Man's Treasure is like walking back in time, only it's a lot of different times all at once. Lyn inhales the shop's unique combination of dust, must, and age, and for a change, he doesn't sneeze right away. Mrs. Tremblay isn't in sight, which is no big surprise. The shop is a warren of hidden corners and blind alleys, and most times when he's come in, she's been down one of those blind alleys sorting books or rearranging clothes. He'll run into her eventually, and she'll probably scare the crap out of him. It's like she's part cat.

The ghost is also missing. Lyn could swear it came into the shop before them. He turns to check if it's still outside.

"Did you see—" is all he gets out before running face first into Ed, who's standing right behind him. Or maybe Ed runs into him. Either way, he bonks his nose against Ed's sternum and stumbles backward. Tall, skinny guy turns out to be surprisingly solid, who knew? He tips back on his heels and flails as he feels gravity pulling him toward the floor.

Oh, this is not going to be pretty.

But Ed catches him. Tall, skinny guy turns out to have good reflexes, too. He grasps Lyn's forearms and pulls him upright.

"You okay?" Ed asks, the amusement on his face tempered with concern.

Lyn looks up at him. *You'd have to stand on your toes if you wanted to kiss him.*

Where the hell did that thought come from? He steps back, regaining his solid footing. "Yeah, fine. Thanks for keeping me from cracking my skull."

Ed gives him a sort-of salute. "Here to help. Did something spook you?"

Besides the thought of kissing you? Lyn shakes his head. "More like something didn't spook me. The ghost didn't come in here with us."

Ed turns around, too. "Is he outside?"

"I don't think so." He moves past Ed to get closer to the door. The sidewalk is empty, apart from the sandwich board sign Mrs. Tremblay puts out every morning.

The sound of someone clearing their throat makes him turn. Mrs. Tremblay stands on the threshold to the shop's lower level, where she keeps bulky, dusty, occasionally rusty items. She wipes her hands on a rag as she walks toward them, her shoes clacking on the floorboards.

"Lyn," she says, "it's been a while. What brings you in today? Looking for anything in particular?"

"Not really," he says, "we're mostly just killing time."

"Poor time, people are always killing it." She smiles at Ed. "Who's your friend?"

The air shifts, and he becomes very aware of Ed standing next to him. He also becomes even more aware of how warm the shop is. Has it always been this warm in here? He clutches his arms closer to his sides.

"This is Ed Sinclair. His car broke down outside of town. We're waiting for a replacement part, but—"

Mrs. Tremblay nods. "Let me guess. The tree down on Highway 11 probably complicates things further." She leans against the counter. "So you're stuck with us for a bit, Mr. Sinclair?"

He nods. "Yes, ma'am."

"I guess it's a day for newcomers passing through. There was another young man in here earlier who was waylaid by the tree." She sweeps an arm toward the back of her shop. "Kill as much time as you like. Just be sure to hide the bodies."

"What do you think we're supposed to be looking for?" Ed asks when they venture deeper into the store. He pauses near a rack of clothes and plucks out a bowling shirt in a tropical print, yellow and green foliage against a bright blue background. "Hey, this is pretty cool."

"I'm sure that's exactly what the ghost wanted us to find in here, yes," Lyn says. Ed gives him duck face and starts to hang up the shirt, but Lyn stops him. "No, keep that. It'll look good on you."

"You think so?" Ed holds it up to his chest and looks down at it, his expression doubtful.

He nods. "Works with your eyes."

Which is only the most completely awkward thing he could say at this point. Any hope Ed will let the comment slip by goes right out the window when, with almost torturous slowness, he raises one eyebrow. Lyn turns away as quickly as possible because if he looks at Ed for a moment longer, he might implode and drag all of One Man's Treasure into the singularity of his embarrassment.

"We still need to figure out what we're meant to find in here," he says, heading deeper into the store. He doesn't have a particular destination in mind. The warren of small, junk-filled rooms seems to shift at random along with the cast-off items marooned within it.

He turns a corner, and there in the middle of the aisle is the ghost.

It's not looking at him, instead staring intently at a paper-stuffed shelf on the left side of the aisle. It's only about ten feet away, probably the closest he's ever seen him—he needs to stop calling him *it*. Close enough to see a shade of stubble on his semi-transparent face before he turns and goes farther down the aisle, turns left, and is out of sight.

There should be a shiver going down his back, but he's more curious than anything else. Why isn't he more freaked out about this? Is it because he's already seen him so many times outside the diner? Seeing him out and about in other places around town is weird, yes, but not *that* much of a stretch from seeing him at all. And this time, at least, he's not staring right at him.

Once it's obvious the ghost isn't returning, he walks quietly down the aisle because it seems appropriate to act like he's in a library. Once he reaches the spot where the ghost stood, he turns to the shelves along the left side of the aisle. It can't have been coincidence that this spot in particular had occupied his attention.

The shelves are metal and open on both sides, like the shelves where they keep spare parts in the garage. They are filled mostly with a mix of hardback and paperback books, some stacked on their sides, piled on top of each other, and wedged in wherever they fit. A few stacks of magazines lie here and there, and on the bottom shelf are bundles of yellowing newspapers. He crouches down and thumbs through some of the magazines—*Maclean's*, *Chatelaine*, *The Hockey News*—nothing really up his alley. Then he pulls the topmost newspaper off the stack. It's *The Hopewell Gazette* from about twenty years ago, the paper brittle and smelling dusty and basementy. He flips through a few more on the stack before unfolding the one in his hands and looking at the front page.

"What're you reading?"

Funny how a ghost doesn't scare him, but Ed's voice shattering the silence sends him nearly airborne. He leaps back, yelps, and hits his elbow against the shelf, which clanks against the adjacent shelf and wobbles precariously. Now his elbow throbs and the pages of the paper scatter to the ground as Ed catches both the shelf and him at the same time and keeps either from falling.

"Whoa," Ed says once everything seems stable, "what's got you spooked?"

Before he can answer, Mrs. Tremblay's voice drifts back from the front of the shop. "Everything all right over there, boys?"

"Sorry, Mrs. Tremblay," he calls. "I ran into one of the shelves."

"Nothing broken, I hope?"

"No, it was just books and magazines."

He can't remember hearing her laugh before, but it's loud, nasal, and sounds like a goose. "I meant you, silly."

He smiles, and Ed lets go of his arm and the shelf. "No, we're not broken either."

"Sorry," Ed says as they both bend to pick up the paper and nearly bonk their heads together. "Didn't mean to startle you."

"I guess chasing a ghost must be getting to me," Lyn says. "I just saw him again."

Ed spins around, as if the ghost might still be lurking nearby. "You mean here?"

"Yeah. He was staring at these shelves before he went down the aisle and around the corner."

Ed slides past him and walks to the end of the aisle. He checks to the left, then right, then left again, like a kid about to cross a street. "He's—"

"Gone, yeah. I know."

Ed comes back and stands next to Lyn, looking over his shoulder as he examines a newspaper that is so old it's practically fossilized. "Local paper?"

Lyn nods. "It's been online ever since I can remember, but I guess they did a print version back in the day."

Ed taps the date up in the corner of the page. "That's like five years older than I am."

"Same."

Ed gets a look of deep concentration, like he's trying to remember something. He gestures toward the books and the papers. "You said the ghost was staring at these shelves?"

"Seemed like it. Why?"

Ed drops to his knees and starts pulling papers from the stack. "It must be a clue. Are there obituaries in here?"

"Obituaries?" It doesn't take him long to get what Ed means. "You think he was trying to tell us who he is."

"Maybe."

"How can we be sure he was trying to communicate with us at all?"

"We can't, but it's the only theory I've got right now."

Ed lifts each page delicately by the corner, but his fingers are soon smudged with ink and dust and time. Lyn looks over his shoulder once he gets to the obits. None of the people listed there are under seventy years old. Ed refolds the paper and picks up the next one.

"How old would you say the guy looks?"

"Hard to tell since he's mostly see-through, but kind of old. Thirty? Thirty-five?"

Lyn checks the date on the next paper unfolded in Ed's lap. Monday, May 4, 1981. It's still anybody's guess, since they don't know when the guy would have died. Ed pulls a few papers from the pile and hands them up.

"Unless you have a better idea, take a seat and start flipping."

Lyn sits on the floor next to Ed and watches him go through two more papers without finding any prospects. The papers Ed handed him, though, remain folded in his lap. He hasn't been able to bring himself to touch the one on top. It's from about seventeen years ago, and the banner headline across the page says *Hwy 11 Crash Kills Hopewell Man, 35*. There's a black-and-white photo of a wrecked car surrounded by emergency vehicles. The car is twisted like a wet rag wrung out by a giant.

"Um, Ed..."

Ed stops flipping through the papers. "What's wrong?"

"Nothing, it's just..." He looks down at the papers as if they might bite him. "I guess this isn't exactly how I expected to be spending my afternoon."

"Oh." Ed sets his hands flat against the paper lying across his legs and goes very still for a moment before he starts stacking up the papers to return them to the shelf. "I'm sorry. I guess I shouldn't have assumed you wanted to investigate this like some great big mystery."

"Oh hey, no." Lyn puts a hand on Ed's arm before he can pick up the now neatly stacked pile. "I didn't mean I minded hanging out with you. I meant that…"

Lyn rests his forehead against one hand. What *does* he mean? He lets out a deep sigh and taps the front page of the paper in his lap. "I think I know who the ghost is."

Ed leans closer, tilting his head so he can read the front page. "You think this is our ghost?"

Lyn nods. For a moment, he flexes his jaw sideways, as if he doesn't trust himself to speak. Finally, he says, "Yeah. So, 'Hopewell Man, 35' was my dad."

Ed's face goes slack. "Shut the front door. You're kidding."

Just like that, Ed punctures the sense of dread trapping him and, laughing, he shakes his head. Ed blinks fast. Once, twice, three times. "Your *dad*? And you didn't think that was important enough to mention?"

"I mean, I wasn't a hundred percent certain, but it seemed likely."

"I can't believe—wait a minute." Ed waves his hands. "Don't you know what your own dad looked like?"

"I never knew him. He died long before I could remember him."

"But you know what he looks like."

"Sort of? I guess. Mom doesn't really keep a lot of pictures of him out on display. She said it made the house feel too funereal."

"'Funereal'? Wow, she really is an English teacher."

"Tell me about it. Anyway, there was a phase where she tried to date again and didn't want guys to think she was still hung up on Dad, so she packed away most of the photos."

"Did it work?"

"Not really. She gave up after a while. Never put back the pictures, though."

Ed takes the paper from his lap and scans the article. Lyn already knows the details—"Single car accident…black ice…killed instantly… pronounced dead on the scene…wife, Adrienne, and a one-year-old son…" Ed follows the story to the jump page, where there's a thumbnail photo of the man who was killed, which he holds out to Lyn. It really is no bigger than Ed's thumb, and it has all the quality of a DMV driver's license photo.

"Does our ghost look anything like this?"

Lyn takes the paper and squints as he peers at the photo, bringing it closer to his face so it almost brushes his nose. "Yeah, could be."

"Wow." Ed leans back against the shelf opposite the books and papers. Lyn lets the paper settle in his lap again and rubs his hands together. "So, what did you want to spend your afternoon doing?" Ed says.

"Pretty much anything that doesn't involve hanging out on the floor of Mrs. Tremblay's shop looking through old newspapers I think are about to make me sneeze."

Which is when he turns his face just in time to avoid letting out a massive sneeze right in Ed's face. A second sneeze follows, less seismic than the first.

"Got it." Ed takes the papers and returns them to the shelf before standing. He holds out a hand to help Lyn get up. "Besides, I think we've gotten everything we were supposed to discover here. Any thoughts on what it all means?"

Lyn shakes his head. "I don't think that confirming he's my dad was the main point. It feels like, I don't know, he wanted to make that point so we'd believe whatever else he's trying to tell us. What he's really trying to tell us, I mean."

"Which is?"

"Yeah, I got nothin'."

They stop at the front counter so Ed can pay for the shirt. It turns out to only be three dollars, which is even more of a bargain after the exchange rate. Once they're outside on the sidewalk, Ed stuffs the shirt in his messenger bag and scans the street.

"Is he around now?" he asks.

Lyn points back the way they came. "He's gone back to the intersection."

"Should we follow him?"

"Sure seems like he wants us to."

"Yeah, but what do you want?" Ed hikes a thumb over his shoulder in the direction of the shop. "You said hanging out back there wasn't on your agenda for the afternoon. What would you be doing if you weren't chasing a ghost with a nerdy American?"

That gets a smile out of him, at least, which feels like an achievement in itself.

"Is there a better way to spend an afternoon than chasing a ghost?" Lyn asks. "Because I can't really think of one."

They fall into a somewhat awkward silence as they follow the ghost down the sidewalk, pausing every once in a while as Ed peers through shop windows. Main Street seems quaint, a little old-fashioned, but sturdy and determinedly cheerful, like a place that has moxie, as his grandmother would put it. When they pass the street he walked down earlier that morning, he squints at it narrowly. How could he have made the two turns that he needed to make to get down that road and not remember them at all?

His phone buzzes. It's a text message from Siobhan:

Wanna see something cool?

"Hang on," he says to Lyn. "I need to answer a text."

Depends on the something, but OK.

A couple seconds later, she sends a photo of herself, holding a slender metallic wand-like device he instantly recognizes as the Thirteenth Doctor's sonic screwdriver.

OMG WHERE DID YOU GET THAT

That comic book shop Joshua mentioned. They have a bunch of them. Want me to pick you up one?

OMG yes please

"You seem happy about something," Lyn says. Ed holds up the phone so Lyn can see the picture.

"They must be at D20," he says.

"D20?"

"Not a gamer, I guess, huh? It's a die used in RPGs. That's role-playing—"

"Games," Ed finishes. "We're going to a con, so I am familiar with the concept at least." Mentioning the con makes him wince. The fact that they'll miss it still stings. "You play?"

"Used to. Not much anymore."

There's more to his response than he's letting on, but Ed's phone buzzes with another text before he can follow up. This one's from Curtis.

So, I have some bad news from the garage.

Yeah, they told me about it too.

Curtis sends a frowny-face emoji.

They also told me the price. And that they probably won't get the part until tomorrow at the earliest.

I guess that means we need to find a place to stay for the night. Pretty sure they won't let us sleep in your car in the garage.

Yeah, probably not. But we got it covered. Got a room at the B&B down near the riverfront.

OK let me know what my share is. Hopefully we can get on the road tmrw in time to make the opening ceremony for SciCon.

After that, Ed can't help but notice Curtis takes a while longer to respond.

Yeah, about that. Btwn repairs n cost of the room tonight, I'm kind of gonna be wiped out for the weekend. Which means I can't afford the room in Toronto. Which means...

And that's exactly how Curtis ends his text. Ed resists the urge to fling his phone into the street. "Fuck."

"What's wrong?" Lyn asks.

"Hang on." Ed types back a quick response—Not your fault. I'll catch up with you all later—and then puts his phone back in his pocket. "Sorry," he says to Lyn, "just looks like even if the tree does get cleared, we're not going to be able to get to SciCon."

"I'm sorry. That sucks."

"Well, what can you do?" He looks ahead of them. "So where's our ghost now?"

"Pretty much waiting for us to keep following him."

"Well, let's not make him wait."

They head down the sidewalk again, the silence more awkward than before, although he's not sure why. The shops on either side of the road give way to trees and bushes, and eventually the sidewalk ends. They fall into single file and stay as close to the edge of the road as possible, but traffic is sporadic.

"Where's he leading us to?" Ed asks.

"Honestly, I have no idea, although once we get around the bend, we'll be close to downtown where—whoa."

Suddenly, Lyn veers off the road and plunges into the bushes.

Ed follows even though there's no path to speak of, and before long, branches and thorns are plucking at the sleeves of his hoodie as tries to keep up.

"Hey," he calls toward Lyn's receding back, "slow down. I can't keep up."

"Sorry." Lyn stops and waits for him to catch up. They're both a little breathless from the sudden detour. "Ghost just decided to go off-road all of a sudden."

"Where's he leading us?"

Lyn shakes his head. He's not looking at Ed when he speaks, his focus instead on some point in the distance where the ghost must be. "I have no idea. I'm not really in the habit of wandering through the woods like this." He pats Ed's arm. "Come on. He's still on the move, and we'll lose him if we don't keep up."

Something feels different about their pursuit now. There's a sense of urgency to their pace that wasn't there when they started. Lyn is crashing through the tangle of branches in front of them, whether from desperation or excitement, Ed can't tell. Thankfully, their trek through the underbrush is short-lived, and soon they emerge onto a rough path of sorts, a narrow track of packed dirt flanked by sun-baked shrubs that plunges into some more trees beyond the clearing. The trail is still only wide enough for them to pass single file, so Ed contents himself with the view from behind and wonders if being a mechanic involves a lot of leg work and squats.

The path slips into the coolness of the woods on the other side of the clearing. The trees on this side are dominated by pines, which have deposited a carpet of needles that muffle their footsteps. It's easier going through here, almost pleasant. As the path through the trees widens, he manages to catch up and walk alongside Lyn.

"I didn't even know these trails were back here," Lyn says.

"You hike a lot?"

"Some. There's a greenbelt path that leads over to the community centre, and some woodsier trails over by the riverbank. If we have time, I'll show you my favourite place to hang out. It's—whoa."

Lyn stops dead in his tracks, and Ed bumps right into him, nearly knocking the both of them over. He grabs Lyn before he can faceplant into the dirt. *What is it with us?* This is at least the third time they've collided today. Is this town trying to give them each a concussion?

Well, score one for him, then, since they're both upright, not head injured. And he still has his arms around Lyn, who is not exactly struggling to get away. All the same, he lets Lyn go before it gets even more awkward than it already is.

"We've gotta stop bumping into each other like this," he says.

"Kind of becoming a habit, yeah?"

Ed puts his hands in the front pocket of his hoodie. "So what made you stop all of a sudden?"

"You know how I mentioned showing you my favourite place to hang out?" They're standing at the edge of the woods now, the trees thinning out to grass and light beyond. Lyn walks forward into the sun, and when Ed follows, they're standing on a wide, grassy bank leading down to the edge of a broad river—maybe not as broad as the Mississippi back home, but definitely bluer.

"This is nice."

But Lyn shakes his head. "This is impossible, is what this is. There's no way…" He leaves the thought unfinished, going back to the edge of the woods and pacing down to the riverbank. He runs one hand through his hair as he peers up and down the river. Not far off to the right is a hotel-like building with trees and a manicured garden in front, along with tables and benches. To the left is a path following the contour of the river—not the path they came down through the woods. Lyn gazes at the path as if he might be seeing things. Besides a ghost, that is.

"What's wrong?"

Lyn stops pacing and comes to stand in front of Ed. "I have no idea how we got here. The way we came, we would have had to pass the community centre and cross at least one major road and walk through two neighbourhoods."

He gets out his phone and starts tapping, then flips it so Ed can see the screen. Google Maps clearly shows where they're standing, along with the blocks of houses, the road, and the community centre they most definitely did not walk past on their way here.

"Okay," Ed says, "so that's weird."

Lyn pockets his phone. "You think? It's beyond weird. It's geographically impossible. It's…" He stands there gap-mouthed but unable to speak. He shakes his head. "People say this town is enchanted, but maybe it's possessed, with bizarre things like this happening."

"I feel like I should remind you we've spent the last couple hours in pursuit of the ghost of your father."

"I *know*." Lyn's really losing his chill now, and the ache in Ed's chest at seeing him in this level of distress is unexpected. "I thought I had things figured out, you know? But now, all this? I just, I have no idea."

He covers his face with his one hand. He's not crying, at least Ed's pretty sure he's not, but the way his shoulders sag, he radiates exhaustion.

"Hey." Gently, Ed takes his hands. "You don't have to have anything figured out right now, okay?"

Some moments Ed wishes would last forever. The moment right before kissing someone for the first time is at the top of the list: the stomach-dropping anticipation, the wondering if they'll kiss you back, the uncertainty of it all. He can count his first kisses on one hand, but that's enough to know they're one of his favourite feelings. And when he bends down toward Lyn, and Lyn rises up on his toes to meet him, he can't imagine he could ever feel better than he does right now.

And then their lips meet, and he forgets he's ever been kissed before.

❖

"Wow."

Lyn's not sure which one of them says it first, but when they come up for breath, it's the first thing they both say. Ed's eyes are still closed, a blissful glow softening his expression, and the only thing Lyn can think about is kissing him again.

Or maybe Ed's just stunned. Lyn shakes his arm a little.

"Hey, you still in there?"

Ed blinks and opens his eyes, squinting as if dazzled by the sunlight. "Yeah, I'm still in here."

"I was worried I broke your brain or something."

Ed laughs. "Almost. If you kiss me again, you might short-circuit something." He pauses and looks Lyn in the eye. "That's an invitation, by the way."

Lyn doesn't need to be told twice.

"So, I'm beginning to think there might be something about this whole 'the town is enchanted' thing after all," Ed says when they take another breather. He looks around them, his expression curious. "Which reminds me, any sign of our ghost?"

Our ghost. Lyn smiles. They already have something to share that feels special, almost secret. He looks around too, and—where *did* the ghost go?

He pauses. The breeze, tugging at his sleeves and whipping his hair into a mess all afternoon, has gentled and sets the leaves overhead to rustling. The mid-afternoon sun glitters across the surface of the river, scattering diamond light.

Here. This has been the destination all along.

"I think I've figured out what he was trying to get me to see," Lyn says.

"What's that?"

"You."

For the longest time, Ed grins like he's waiting for the punchline. But Lyn really means it. Eventually, Ed's expectant grin subsides. "Wait, seriously?"

"You're what's different about today. I might have missed it if—" For a moment, he's tempted to say "Dad," but instead says, "If the ghost hadn't led us here."

Ed steps past him, closer to the water's edge. "And where are we, exactly?"

"My favourite place. Whenever I just need some peace and quiet, this is where I come. I've fallen asleep under that tree a zillion times."

Ed turns back toward the tree. It's a broad, old maple that's neither the biggest nor the fanciest tree around, but Lyn remembers the contour of each groove in the bark pressed against his back. He's been coming to this tree for years, and as much as he's changed, it's stayed reliably the same.

"How did you find it?" Ed asks. He walks over, turns his back to the tree, and sits on the grass, leaning back against the trunk.

"Pretty much like that." Lyn sits next to him and points over at the retirement home. "It was probably the first time we came to visit my grandma after she moved into the senior home. She and my mom were unpacking and told me to go outside and have fun. I'm pretty sure I was just in the way or they were unpacking my grandma's underwear or something. Anyway, I wandered over to the river and hung out here and pretty much fell asleep. Kind of freaked my mom out when she couldn't find me once it was time to leave. Anyway, I've been coming back here ever since. Whenever there's something on my mind or something that's worrying me, I can think about them here and then imagine letting them go and watching them float around the bend in the river." He gazes up into the canopy of leaves, their contours glowing translucent green in the sunlight. "I've had some pretty great dreams under this tree."

When Ed doesn't respond, he glances over to find his eyes closed, his chin tilted down toward his chest. Smiling, he threads his fingers through Ed's. "I can't wait to hear yours when you wake up."

❖

Ed wakes with a start and, for a moment, doesn't know where he is. It comes back to him—the tree, the river, the breeze—and it becomes clear from the angle of the sun, now scattering gold across the water where before it was diamonds, that he was asleep for a long time.

It also becomes clear that at some point he leaned over and wound up with his head in Lyn's lap, which he's absolutely not going to complain about but which might be awkward when Lyn wakes up, considering the proximity of his ear to Lyn's junk.

Fortunately, there's not much time for things to get awkward. Lyn wakes up, and after a brief, dreamy smile, his expression slides into panic and Ed's head slides off his lap and bonks against the ground as Lyn gets up.

"Oh shit, what time is it?" Lyn pulls out his phone, taps the screen, and then taps it again, frowning. "Do you have any battery left?"

He's already got his phone halfway out when Lyn asks. Nothing. "That would be a no." When was the last time he looked at his phone, anyway? Hours, at least. Granted, he was asleep for several of those, but given that he's used to checking it every fifteen minutes these days, going so long without thinking about it tells him something. Something good.

"We'd better head back," Lyn says, brushing grass from his jeans. "Your friends probably think I've kidnapped you, and my mom is probably freaking out a little by this point."

"Good idea." Ed starts toward the woods, but Lyn taps him on the shoulder and points along the river to their left.

"The path's not far down there. Probably easier than trying to find our way through the woods in the dark."

From the tree, the woods appear to extend all the way up to the riverbank, like they would be forced to walk through the water to get around them, but as they approach, the river angles away enough for them to get by without having to go single file. When he turns around, the illusion is repeated, and maybe ten yards away, the footpath begins.

"No wonder that's such a quiet spot," he says. "From here, you'd never know it was around the corner."

Lyn glances in the same direction. "Yeah. And not a lot of people bother to go past the end of the path, anyway."

They don't hurry back, but it's not long before Lyn is unlocking the door to the garage and they're going inside. He makes a beeline for the counter, opens the drawer beneath the register, pulls out a tangle of phone chargers, and hands one to Ed. Once they've both plugged in, Lyn picks up the landline while Ed waits for his phone to get enough charge to reboot.

When it does, it vibrates so hard it almost bounces off the counter. Ed catches it before it can dive off the edge. Notifications scroll through the lock screen faster than he can read them—all text messages from Siobhan or Curtis, it seems. When he opens up his messages, their texts go from amused—did the cute mechanic turn out to be a serial killer who dumped your body in the woods and this message is making the phone buzz on your cold, lifeless corpse?—to seriously concerned—Dude, Siobhan's this close to calling the RCMP, and if she's willing to do that you know she's freaked. Pick. Up.

Drama queens, both of them. He fires off a group text: Geez, I'm fine. He didn't kill me.

Siobhan answers first: Whew.

He hesitates before sending a follow-up: Although he might have kissed me.

Siobhan: !!!!!

Curtis: Aw yeah, Ed's got game.

Ed rolls his eyes. Chill, you two. Where are you?

Siobhan: We're at the B&B. Room's big enough for all three of us.

Curtis: Although maybe you and the hottie mechanic want to get your own room. #chickabowwow

Siobhan: Babe, this isn't Twitter.

Curtis: We're gonna order pizza and watch Phantom Menace on Siobhan's iPad. Wanna head over?

Ed: Lemme text u later. I'll ask Lyn when he gets off the phone.

Siobhan: Yeah, right. We won't be seeing you tonight...but you might be seeing some man-on-man action.

Ed: OMG please stop

The first thing Sloan says to Lyn when she picks up is, "Your mom's been looking for you."

Figures. "Did she sound freaked out?"

"More like annoyed. Which is better?"

"I guess I'll find out. Any word on the alternator?"

"Should be here tomorrow afternoon."

"Shit." He glances down at his phone, where the sad empty battery icon has been replaced by the time—seven twenty-eight. "Has Hydro cleared the tree?"

"Not yet, but they're on the scene. Shouldn't be long."

"Let me go pick up the part." Before Sloan can protest, he adds, "They open at seven, but you know he's always in at six. I can be there first thing in the morning, pick it up, and be back at the garage before it would have even left if we waited for them to courier it."

"True." A pause. "Is there some reason you're in such a hurry to get rid of these people?"

"It's not that." He explains about the convention, about Matt Smith—Ed looks up at the mention of that name—and why it's important to them. "If I leave at three thirty, I'll be there right when he gets in and back here before nine, and they'll be able to get on their way before lunchtime." He leans one hand against the counter and watches Ed, who's focused on the screen of his phone but is so obviously listening that it's not even funny.

"So," Sloan says, "you spent the entire afternoon with this kid, right? You sure you want to help him leave town so quickly? He seems kind of—"

"Nice?"

"Well, highly strung was the phrase I was thinking of, but I'm getting the impression he might like you. Do you like him?"

Oh yeah, very much. "Maybe."

"Maybe don't be in such a hurry to send him on his way, then." Another pause, and in the background he hears a muffled question as if Sloan has put her hand over the phone. An answer leads to another question and another answer, before the line clears and Sloan says, "Dina says hi, by the way."

Lyn smiles. "Hi, Madam Mayor."

"Yeah, no chance I'm calling her that. But anyway, seems like coincidence has conspired to bring these folks to town here, and you know—"

Lyn sighs. "Not you, too."

She laughs, the sound over the line like nuts and bolts rattling in a bucket. "No, but Dina's a true believer, and if it helps make her happy to give Hopewell the benefit of the doubt that it's got a little magic about it, I'm not gonna argue. Maybe you shouldn't either."

When he hangs up, Ed's got his head bent over his phone, thumbs tapping at near inhuman speed. Something about his frown of concentration makes Lyn feel helium-filled. What's he supposed to do with this feeling?

He's not sure. But for now, he likes it.

Ed pockets his phone and smiles at him. Lyn leans across the counter, takes hold of Ed's hoodie, and pulls him closer. How many people has Ed kissed? It's so tempting to ask. More than he has, most likely, but asking would mean stopping the kiss already in progress, and he's not about to do that.

"How much will you knock off the repair bill for each kiss?" Ed asks. "Because I'm willing to do this a lot."

"Not if I want to keep my job," Lyn says. "Sloan says I do too much pro bono work for my friends as it is. Speaking of friends, what are yours doing?"

"They got a room at the B&B and are ordering some pizza."

"What do you want to do?"

Hopefully, Ed's answer will involve spending more time together in some way, but if he wants to go hang out with his friends, that's understandable. And besides, he's going to be on his way as soon as the car is fixed. He has to remember not to get attached. But it's also as good a reason as any to spend as much time together as possible.

He's about to mention this—maybe it'll seem desperate, but who cares—when Ed says, "Got any plans?"

Play it cool, he tells himself, but he can't resist grinning. "Not until I drive to Hodges tomorrow morning to pick up the alternator. How do you feel about—"

His phone buzzes before he can finish. It's his mother:

Sloan says you've resurfaced. Are you planning on being home any time soon?

On my way. With company.

Intriguing.

She adds a raised eyebrow emoji, which is about her only concession to less than grammatically perfect prose even when texting. He pockets his phone, looks up at Ed, and hopes his smile is convincing.

"How about dinner at our place?"

It's not until they're standing on the front porch, his hand on the door handle, that it occurs to him: *I'm about to introduce him to my mother.*

Shit, he's about to introduce me to his mother.

It's not until Lyn is putting the key in the door that he asks, "Won't this be weird?"

Lyn pauses to look back at him. "Why would it be weird?"

Lyn's tone and the spooked look in his eyes make it clear, though. Yes, this is going to be weird. He forgets about that when Lyn opens the door and the scent of dinner practically drags him into the house, reminding him that, no matter how good that grilled cheese was, he ate it a *long* time ago.

And to his surprise, it's not weird. His mom turns out to be super nice, and she made lasagna, and her banter with Lyn is pretty funny.

"So you're going to Toronto?" she asks after all of them decided that seconds of the lasagna would be fantastic and are now sitting around the table feeling way too full.

"Well, we were. But between the cost to fix the car and the room they got at the B&B, Curtis can't afford his share of the room in Toronto. And if he can't afford it—"

"Neither can the rest of you," Lyn's mother finishes. She props her elbows on the table and frowns over her clasped hands. "Do you all still have your tickets?"

He nods. "For what it's worth. Those aren't refundable, unfortunately."

She looks like she's about to say something, but instead she gets up from the table and starts clearing their now-empty plates. "When do you have to head out to pick up the part?" she asks Lyn.

"Three thirty." He looks at his phone and grimaces. "About six hours from now."

She pauses after picking up Ed's plate. "Why don't you get a few hours' sleep in our guest bedroom before you and Lyn head out?"

He can just imagine what would have happened if she'd asked him that while they were still eating. Thankfully, she didn't, and no one has to give him the Heimlich maneuver. "Here?" he asks, which is not the way to get on his host's good side, but if his completely boneheaded question falls flat with her, she doesn't show it. She just smiles a little wider.

"We've got plenty of room, and this way you'll have a room to yourself and you won't wake up your friends at three thirty when it's time to go."

He only misses half a beat this time. "Sure. Thanks, Mrs. St. Francis."

Another smile, and then she takes the plates into the kitchen. Which leaves him and Lyn staring at each other across the table. Judging from Lyn's expression, there's plenty of surprise to go around. He leans forward so he can keep his voice down.

"What just happened?"

"I think my mom just invited you to spend the night."

"Whoa." He waves both hands and shakes his head. "Phrasing."

"Well, she didn't say you could stay in *my* room. Besides, that would be like moving at warp speed." His tone's more serious, though, when he adds, "I can take you over to the B&B if you really want."

He shakes his head. "Your mom had a point about waking up Curtis and Siobhan later. They're *not* gonna want to get up that early." *I'm not sure how thrilled I am about it* is a thought that remains unspoken. He gets out his phone. "I'd better text them and let them know what's up."

Their responses are predictable. Curtis sends an animated GIF of some cartoon character twerking, and Siobhan, at first, just sends three words:

"Guest bedroom." Right.

I don't think his mother's lying about having a guest bedroom.

And I don't think he's gonna pass up the opportunity to take you to pound town.

OMG SIOBHAN

She sends him a skull emoji after that. Well, he's been fished in. He types back:

I hate u

U love me. Your duffel bag is still in the car if you wanna go get it. Unless you're planning to sleep nekkid, you wicked temptress.

I'm turning off my phone now.

As if. You never turn your phone off.

She's right, and he doesn't turn it off now, either. But he doesn't look at it the entire time they're going to the garage and getting his bag. He certainly doesn't look at it when he and Lyn pause to make out on at least three occasions while they're at it—once under a lamppost, once against the wall of the garage, and once more just outside the circle of light cast by the fixture above his front porch. The only time he looks at it is when he sets his alarm for three thirty and places the phone on the nightstand in the guest bedroom and turns out the light.

Naturally, Lyn can't sleep.

He stares at the ceiling, then he stares out the window, and he tries not to think about the fact that Ed's lying in bed on the opposite side of the wall behind him. He's like two feet away.

His phone buzzes. It's Ed.

Well, I can't sleep.

Yeah, me neither.

I've never tried counting sheep, but at this point I'd be willing to try. Think it works?

He searches for an amusing reply and comes up blank. The best thing to do when you can't sleep, he remembers his mother saying, is to get out of bed and don't go back until you do feel sleepy. He turns on the light and flings the covers aside.

This is ridiculous. Meet me in the kitchen. I'm making hot chocolate.

By the time Ed comes down, Lyn has the kettle on and two mugs with cocoa mix on the counter. Despite his smile, Ed looks worn out. It's a cute look, and makes Lyn want to pull him toward him, but instead he motions for him to go sit on the couch while he finishes the hot chocolate. When he brings the mugs over, Ed's got his legs stretched underneath the coffee table and has picked up the remote, which he squints at as if he's never seen one before.

"Want to watch something?"

Ed swaps the remote for a mug. "Dealer's choice."

Lyn grabs a DVD from the box sets on the shelf under the TV, drops it in the player, then goes back and settles on the sofa next to Ed, who scoots in closer. Before long, the screen is taken up by the trippy 1970s time tunnel effects, and Tom Baker's basset hound face appears on the screen.

"Going old school," Ed observes.

"Have you watched many of these?" Lyn asks. Ed shakes his head. "This was the first episode I ever saw of the show."

"What's it called?"

"'The Invasion of Time.' I must have been like six years old. I had no clue what was going on, but I thought Leela was cool, and the Sontarans looked like a bunch of giant Mr. Potato Heads invading Gallifrey." Whoops. He glances over at Ed. "Spoiler alert, sorry."

"Considering this probably came out like forty years ago, I have no one to blame but myself." He sips from his mug. "In any case, a much safer bet than choosing Tennant versus Smith."

Lyn's not sure how much of the episode they get through. He

wakes up when he feels the mug being taken out of his hands and blinks his eyes open. Mom smiles down at him.

"It's about time for you boys to get ready."

Lyn lets Ed use the bathroom first while Mom gets the coffee going and makes oatmeal.

"So, I talked to your Aunt Michelle last night," she says. "It's been a while since you got a chance to see her, and she and Uncle Mike have that big place in Toronto you've never visited."

Convenient timing. "You called her, didn't you?"

She holds up a hand. "Guilty. Anyway, Ed and his friends are welcome to stay at her place if they still want to go to SciCon."

This is all adding up to a very strange sum. "Won't that be weird, staying with total strangers?"

She hands him a travel mug of coffee and takes a sip from her own mug. "Not if you go with them."

"Wow. That's"—he searches for the right word—"wildly presumptuous."

She purses her lips and looks sidelong at him. "Spending more time with the thesaurus or just picking that up by osmosis?"

"Hazards of having an English teacher for a mother."

"Fair." She takes an obviously strategic sip from her coffee, letting the silence draw out. How has he not jumped out of his skin already?

"Mom—"

She holds up a hand. "I've bought you a weekend pass, but if you don't want to go, just say so. I wouldn't make you do anything you didn't want to."

"Even if you thought it was something I should really do."

This time there's no strategic sip. "Even if I thought you would regret it, I'd never make you do it."

He leans against the counter. "He lives, what, three hours away?"

"Five. I checked."

"You're not exactly selling me on the prospects here."

She sets her mug on the counter and puts a hand on his shoulder. "Did I ever tell you how your dad and I met?"

He tenses up, which she must sense, but can she guess the real reason? He'd bet not. Still, he stifles that. "Let me guess. Car trouble?"

She nods. "You know how far away I lived at the time?"

"If I had to guess again, I'd say farther than five hours."

"Try more like five provinces. I had just finished my last year of grad school at UBC in Vancouver, and for some reason I thought it would be great to drive across country to see my sister in Toronto. I had a crappy little car and more courage than sense, all of which got me this far before it broke down. I didn't have a cell phone, either, so I just walked into town until I found a mechanic and that's how I met Sloan, who told me to go to the diner while I was waiting. Guess who was having lunch there at the time?"

She smiles, but her eyes turn down at the corners a little. That bit of sadness is always there whenever she talks about Dad, even now. Maybe it always will be.

"So you didn't get to Toronto?"

She shakes her head. "Not for a while, no. And by the time I did, I was engaged."

"How long were you here?"

Lowering her coffee mug, she tilts her head, thinking. "A couple weeks, at least."

"And you were already engaged by then? Impulsive much, Mom?"

"I'm telling you, this town is like that."

He leans against the counter and looks over the kitchen island toward the family room. The opposite wall is where all of their family pictures are hung, from school photos and vacation snapshots to birthday parties and visits to grandparents. They're arranged in a constellation around his high school diploma alongside her bachelor's and master's degrees. He balked when she wanted to hang his diploma there, but she said it was important to remember milestones like that.

"What if I told you I was starting to come around on that whole 'Hopewell is magic' thing?"

"I'd probably ask who are you and what did you do with my kid. What changed your mind?"

He stares down at the lid of his mug. He won't tell her about seeing Dad, not yet. Maybe someday. Instead, he looks over toward the stairs. She seems to get his meaning clearly enough.

"Well then, I rest my case."

"Assuming he wants me to come."

"Believe me, he wants you to come."

From upstairs, he hears the clack of the bathroom door handle opening, followed by Ed's footsteps. The guy has a heavy tread. He and Mom share a look of amusement.

"Better start getting ready. Want me to start throwing some stuff in a bag for you?"

He's tempted to say no, but nods yes instead. If all goes well, he probably won't have time.

"Hey, Mom?" He pauses at the foot of the stairs. "Do you think it's time to start putting some of Dad's pictures back up?"

She turns and looks toward the family room wall, that same smile turned down at the edges settling on her face. "Yeah, it probably is."

"So why didn't you tell your mom about the ghost?" Ed asks. He looks over at Lyn, who has one hand on the wheel at twelve o'clock and the other resting on the seat in between them, where they've got their fingers interlaced. They've been on the road for about an hour, and it's not light yet, though the promise of it teases on the horizon. Every once in a while, Lyn runs his thumb back and forth along Ed's palm and makes this contented sigh that's easy to miss over the drone of the engine.

"I thought about it," Lyn says. "I guess the main thing was I didn't want to lay that on her right before I headed out the door. 'Hey, Mom, I think I saw the ghost of your dead husband. See you in a few hours!' I didn't think that would go over so great."

"Yeah, maybe not."

One thing that did go over well, though, was Ed's text to Siobhan and Curtis telling them they had a place to stay in Toronto if they still wanted to go:

Siobhan: **Still want to go? You're kidding, right?**

Curtis's reply consisted of an animated GIF of the fireworks over Coruscant after the destruction of the Death Star. Point made.

Siobhan: **Does this mean you have to put out in exchange for getting us a place to stay?**

Ed: **OMG SIOBHAN**

"Are you going to tell her eventually?" Ed asks.

Lyn doesn't answer right away, but he slides his thumb over Ed's palm again. "Yeah, I think so. I'm good with this just being our thing right now."

"So we have a thing, huh?"

Lyn smiles but keeps his eyes on the road. "We definitely have a thing."

A half hour later, he gets another text from Siobhan: You're not going to believe this.

She follows up with a link to the news page on the SciCon website. Matt Smith's panel and autograph sessions have both been postponed until Sunday on account of flight delays.

Ed punches the air. "*Yes.*"

"Good news?" Lyn asks.

"The best. Matt Smith's flight is delayed so he's not appearing until Sunday. I'll still get to see him."

"Huh. He must be flying Air Canada."

Ed puts his phone away, and it occurs to him he hasn't checked it reflexively ever since he and Lyn collided in front of the diner. He hasn't wondered about Samar texting him back, he hasn't been tempted to text Kyle. He hasn't thought much about things back in St. Louis. Why doesn't that worry him the way it did just a little while ago?

Lyn slides his thumb across his palm again, and he knows.

Three hours later, when Sloan's closing the hood of Curtis's car, it occurs to Lyn how perfectly things have worked out. He never would have met Ed if their car hadn't broken down at just the right spot, he might never have spent the afternoon with this intense and intensely nerdy guy if he hadn't ended up wearing his lunch, and he definitely wouldn't have kissed him if his dad's ghost hadn't led them on an impossible detour through the woods.

So much of everything comes down to timing, and luck.

They pile into the car. Curtis pauses, slides his hands over the steering wheel, then cranks the key, wincing in anticipation. The engine roars to life and settles down to a throaty gurgle. He sighs.

"Music to my ears."

"Thank the maker," Siobhan says. She leans across the center armrest and slides her arm through Curtis's before turning to the two of them in the back seat. "I apologize in advance for anything snarky I might say this weekend."

"Snarky?" Ed says in mock disbelief. "You?"

She gives him duck face but doesn't contradict him. Curtis puts the car in drive. "Ready?"

"Hit it," Siobhan says.

As they pull away from the garage, Lyn reaches across the seat for Ed's hand and finds it without looking.

THE SCAVENGER HUNT

J. Marshall Freeman

CHAPTER ONE

Discord Server: scavengers
#clue_factory

rome_in_a_day
Zone 2: "It lives inside but its face peeks out the window."

betrayed_by_jo
I have no idea. This is where? Yorkville?

rome_in_a_day
No! Zone 2 is Sherbourne

betrayed_by_jo
Oh yeah. You following registrations? We're up to 752 this morning! The volunteer room is panicking.

rome_in_a_day
Not our department. We just need to focus on clues and clue sites.

betrayed_by_jo
You find the perfect grand prize yet? Let's just use the game tokens for Rowdy Player One.

rome_in_a_day
No! It has to be special. I'll find something!!

"Is that a good barn?" his mom asks as their car arcs around another rocky outcropping onto a farm-dotted straightaway. Rome looks up from his phone at the decaying structure, the weathered wood, the beams that once met cleanly but now gap and sag. He lines up the pic and snaps it, drops on a sepia filter, and captions it for his Instagram: *The old world coming apart at the seems.*

"Let me see the pic," his mom says, taking her eyes off the road long enough to make him nervous. "You mean s-e-a-m-s." Brow furrowed, Rome makes the correction and shares the post.

A notification dings. Kai's DM bubble reads: My heart is open but there are no customers.

Rome types back, you're still in bed aren't you? Writing depression poetry.

Kai: where ru?

Rome: about an hour from the hospital i think

Kai: I hope your grandma's okay. What's the Jewish word?

Rome: Bubbie

Rome snaps a pic of three teens, two boys and a girl, smoking in the parking lot of a tractor dealership. They give him hard stares as the car drives past them, and he captions the post *homophobes in their natural environment.*

Kai responds to the post almost immediately: You don't know anything about them Rome.

Rome: You should see it out here. If they saw us holding hands we'd be crucified on a fence.

Kai: you only ever hold my hand as a political statement.

Rome: you're my bf.

Kai: but am I really?

"Who are you chatting with?" his mom asks.

"It's just Kai."

"It's been a while since you brought him around for dinner," she says and swings into the oncoming traffic lane to accelerate past a truck. A van is heading their way. Rome, imagining the fatal impact, tenses and pushes down on an imaginary brake pedal in front of him. Their car roars with overreaching ambition before his mom swerves back into the proper lane. Rome's phone dings, and she says, "You'll get carsick if you keep staring at your screen." Another ding. He puts the phone into the pocket of his jacket without looking at Kai's new messages.

He stares resolutely forward, ignoring the curious side-eye she's giving him. "Are you still dating?" she asks.

"*Dating*," he says. "No one says that. He's just my boyfriend."

"Back in the day, gay people always called them 'lovers.' When I started volunteering at the community centre, I said it, too. Because I was an ally. But it always made me think of some doomed romance in a movie. Two cheating spouses in a motel room."

He gives her a weary sigh. "Oh, Susan, you heterosexuals are so messed up."

His mom signals and pulls the car into a highway rest stop. "Pee break."

The anxiety crawls right into his stomach. "Can't we just pull up a side road? Rest stop washrooms are disgusting."

"I'm too old to squat in a ditch. Let's make this fast. I want to get to the hospital before morning rounds are over and Edith's doctor disappears."

With great efficiency, she pulls into a parking place, unbuckles, and leaves the car. Rome sits tensely in his seat. He really does have to pee. Having two cups of pod coffee in their motel room was a mistake. He flips down his visor and checks his makeup in the mirror. He left it subtle this morning—just a bit of cocoa eyeliner and an almost nude lipstick—but he was damned if he was going to let the rural rednecks push him back into the closet.

He stands and checks the fall of his jacket, a beautiful semi-shine black with narrow lapels that he found in a vintage store, and marches to the men's room defiantly. He's read trucker porn. His research is nothing if not broad. But the stink of old piss and the shadowed recesses of the concrete room make this about the least erotic place he could imagine. Do men really lurk behind the ill-fitting stall doors, waiting for action? The idea is revolting. And now he's trying to pee at the dirty urinal, glancing back over his shoulder toward the outer door, imagining it being filled by some tough in a greasy T-shirt who blocks his way and calls him a faggot.

Finally overcoming his pee shyness, he does his business, zips up, runs his hands under the thin trickle of cold water at the sink, and escapes the men's room. A soft-bodied dad on his way in with his five-year-old looks up at Rome and drops his mouth in surprise, obviously at his modest makeup, as if Rome's the freak.

"What?" Rome barks back at them and breaks into a run, circling the parking lot once to shake off the nerves before returning to the car where his mom is already behind the wheel with the engine running.

"All good?" she asks.

"Just drive, Susan."

"Hey! This day is going to be hard enough without you being a big a-hole."

"Sorry."

"You were the one who wanted to come, Rome."

It's true. Even with SciCon and the scavenger hunt just days away, he felt it was his duty to his mom and to his bubbie to be there at this time of crisis. The decision made him feel like a man instead of a dumb kid just finishing grade eleven.

The giant regional hospital stands at the outskirts of the town where his bubbie lives. No, not "town." They call it a city, though it doesn't live up to Rome's definition of the word. Even Toronto isn't New York, or Tokyo, or his namesake, Rome. Not that he's been to those places yet. But at least Toronto has the culture and the diversity. Anyone can find their place if they look. And if the haters want to hurt you, your friends are there to stand up to them.

"I'm looking for Edith Sugarman," his mom says at the nursing station.

"Room A57, down the hall on the left," the nurse answers. He looks at Rome and says, "Nice jacket." He's cute, with a few brown curls peeking out the V-neck of his uniform. Rome blushes, nods, and hurries after his mom, who is already halfway down the neon-lit corridor.

He watches her make a left turn into the distant room, but takes his time following, weaving a slow, meandering course around food carts, wheelchairs, and portable system terminals with big rubber wheels. Rome peeks into rooms he passes. A middle-aged man, greying hair like a bird's nest, sitting up in a chair with a tube between his legs that disappears under the skirt of his hospital gown. A Chinese girl his age in bed, eyes half-closed, being fed something soft by her mother. An ominous empty bed, its plastic mattress being sprayed and wiped down by orderlies, an unidentifiable red glob glistening on the floor by one wall.

Rome hesitates outside room A57. It's been six days since the stroke, and he doesn't know what to expect. His mother warned him about weakness on his bubbie's right side and problems with her speech, but he has found it impossible to reconcile the idea of weakness with the tough old woman who loves him so hard.

When he finally enters the room, the reality is much kinder than his imagination's conjurings. His mother has her back to him as she begins to empty the contents of the closet and the drawers beside the hospital bed into plastic bags, but his bubbie sees him as soon as he enters. Her long, grey hair is out of its usual pins, falling to her shoulders, combed as straight as the frizz will allow. Her dark eyes peer at him with undimmed intensity, and she lifts her arms out for a hug, the right not nearly as high as the left.

"Jerome!" she calls, though with an unaccustomed huskiness and a pause between the syllables: *je...rome.* But it's definitely her, not the zombie he'd feared. Relieved, Rome runs forward and falls into her arms.

His mother cautions, "Be careful, she's weak."

"Non...sense, I'm f-fine!"

"Yeah, Susan, she's fine," Rome says, sitting up on the bed as his bubbie strokes his head with her unaffected left hand and gives a customary "tsk" about his makeup. Somehow, he doesn't mind this from her. He suspects she enjoys his being a rebel. They are a line of troublemakers—Edith Sugarman, who unionized her factory, and Susan Epstein, campus feminist leader. Rome doesn't feel like he does enough to make the world better. Sure, he's out and visible, he volunteers at Pride and marches at protests, but none of it is significant. He worries he's not as brave as these women.

As they get her ready to be discharged, Rome has to admit to himself that his bubbie is not really fine. Everything is an effort—going from bed to bathroom, getting dressed—all made worse by her insistence that she doesn't need help. His mom is grim-faced and efficient and won't meet their eyes. Edith sits in the armchair with the slippery cover, and Rome lies on the bed while his mom goes back to the nursing station to get instructions.

"Wh...hen are your ex...ex...ams?"

"Finished the last one on Friday. I think I aced everything but chemistry."

"Sm...mart b-boy. When aa...yu going h...home?"

There is an edge of need in her voice he's not used to hearing. It makes him uncomfortable. "Me and Susan will make sure you're all settled at your house, and then we have to get back on Wednesday morning. It's SciCon22 this weekend, and we're doing the biggest scavenger hunt ever. It has mini-prize finds, video performance scores, geo-caching, everything. There's more than thirty-five teams, and I'm in charge of the clues and prizes committees. It's going to be next level."

Edith is nodding and smiling with uncomprehending pride, her head ratcheting down step by step until she's fallen into a snoring doze. Rome takes out his phone, again ignores Kai's DMs, and checks email.

"Yes!" he says in a sotto voce cheer, peering up to make sure he hasn't woken his bubbie. He opens the scavenger hunt Discord.

#clue_factory

rome_in_a_day
The Fox and Peach just wrote. Agreed to give us the back room for 3 hours. We'll have the living statue guy there. Hunters have to ask him the right question or he won't give the next clue.

Rome isn't expecting an immediate response, but someone whose screen name he doesn't recognize throws up a party emoji. It makes him feel a little less alone here, on the north shore of Lake Superior, at the end of the world.

His mom returns, loaded with pamphlets and doctor's notes. They are ready to go, but everything moves with excruciating slowness— waiting for the orderly with the wheelchair, elevators one after the other too crowded to hold them, more forms and signatures on the ground floor. Eventually, Rome is standing outside in the heat of the June day while his bubbie hums grimly beside him in her borrowed wheelchair and his mother retrieves the car.

"This is warm for June up here, isn't it?"

She has no energy to waste on small talk. "You got...a sss... moke?"

Rome grins at her. "Behave, Bubbie. Anyway, I don't smoke. Well, just some weed sometimes." He looks back over his shoulder in case his mom has snuck up on them. Not that she doesn't know, but she's already on edge today. He doesn't need to make her perform motherhood.

"I'm going to sit with Edith in the back," Mom tells him. "You drive."

"No, wait," Rome bursts out. "I can sit with her. I don't know the way to her house."

"It's 632 Rowena Drive. Put it in your GPS."

She knew what he meant, he's sure. So much is expressed between them without words. *I don't like driving streets I don't know, Mom, especially highways. Yes, Rome, but this is a crisis, and I need you to step up and not whine about it.* As he settles himself behind the wheel and starts making adjustments to the seat, he looks into the rear-view. His mom's face is the closed gate of a castle under siege. She stretches across the back seat, working Edith's seat belt, mopping sweat off the old woman's brow with a tissue.

"Get the air conditioner going as soon as you can," Susan tells him. "Do you need a drink, Mother?"

"Wa…ter, yesss."

Rome does okay on the unfamiliar roads but hates how the highway is cut through the granite and shale of the Canadian Shield. Sometimes the road separates eastbound and west around a mound of rock, and the striated rock face, revealing layers of history millions of years old, looms beside the car, so close he feels like he could slap it through the open window. It's too easy to imagine losing control, the car scraping along the rock, sending up sparks, and finally the explosion that ends them. Roll credits. Of course, the only almost-accident he causes is when he forgets to check his blind spot before making a left turn. He glares back at his mother in the mirror.

But finally he pulls up the familiar steep driveway of his bubbie's house and jerks the car to a sudden halt. With no wheelchair of their own, they have to help Edith out of the car and walk her up to the house, one on each side. The nine steps leading up to the front door feel like a mountain. How will this diminished figure ever manage them again? Rome wonders.

"We need to get you a walker," his mom says.

"I don't w…want a waa…wa…ker," comes the predictable

answer, and Rome sees that it's going to be a long couple of days. Edith refuses the couch and insists on lying down in her own bed, so they begin the stubborn schlep up another sixteen steps to the second floor.

When they finally have her tucked safely into bed for a nap, Rome escapes back to the front porch. The neighbourhood rises and falls on stony hills. This house, which he has known his whole life, sits almost at the top of the street, commanding a majestic view, though it's only a view of more suburban homes. In truth, the view he's taking in isn't just the local sights as they are now, but his own past, layered onto them like the exposed rock face on the highway. Rome sees his zaidie, long since dead, carefully setting up the sprinkler on the small lawn according to some mystical geometry of his own. He sees his father, out here on a break from the Passover seder, his face obscured by both the smoke of the cigarette and his own clouding breath on the cold, clear April evening. This is one of his earliest memories. His father, looming high above him, has long since disappeared into the mist, into mystery.

And Rome remembers being out here on a summer evening at thirteen, watching the shirtless skater boys roaring down the steep road. Their long hair and long, hairless torsos made him burn with desire, like he was standing recklessly close to the Canada Day fireworks as they went off, his flesh branded by the heat, afterimages dancing in his eyes.

At his mom's insistence, Rome has had his phone in airplane mode since they left the hospital. He could have turned it on once they arrived, but to tell the truth, he's scared of seeing more messages from Kai. Now he reconnects himself to his world, half-squinting his way to Discord, deliberately not noticing the rising numbers on his DMs. He spends the next half hour on scavenger hunt business. The group is operating well. Most of the people on his committees are older, and he's surprised himself by his ability to command their respect. It's something he learned from watching his mom, or maybe it's genetic.

If only he could find that "perfect" grand prize. It's ridiculous and narcissistic that he needs this piece of validation to feel good about himself, but he can't help it. As the neighbourhood buzzes quietly around him with the sound of kids, lawnmowers, and barking dogs, Rome imagines himself on the stage of the Masonic Temple at the end of SciCon, handing over this magical object to the winning team, the glorious culmination of months of preparation. He also imagines the crisp black suit he will wear and the glorious makeup he will achieve that day, the eyes based on Elizabeth Taylor's first entrance in *Cleopatra*. Goals.

His mom is on the phone when hunger sends him inside in search of food. He finds her in the kitchen, the only room in the house that isn't all dim lighting, heavy dark furniture, and thick brown rugs. The kitchen was modernized with colour and shine and artificial materials when he was a kid. It was supposed to be the beginning of a new era for the old house, but Zaidie's death brought the project to a halt. Susan waves at the makings of dinner on the counter, and Rome gets to work preparing the tuna salad sandwiches and heating the vegetable soup. He listens to her side of the conversation with the social worker: home care, how to apply to the provincial agency for a subsidy on the price of the walker, moving Edith to the ground-floor guest room rather than her bedroom at the top of the stairs. His mom is making lists. She is *always* making lists, checking off items one by one, the way Rome has with the scavenger hunt.

Susan leaves it up to him to get Edith back downstairs. Rome is on his bubbie's left side as they descend step by step. She has both hands on the rail and lowers herself onto each new stair with her left foot, twisting so that it takes most her weight, then straightening her stance before the next step. And thus they corkscrew their way down to the table, where she collapses into her chair, breathing heavily. Rome is startled to hear the word "shit" escape her previously pure lips.

He and his mom make small talk, putting off discussing the ways Edith's life will have to change forever, starting the very next day. Edith only gets involved when asked direct questions, and then answers monosyllabically. Too tired to try harder, Rome and Susan just let the conversation flow around her like she's a rock in the stream.

"You should go for a walk after dinner," Susan tells him. "Down to that park at the bottom of the street."

"Here in small-town Ontario?" Rome asks. "That's great until they surround me and play a traditional game of kick-the-fag."

"This isn't a small town, and you can't assume it's all bigots here."

"It's not Trinity Bellwoods Park either, Mom."

"Which is all drug dealers at night."

"No! Which is *everyone*. That's why cities are better. We're all freaks together. I don't feel safe here. You wouldn't understand."

"You're saying a woman doesn't understand not feeling safe on dark streets? Remind me to tell you what Take Back the Night marches were about."

They are surprised when Edith speaks up. "Back then, wa...asn't safe for J-jews to walk here at night. Some...t-t-times they attacked us. Long time a...go. Mama was so...wor...ried if we went...out, but we were...*mmm*. Y...oung. Brave."

Back on the front porch, in the long twilight of the June night, Rome finally reads through Kai's posts.

Kai: when was the last time we did anything together?

Kai: do you think about my feelings ever??

Kai: you get this weird look when you tell ppl This is my bf, Kai, like your saying Do you like my new shoes

Kai: WHY RU IGNORING ME?!!!

Kai: look i know about your bubbie sorry but pls just let me know ur seeing this

Kai: Rome?

Kai: seriously? Still nothing?

Kai: Rome should I be worried

Rome's chest has been tightening steadily as he scrolls through the messages. He types quickly:

Rome: I'm fine ttyl

The sounds of barking dogs, laughing kids, crickets, and birds have merged into a busy summer silence. Beneath it, he's sure he can hear his heart pounding. The ring of his phone shatters the air, and he almost fumbles the device down the stone steps.

"Hello!"

"Rome? What the fuck!"

"Kai! Are you a psychopath? Why are you calling me?"

"Oh, sorry. I thought I was your boyfriend or something. Guess I'm just a telemarketer."

"Shut up. You *are* my boyfriend. I mean we usually just text!" A middle-aged couple walking a fat cat on a bejewelled leash look up at him curiously. He pulls the phone tight to his ear and runs inside, passing Susan and Edith as they sort pills at the kitchen table, and slips into his bedroom. Tomorrow it will become Edith's, until she dies or moves out.

He slams the door harder than he meant to and throws himself onto the bed. "You're not the only person demanding my attention, Kai!"

"Oh my God, Rome, you're going to have to shut up really soon."

"If you want me to shut up, why are you even calling me?"

"No, *you* tell me why we're even a couple."

"Why? You read my essay on representation, didn't you? You claim you did. Queer people used to miss out on their whole adolescence. They didn't get to do the ordinary things teens do, like date and go to dances and learn about sex. And that's been linked to promiscuity in their twenties because they came out so late."

"What the fuck does that have to do with—"

"Listen! You and I, we *represent* something. When we walk through the school holding hands, we're an example to queer and straight kids alike!"

"So you go out with me because we represent something. Is that what you're saying?"

"Yes! I mean, no, not just that."

"Then what else? When we're alone, we have nothing to say to each other. And we don't have sex."

"Stop pressuring me to have sex, Kai!"

"Fuck you, I don't do that. I think we should break up, Rome."

Rome's chest tightens. "You don't mean that. Look, I'll do better. Tell me what would make me happy, and I'll do it."

"You'll do what makes me happy? Really? You don't mean that, Rome. Just be honest with yourself."

"So I was right. This *is* about sex! Maybe we *should* break up!"

He hits the disconnect button and immediately bursts into tears, like a water balloon hitting the pavement. He gets his breathing under control and stares at the screen, sure Kai will phone back. After two minutes of waiting, he blocks Kai's number and pulls a pillow over his face. Time passes, and then he's too sweaty and tosses the pillow across the room. It's fully dark now except for the screen of his phone. He scrolls Instagram for a while, then gets up and goes to the bathroom, where he checks the ruin of his mascara. He's probably stained the pillow, but he'll worry about that later. When he's presentable, he heads out to find his family.

They're in matching armchairs in the dark, heavy living room, where many sconces and floor lights cast a stifling glow.

His mom raises her head from her book, sees his red eyes, and knows instantly. "What happened?"

"Kai broke up with me."

This thaws the hardness that's frozen her face all day. "Oh, sweetheart…"

"Or I broke up with him. It's fine." He feels guilty making a play for sympathy when she's already so stressed. He *is* fine. He will be.

Edith's head is drooping, but she says, "L…love isn't eas…easy."

Susan stands up. "Mama, let's get you to bed. Come on, Rome."

They climb Everest again, and Rome hurries back downstairs as soon as Susan takes her mother to the bathroom, terrified he'll be asked to help with bathing or dressing duties. Wandering back to the living room, he spots something whose familiarity brings a stab of joy to his heart. There on the mantel is the porcelain dancer that fascinated him as a little boy.

She's barefoot, her long skirts flying in a twirl. The crocus blue of the dress is fading transparent in the gradient of time, but that somehow adds to the magic. It's a wonder the delicate statue survived his attempts to play with it as a child. How many times was it snatched from his greasy hands with a stern rebuke and replaced on its perch? So he had just twirled in front of it, emulating its grace, around and around in ecstasy until he grew dizzy and fell to the thick carpet.

As a child, he needed to drag a chair over to the mantel, but now he just reaches out and takes it, feels its antique weight, and has an inspiration. Is this the scavenger hunt prize he's been searching for? Would his bubbie even let him take it? He'll ask so nicely in the morning, when he's helped her change rooms. After everything he's done for her, she won't be able to refuse. With this plan in place, he finally feels a sense of closure to this train wreck of a day. It's all going to come together—Edith's health, his mom's stress, his new single status. It will all be fine. He takes the dancer with him to his room and undresses, jerks off thinking of anyone other than Kai, and falls asleep.

❖

Susan leaves right after breakfast to go pick up a walker. Rome is supposed to be rearranging the furniture in the guest bedroom according to his mom's new master plan, but he stays at the kitchen table to talk with Edith, figuring that has to be at least as valuable as the heavy lifting.

"Bubbie, when did you first meet my father?"

She's better today, more alert, though that somehow makes the effects of the stroke more apparent. On her left side, she is the grandmother he knows, but the right seems like a traitor to the cause. "Um...hmm. Sh...she brought him here. For...forthe weeknnd." She makes an ineffectual whistle and a rakish half-smile. "So...hands... some. They wrr jus twenny...one."

Rome laughs, but his mind is sorting through photographs in his head. He has so few images of the man to draw from. Now he tries to reconstruct this phantom as an object of desire, creeping himself out in the process. His father on the front porch, hidden by mist, saying something just beyond memory's reach.

"Was he in love with Mom?"

Edith has been leaning her chin on her left hand, and now uses both hands to push herself upright in the chair. A strand of grey frizz hangs across her face, and she is looking into the distance, into nowhere, through a closed door into the past. "Lo...oovvve," she sighs, as if that single word contained all the answer she could possibly give.

He's out on the porch again when his mom returns, and he heads down to the driveway to help her with the walker and groceries.

"That's a lot of stuff, Mom. Remember we're leaving tomorrow."

"I obviously can't go home yet, Rome. Not for a while."

"Mom! I have to get back to Toronto. There's only a few days until the convention."

"I know. And if that's what you want, you'll have to take the car back yourself. I can use Edith's Toyota. Leave first thing tomorrow, and stay in the same motel as on the way up."

Rome is speechless, his right hand bunching into the material of his Robyn T-shirt. His pride doesn't want him to admit he's scared, but his mom is the one he goes to when he is. "I can't do that on my own. It's too far, too much highway driving."

"I believe you *can* do the drive, Rome. You'll go the speed limit, get out at rest stops and go for a walk. You'll remind yourself you're a careful and competent driver."

"But I can't control everyone else!" He imagines some drifting drunk or someone incoherent with road rage slamming into him, sending the car into a fiery crash.

"Then stay here and let your friends run the scavenger hunt." Susan is looking at him with a steady gaze, neither intimidating nor cajoling, but offering him no honourable way to back out.

"You're right, I'll be fine." He doesn't believe it, but he has no choice. He has responsibilities to SciCon, as well as the family emergency they're living through.

"Here's your credit card," Susan says, pulling the magic piece of plastic from her wallet. He had carried it himself until a few too many spontaneous purchases had appeared on her monthly statement. He puts it away in his own wallet, feeling its power throbbing there. She continues, "If anything goes wrong, I'm one call away."

They get down to work moving Edith's room downstairs. When they're done, all sweaty and tired, Rome brings his bubbie in to see it. He grins at her, like she should be pleased, but her face is grim.

"Th…this is th' g-guest rooom. I'm not g-guesst. S'my house!"

He helps her to bed and she lies there, staring at the ceiling. Rome tries not to think of how he jerked off in this same bed not so long ago.

His mom brings them tea, and Rome stays to keep Edith company, doing scavenger hunt business and scrolling Instagram. He hasn't blocked Kai there yet. Seems Kai had breakfast at the Grapefruit Moon Diner with his uncle, posting slices of french toast glistening with syrup, now long devoured.

"Hey, Bubbie! You know your porcelain dancer? Can I have it? You know, for my scavenger hunt. It would be an amazing prize!"

He wonders if she is asleep, but then she says, "M…my." Is she telling him that no, it belongs to her? Has he offended her with the request, like he's robbing her tomb before she's even dead? But she continues, "My dansssrr. Yes, y…you always liked that. Take it."

She isn't at the table when Rome comes downstairs the next morning.

His mom says, "Edith's tired. She'll eat later. Are you all packed?"

"Yes." He is surprisingly hungry, eating two-thirds of the omelette Susan has made them, along with three fat slices of toast and an orange. After breakfast, he goes to say his goodbyes.

"I'll come up and visit soon, Bubbie."

"Who knows?" she answers, as if to a different, unspoken question. He puts an arm around her frail shoulders and kisses the grey hair, pulled back tight by his mom and clipped with a beautiful ceramic butterfly he also remembers playing with.

He grabs his little suitcase and his backpack, checks to make sure he has his phone and wallet, and heads down to the driveway, where his mother is already waiting. He is carrying the porcelain dancer in one hand.

"Did you ask Edith if you could take that?"

"She said it's fine."

Susan takes it from him and examines it with a critical gaze. "One day I noticed the eyes were painted crooked, and I could never unsee it after that."

Rome snatches the dancer back and examines the face for himself. Sure enough, the black semicircle of the left eye sits lower than the right, visibly off from the sculpted bump of the eyeball.

"Shit," he says, feeling some small piece of himself break off and fly away in the breeze.

"Why do you want it, anyway?"

"I don't. Take it back inside."

"I need to start going through all her stuff, start getting rid of the garbage. If we wait until the day she has to move, we'll have a hell of a job."

This casual announcement hits Rome in the chest like a punch. "Mom, don't! Just…just let her have what's left of her life. For a while, anyway, okay?" He feels tears rising, and he takes a big breath to stop them.

Susan shakes her head. "Hanging on to the past is just as exhausting, Rome." But at the same time, she reaches out to comfort him, pulling him into a hug, bringing his head down to her shoulder where he catches a whiff of Edith's favourite perfume. He's not the only one collecting bits of the past.

He's on the road by ten, reminding himself not to grip the wheel so tight and to relax into the seat instead of holding himself rigidly upright. He doesn't accelerate fast enough as he merges onto the Trans-Canada Highway, and a camper van leans on its horn and swings abruptly into the left lane to get around him. Blond faces glare at him as they pass, and he feels too Jewish, too gay, too urban. But soon he has the car zipping along smoothly at 100 km/h. The sun is sweet, and take-no-prisoners girl pop is blasting away his depression. Maybe this trip won't be so bad after all, he thinks.

As the road opens before him, he understands for the first time the joy of driving, the freedom promised in those bullshit ads where shiny SUVs zoom down empty mountain highways. In truth, you need to be this far from a real city to enjoy this kind of adventure. He is halfway through the first verse of "Little Boxes" before he realizes he's singing it over the dance break of an EDM remix. It's a song his bubbie taught him long ago on a long car drive. Where were they going? Montreal? Florida? His brain is pulling together disparate pieces of history, stringing them like pearls. Edith would teach him a melody, then tell him to hold tight to it as she sang the descant, floating above his boyish alto in her own breathy soprano. He would inevitably mess up, slip from the note, and she would start the song again with infinite patience, over and over until he heard the magic of harmony bloom like a spring garden.

While he's been with her in the last two days, he's tried hard to stay positive, to think of her as the same woman he's always known. But reality sets in with distance, and he doubts he'll ever sing with her again, wonders if she'll even be alive a year from now. "One stroke can lead to another," his mom said with heartless objectivity last night. "I just don't want you to get your hopes up."

Images of Edith flood his mind, suffuse his heart with choking sorrow. Laughter, song, but also shouts and accusations, hard truths desperate to stay hidden.

"Just leave me alone, Bubbie!"

"Something's wrong, Jerome, I can tell. Is someone at school giving you a hard time for—"

"No! It's nothing. And I'm called Rome now."

"Burdens need to be shared, Rome, or they break our backs."

But he couldn't speak. And if he had told her what was happening, would it have made a difference? Could she have stopped it? Him? Maybe. Or maybe other kids would have taken up the job, and Rome would have been screwed even worse. He was fourteen then. Just three years ago, but it seems a lifetime.

He stops for lunch at a small park overlooking a clear, still lake.

The roast beef sandwich his mom made him is perfect, with hot mustard and bean sprouts, but he wonders again if it isn't finally time to go vegan. Kai is vegan. Kai would tell him that with every bite of cow, he is devouring his own future. But it's so good! There's a sharp, clean breeze coming off the lake, a perfect antidote to the strong sun and the mosquitoes that swarmed him in the parking lot as soon as he left the car.

Back on the road, the signs tell him how far it is to each town, none of which Rome has ever heard of: Rowendale—5, Hopewell—16, Gunn Point—27. Why do people still live in these remote outposts, he wonders. What could be here that isn't better in a city? A sudden electronic squawk disrupts his playlist, which has been serving him a tasty lineup of dance pop, French hip-hop, and diva ballads. The music is replaced with what sounds like a podcast he doesn't remember downloading, volume turned up way too loud.

"He was alone when he died. Coroner said he'd been there for days. Neighbours complained about the smell, right?"

A second voice responds. *"I can imagine."*

"And it was all there. All the artwork he'd been making since his last show."

"So, like, twenty-five years of canvasses?"

"At least! Some of it half-eaten by the rats."

"What the hell?" Rome says, reaching to turn down the volume. But before he can, there's another squawk, followed by something even louder—blistering, throbbing, atonal guitars and a howling punk voice, shattered by too much high-decibel abuse: "STICK MY HEAD IN THE FIRE AND *SCREEEEAAAAAAMMMMM!!*"

The sound cuts dead, and it takes him a second to realize the engine has, too. The car is dropping speed rapidly. The driver behind him honks and pulls out to pass. Rome pushes the start button, but the only response is dashboard lights that blink an inscrutable semaphore. The power steering is dead, and he wrestles the car to the shoulder, straightening the wheels just before the car rolls into the deep ditch beside the highway.

He pulls up the emergency brake, then sits gripping the steering wheel and panting in the sudden silence. A truck flies by him, and the whole car shudders in its backdraft. He tries again to start the engine, but nothing happens. His heart pounds as he tries to think what to do next. He is on a thin strip of gravel between the highway and the ditch. Beyond it is a meadow, uncultivated unless the crop is big post-glacial boulders. The word "moraine" pops into his head from back in grade nine geography.

There are rules and procedures, but his head is all white noise. Okay, somewhere in the glove compartment is a manual and some kind of legal papers that prove he didn't steal the car. Not that they're in his name. If the cops show up, would he be able to prove he didn't steal it? Also, glove compartment? When was the last time *anyone* kept gloves in there?

The manual tells him nothing useful, and he's not about to pop the hood and poke around in the car's dirty innards. So he reaches for his phone, feeling like this is a rebuke to his manhood, especially since the only person he can think to call is his mother.

"I'm texting you a pic of my roadside assistance card. The membership and password are right there."

"I'm sorry about this, Mom."

"You didn't do anything wrong, Rome. Download the app. They can use GPS to get a fix on your location."

"Okay." The cell strength is mediocre, and his annoyance grows as the download creeps along. He asks, "Shouldn't you have had the car checked before we went so far from home, Susan?"

"Jerome!" Then softening. "Would you please not…" The sound of her holding her breath and letting it out slowly. "I have the occupational therapist here. Just handle it, okay? And call me when you get to the motel." And she hangs up on him. The silence returns, weightier than ever.

The app is ready, and he inputs the credentials. He clicks the chat icon, and a message comes up: How can I help you today, Susan? He doesn't bother to correct them. He describes the problem, wishing he had some more technical words so he didn't seem so clueless. GPS puts you just outside Rowendale. Is that right? He confirms this. Closest certified garage is in Hopewell. Please stand by while we put in the call.

Trucks blow by on the Trans-Canada, shaking the car like it's a seashell and they're the hungry seabirds hunting for lunch. He wonders if Kai has messaged him, then remembers he blocked him.

The app pings. A tow truck from Braxton Auto is on its way. ETA 20 minutes. Is your car safely out of traffic?

Rome types: On the shoulder

Can you put out safety cones, Susan?

I don't think we have those.

Then if it's safe to leave your car, open up the hood.

He's not about to step out on the driver's side while traffic is flying by, so he climbs over and out the passenger door. With the hood up and his hands filthy, he considers crossing the ditch to go exploring in the moraine. He'd jump from rock to rock like a kid and watch grasshoppers scatter. But he just sits with his feet dangling out the open passenger door, waiting at his post. Because he's responsible, practically an adult when he needs to be.

He's reviewing clue location posters from the graphic design committee when the tow truck arrives and pulls in ahead of him. It's weighty and greasy and means business. The driver hops out and checks something on his phone. Rome imagines what a small-town grease monkey might make of his makeup, so he puts on his sunglasses and braces himself for the encounter.

"Hey," the kid says, approaching. "I'm Lyn from Braxton Auto. I'm guessing you're not Susan?" He's blond, face cute in a bland way, though looking very good in the tight jeans.

"She's my mom."

"You're paying through the Roadside app, so it doesn't really matter. Go sit in the truck while I hook up your car. We'll be out of here in no time."

Rome watches Lyn at work. He's probably not much older than Rome, but his competence makes him seem a lot more adult. Lyn hops in beside him and slides onto the highway with practiced nonchalance. Rome panics at the thought of having to make small talk, so he sticks in his earbuds and cranks the tunes. He knows he's being rude, but it's better than saying something utterly stupid or facing down the boy's undoubted prejudices. Still, he does get a thrill from Lyn's masculine presence beside him. There's a Pavlovian reaction to a mechanic, deeply ingrained from porn.

They cross a sturdy bridge over a river, only a hint of the dark water below visible from where he's sitting. Just before the bridge, a sign reads: "Welcome to Hopewell. Well North, Well-Being."

"What does that mean, anyway?" Rome asks out loud, realizing he's accidentally started a conversation. Annoyed with himself, he removes his earbuds.

"I don't know," Lyn says as he takes a left onto a smaller road. "Something town council came up with. I would have written it different."

"Like what?"

"'Hopewell: Something Must Have Brought You Here.'"

"You mean like, 'Everybody has to be somewhere'?"

Lyn laughs. "Sort of. I don't know. The old-timers say that Hopewell has a way of giving people what they need. People see things here, get intuitions, turn their lives around. So they say."

Rome is intrigued by this. He likes the idea of a town that takes care of you. "Do you believe it?"

"Not sure. Now that we've graduated, my friends are all leaving, but I think I'm going to stick it out."

The conversation is veering into the personal, and Rome doesn't want to start answering questions about himself. So he gives Lyn a noncommittal grunt of acknowledgement and puts the earbuds back in. As they head north, the town emerges around him, first in widely spaced houses, then a gas station and other small businesses. He sees the sign for Braxton Auto. Lyn backs into the parking lot, expertly delivering Rome's car to the open garage door.

Lyn directs him to the outer office where a woman in her forties stands behind the desk, looking through a car magazine. She checks the status of Susan's account on her computer, goes into the auto shop to consult with Lyn, and returns.

"What time do you close?" Rome asks her.

"Six o'clock tonight."

Rome does the math. He'd get into Toronto after two in the morning, with hours of highway driving in the dark. Then the woman says, "But your car's probably not going to be ready today."

"Tomorrow afternoon, I'm guessing," Lyn calls through the door, mentioning various auto parts and their particular disruptions, none of which means anything to Rome.

"But what am I supposed to do until then?" Rome can hear the whine in his voice and tries to control himself. "I mean, where do I stay?"

"I could drive you to the motel just up Highway 11, but you want my advice? Stay at the Honeyrose B&B on Horace Road. Bit more expensive, but it's just off Main Street, right in the heart of town, close to all the sights."

Rome scoffs silently at the idea that Hopewell might have any sights worth seeing, but she is already writing the address and drawing a little map on a thick cream-coloured card, a little smaller than a standard postcard.

"Here you go. Five-minute walk. Tell Candace that Sloan sent you."

As Rome steps outside, he makes the bell tinkle and rolls his eyes at the cutesy small-town affectation. Still, if he's stuck doing the Hopewell Experience, he shouldn't complain about it. He looks at the hand-drawn map and orients himself. Flipping the card over, he sees, written in a bold, decorative serif font, "Hopewell: Decent and Kind." *How many mottos does one town need?*

It's a beautiful afternoon, just this side of too hot. Calm and clear, the only clouds in the sky are artfully decorative and unthreatening. Rome walks up the hill, his suitcase rolling beside him like an obedient dog, and hangs a right onto Main Street. He immediately knows this stretch for the tourist bait it is. There's the ice cream stand, the souvenirs shop, and One Man's Treasure, the inevitable antiques and curios emporium, along with Tireless Wireless, where you replace your lost charger cable and earbuds, or buy a raccoon-themed phone case.

At least the shops are not just international chains, other than the 7-Eleven, and everything is well-maintained and not too tacky. Hopewell has gained another point on his Yelp review. However, restaurant options seem few. Sketchy Italian and Chinese, and across from the auto shop, Softshoe, which bills itself as a "classic diner" and might be his best bet.

It being a Wednesday afternoon and not quite tourist season, hardly anyone is around. He sits at a picnic bench under the cool trees of the neat public park and texts his mom. **Stuck in Hopewell until tomorrow. Staying at B&B. If you don't hear from me, I died of boredom.** He was going to write I was murdered by small-town phobes, but Hopewell has charmed him, and he doesn't have the energy to resist its charms.

She texts back a minute later: Buy yourself a good dinner and breakfast. Surprise vacation! Reward for finishing exams.

"Not that we've seen my grades yet," he says to a chickadee that has landed on the far side of the bench. The bird flies off.

Horace Road is a left turn off Main Street between the park and the electronics store. The Honeyrose Bed & Breakfast at number twenty-five turns out to be a large and neatly renovated house, a little too small to be called a mansion. There's a plaque from the Hopewell Historical Society providing a lot of information on Milton Horace and all the trees he knocked down to get rich and carve out "a home in the uninhabited wilderness."

Another tinkly bell announces his entrance, and after he stands a bit in a foyer stuffed with overstuffed antique furniture, a woman's voice calls out musically, "One minute!"

She enters with her orange curls partly covered by a polka-dot bandana, tied in the front like Rosie the Riveter. She wears a denim work apron full of tools tied over her jeans and yellow rose-print blouse.

"I'm so sorry to keep you waiting. I'm putting up a shelf in the dining room and finding out more than I want to know about the state of decay in the west wall." She lifts a section of the front desk and gets in behind the counter. "Hello, I'm Candace, owner and chief handyman." She laughs at her joke. "How can I help you, young man?"

"I need a room," Rome says, and as if he's required to explain himself further, "My car broke down on the highway."

"Oh dear, what an adventure. Well, you're in luck. We're full up this coming weekend, but if you just need a night or two—"

"Just one night," he says quickly, like she's trying to trick him into moving to Hopewell. He passes over his credit card, remembering he should have asked about the price first, feeling like now it's too late.

"Well, I have a lovely room for you. Second floor, beautiful view of the Horace Gardens. Won Best Horticultural Design in Barstow County in 2003 *and* 2006."

"Uh, I don't know anything about gardens, but it sounds nice." She hands him a paper to sign, and he can basically see nothing, so he takes off his sunglasses. The woman tilts her head to examine his makeup, and Rome is really annoyed with it being a big deal. It's just some eyeliner, the subtlest hint of lavender shadow and a bit of mascara. *Fuck.*

"From Toronto, eh?" she asks, like she can guess that because of his big ol' faggotry. Then he remembers he just wrote down his address for her. He determines to work on not expecting the worst from people. She tucks away his registration in a drawer. "Well, Jerome, you've picked the loveliest time of year for your visit. Sun's not setting until after nine tonight."

"Cool, but I have work to do now. What's the wi-fi password?"

"Sorry, internet's out until Friday. Something to do with laying new fibre." Rome gawps like he's been slapped. If Candace notices this, she ignores it like a pro. "Let me show you to your room."

He tries, too late, to grab his suitcase, but she wins the contest, probably determined to keep him from bolting despite the prehistoric state of connectivity. He follows her up the stairs, where she opens the door with a flourish. The room also has no television. He curses himself for not taking the garage guy's offer to drive him to that motel on the highway. He imagines robust wi-fi, a TV on which he'd watch shit like soap operas and game shows. They probably even have a corny vending machine with deeply Canadian oddities he hasn't eaten since childhood.

But as Candace leaves him to "get back to the grind," he calms himself down and begins to appreciate the beauty of the room, with its exposed beams, actual art on the walls, queen-sized bed with frilly covers, and a fireplace. He opens a complimentary bottle of local ginger beer, pours it into a cut glass tumbler, and sits himself at the dark wood desk in front of the big window. The gardens, he has to admit, are beautiful, full of spring flowers he can't name and a bed of roses in bloom.

His phone rings and he checks the display. SUSAN. He declines and texts: **Sorry just heading out ttyl**. The lie makes him feel bad for a moment, but he wants to fly solo, not feel like his mom is pulling the strings. He opens up Discord.

Discord Server: scavengers
#Prize Group

Done_and_dusted03
Picked up hunt stickers from printers

rome_in_a_day
Did we go with 100 or 500?

Done_and_dusted03
500

rome_in_a_day
Then put them on everything! Posters, mini-prize boxes. Glow-up the whole convention!!!

Truth be told, sitting in his well-appointed room, handing out assignments and orders, he feels pretty damn grown up. But by five o'clock, his attention is wandering. There's a boy and girl, maybe fifteen, making out in the shadowed bushes in the garden. After she slaps the boy's hand off her breasts for the second time, the girl storms out of the garden. The boy stands there red-faced, kicking divots out of the award-winning lawn. Rome reaches back into the shopping bag on the chair beside him and realizes he's finished off all the snacks his mom packed for the trip. He's not hungry now, but a visit to that diner will be a necessity.

He could lie down on the bed until he's hungry again and watch videos on his phone, but without wi-fi, he'll blow through his data too fast. He wishes for the thousandth time his mom would give him unlimited. There's nothing for it but to go outside and "do" Hopewell. He changes into a wine-coloured polo and puts his semi-shiny blazer over it. He touches up his makeup, decides to dare a rich plum lipstick, and heads downstairs.

Candace is at the front desk with an old-fashioned calculator, adding figures from piles of receipts that surround her. "Well, you look smart. Is the room okay?"

"Yeah, thanks, I like it. Do you run the B&B all by yourself?"

"I have two students starting tomorrow as summer staff, but otherwise, yes. Made the most of my divorce settlement and bought this place. And if I work twenty-four hours a day, I can almost make it pay!" She gives a little barking laugh.

Candace reminds him of his bubbie, Rome decides, a pioneer woman of the north. "Okay," he says. "I'm going to check out the town a bit."

"Take a map," she says, pointing with her chin at a pile of colourful sheets on the corner of the desk as she resumes adding numbers. "It has everything on it, as long as you don't stray too far from Main Street. If you do want to go farther, you can park in the east lot out by the municipal building."

"Car's broken?" he reminds her, as he takes the cartoon-bright map and folds it into a jacket pocket.

"Oh right, then maybe you'd like one of our bicycles." She opens her drawer and pulls out another of the cream "decent and kind" postcards. She copies a series of numbers from a note behind the counter and hands over the card. "This is the combination for bike #4. They're all parked just behind the building."

"What are those cards anyway?" Rome asks. "They had them at the garage, too."

"Oh, they just discovered *boxes* of them in the basement of the old city hall. They were printed in the 1930s, according to the town archivist."

He takes the card. "Thanks." But when he puts it in his jacket pocket beside his room key and the map, he realizes he's forgotten his phone. "Be right back."

He finds his phone sitting on the bathroom sink, pockets it, and turns on his heel to leave again. But when he turns for a last look at the room, he notices something in the middle of the dark desk. It's another of the cream cards, positioned dead centre, like he swears if he had a ruler to check, it would be perfect.

"Where did that...?" It couldn't have been Candace who put it there, and there's no one else in the building. This artifact of the past stares at him, proclaiming the virtues of Hopewell in bold but decorative serif font. Something goes *wooooooo* in his chest as he turns it over.

Find Arch-ie and Fir-onica.
Betty'll be glad you saw it.

The text is written in the same font as the motto, but the ink is a plummy purple. Rome stares, the hairs on his neck standing up because he recognizes this for what it is. It's a clue from a scavenger hunt. But who left it for him? Whose hunt is this?

"Taking a bike?" Candace inquires as he passes through the lobby.

"Thanks, yeah," he says, not slowing down.

The bikes are locked to a wooden frame with thin coils and flimsy locks that wouldn't slow down a Toronto thief for a second. Rome unlocks #4 and rides the blue hybrid out of the driveway onto Horace Road. The seat is too high, and he has to point his toes at the bottom of each circuit. He could stop and adjust it, but his brain is whirling with the clue. *Arch-ie and Fir-onica.* It means nothing to him now, but he's used to that feeling, knows not to let it get him down.

He rides a circuit around Main Street, dismounting in front of the antique and gift shop. The grinning beaver figurines with their Toronto Raptors sweaters are enough to make him decide to give the store a pass. Maybe tomorrow morning, if he's run out of other attractions by then. Two buildings over, he finds the Hopewell Historical Society with a big sign advertising a photo exhibit: "Canada Day in the Boom Years."

He locks the bike to a garbage can featuring big friendly eyes above its gaping maw and a word balloon saying, "I'm hungry for your litter!" and goes inside, reaching for his wallet as he approaches the teenager at the counter, who pulls out one earbud, annoyed.

"How much is the exhibit?"

She has a bad bleach job and poorly applied eyeliner but looks at him like *he's* from the moon. "It's free," she says with a disgusted shake of her head and returns to scrolling her Tik-Tok. He wants to take a picture of her scrolling and post it to his own Insta with the caption *Local wildlife.*

The photographs are from Hopewell's 1952 celebration of Dominion Day, as Canada Day was then known. Some dignitaries stand onstage in summer suits, their wives in frilly summer dresses over lots of foundation garments. There's a brass band, the handwritten caption reading, "The Maple Leaf Forever!!" Two exclamation marks. Portraits of individual family groups posed casually around their picnic tables, the older generation with stony faces because in their day, photography was serious business.

Scott, McDonald, Devon, Wright—a whole world of Anglos

with no Berkowitzes, Sabatinis, or Cheungs in sight. One family with strong, dark features is labelled LeBeau, and Rome wonders if maybe they're Indigenous. Possibly Métis. Either to confirm or contradict, the next picture is a troupe of First Nations dancers in ceremonial garb doing a circle dance. The caption reads, "Local Indians performing a traditional dance of blessing for our patriotic day." He can't help but think if he was curating this exhibit, he would have pointed out the blatant colonialism and included an Indigenous perspective.

He walks back out into the early evening sunshine and thinks about his bubbie. How could they have done it, her and Zaidie and the other Jews? How could they survive up here in a land of *goyim*, without delis, synagogues, or culture? He knows they had kosher food shipped in from Toronto, but was that really enough to offset the feeling of being an eternal outsider? The idea makes him shiver, and he leaves the gallery to stand for a while in the sunshine. Across the park, a series of sculptures carved out of tree stumps lines the road. Animal figures, dancers, an angular sun rising over rocky hills. Having been practically raised in museums, Rome thinks to look for signage and finds it at the end of the row, a metal plaque bolted to a low boulder:

The ice storm of 1998 caused the tragic loss of almost thirty percent of Hopewell's tree stock. Local sculptor Maud Moreau used her chainsaw artistry to carve these works from the stumps of the majestic Manitoba maples that used to line Main Street.

Rome looks up, imagining the former cathedral of trees, and figures he must resemble the gawking tourists in Toronto, craning their necks upward at the glass towers. He climbs back on bike #4 and rides off, heading east along Main Street, picking up speed once he's left the tourist centre where Main transforms into the even less evocatively named County Road 72. More houses on generous properties, new suburban monstrosities standing beside older buildings that wear their decades and layers of paint like a comfortable old coat. The road has a good downward slope, and he is riding faster and faster, shaking off two days of tension in his exertion.

Beyond the neighbourhood, the boreal forest reasserts itself. Kai is into trees and Rome recognizes species he was forced to learn on their walks through High Park: spruce, birch, aspen, poplar, fir…

Fir. *Fir-onica.* He is passing a stand of fir trees, looking like an overambitious Christmas display, when he sees the arch. *Arch-ie and Fir-onica.* He squeezes the brakes, and #4 comes to a sudden stop. The curved entrance cut through the wall of green marks the start of a forest trail. Rome dismounts, leaves the hot pavement, and pushes his bike uphill along a path of cedar chips into the forest's cool, dark embrace. He raises his sunglasses to his forehead just as the mosquitoes, waiting in ambush, descend. They buzz a monotonous song in his ear as he swats at the back of his neck, pushing the bike faster as if that will stop them.

After a couple of minutes, the path turns and then almost immediately opens into a small clearing carpeted with pine needles. At its centre is a wide flat rock, red stone veined with black, sparkling highlights of mica that accent its face like glitter. The base of the rock is trimmed with green and black moss, and Rome wonders how long humans have gathered here. It is a natural place of worship, a central stage for ritual, from which the trees stand back in respect. Maybe in the past, animals were blessed and dressed for sacrifice here. But now what stands on this natural altar is a metal sculpture.

The sculpture is both impressive and crude. More than a metre high, its central structure must have started life as some piece of heavy factory equipment, with purposeful curves and tracks for rotating gears. Onto this solid construction, stars and moons of shining metal have been welded, a constellation hanging above a bare northern hill. On the top, under this shiny night sky, stands a tarnished silver bear facing off against a hockey player who was probably plucked from some high school MVP award. The copper sheen of the welds is sloppy but still beautiful against the grey and chrome, like the tears of a golden god. Rome pushes his bike slowly around the altar. The sculpture, for all its raw execution, moves him, like he can feel something of the unknown sculptor's soul.

But this place of worship has been desecrated. Cigarette butts, beer and pop cans, condoms and chip wrappers litter the clearing. Across the flat top of the ancient rock, tags and dick pictographs have been spray-painted, including one that makes his stomach lurch: INDIAN TOYLET. He feels his anger rise, but also his fear. This place of peace has transformed in a moment to one of menace. Surprisingly, the sculpture itself has been largely left untouched. Perhaps this is superstitious caution—it's one thing to desecrate the temple, another to attack the god on the altar. Rome wishes he could stay and clean the space, apologize to the sculptor, to the ground, to the trees.

The mosquitoes renew their attack, taking stinging drinks from his neck and hands. It's time to go back. He takes hold of the handlebars and looks back the way he came, only to find a boy standing on the path leading back to County Road 72. He's twenty at most, blond fuzz under a backward baseball cap, T-shirt that only flirts with his waist, offering tantalizing glimpses of skin. Slender but worked out, with well-defined arms, he sports a tattoo on his forearm, the hyper-muscled manga character, Berserk.

"Hey," the boy says. "What do we have here? All makeup and high fashion, eh? You a celebrity from Toronto or something?" Impressed by his own joke, the boy laughs, executing a series of poses like he's in a fashion shoot. Rome's heart is already pounding, and he's glad to have the sculpture between him and this intruder. He wants to put his sunglasses back in place, but it's already dark in the clearing, and he needs his vision if escape becomes necessary.

"I'm just visiting," Rome says, voice shaking despite his best intentions. He should look around for other escape routes, but he is unable to take his eyes from the imminent threat, and taking out his phone might provoke the boy to attack.

"Maybe you're one of those transgenders. Do I call you 'lady' or 'bro'?"

"I'm not trans," Rome says and knows he's a bad ally. The boy looks so much like that other one, Rome thinks. The other one, but grown up a few years. Or is it just the hatred in the eyes they share? "Listen," Rome tells him. "I don't want trouble. I'm just going to…go."

The boy takes just one small step off the path and waves Rome through. "Sure, go ahead, tourist lady boy. Glad to have you here in Hopewell."

Rome takes a deep breath. Is he really going to just walk past the kid and back up the path? It's a test of will. If he can manage to show he's not scared, he'll be allowed to pass. He takes a fast look around the clearing, and sees that there is another path, deeper into the woods. But as his eyes return to the blond kid, he sees another of the antique cream cards sitting right there on the altar in front of him. *Decent and kind.* Its motto mocks him. But above the printed text, with stunning obviousness, it says "Clue" in the same purple ink as the previous message.

A loud rustling in the trees draws his focus back to the danger at hand. Two more boys have broken into the clearing. One, with a heavy build and a Megadeth T-shirt, has a joint in his hand.

"Xander! You take my fucking lighter?"

"Hey, who's that?" says the third kid, who has long blond hair and is dressed in all black with unlaced construction boots.

"Transgender influencer from Toronto," says the first kid, whose name is apparently Xander. "Posing with the toilet for his Instagram. Want to take a selfie with us, lady?" Xander asks, taking a step forward.

"I'm good," Rome replies with as much nonchalance as he can muster. He takes a breath, and then in one motion, he grabs the clue, turns the bike, and runs down the new path away from the kids. He hops onto the bike and rockets forward over the uneven ground, almost plowing into a tree before he gets himself under control. He doesn't look back to see if they're following.

The path is climbing, and Rome stands on the pedals to push himself uphill and not lose speed. The ground levels out at a narrow pedestrian bridge, the bike's tires juddering over the boards. Rome looks down at the meagre creek below. Then he's across the bridge, and the path is descending as steeply as it rose, the bike accelerating until he feels well beyond control. Bumping over a little ditch, he bites his lip hard, but then he's clear of the forest and on another paved road. In his panic, he isn't sure which way to go. But he forces himself to think; Main Street must be to the right, so he rides on.

The road follows a broad curve, and before he completely loses sight of the entrance to the forest path, he pulls to a stop and peers back. The boys are not chasing him. Rome tastes blood from his cut lip and spits. The clue is under his sweating palm, half-crushed around the handlebar. He pockets it without reading the message. A breeze is coming down the road, and it cools his sweat. His mosquito bites itch.

It's evening, though the sun hasn't set. It casts long, oblique shadows into the forest, playing light and dark hard against each other. Set back in the brush on the far side of the road is a hut of wood and sheet metal. A figure is sitting on the shadowed porch, long legs in tight jeans the only part of him in the light. Smoke rises around his head—the exhalation of a vape. Rome smells its sweet tang, and his heart quickens again.

"Is this the way back to Main Street?" he calls, though he's not sure why he's drawing more attention to himself.

"Uh-huh," says the guy. His voice is gruff, but he sounds young. Rome has no good response to this monosyllabic reply, but he stands still for many seconds, trying to see through the obscurity that surrounds the mysterious figure. He turns away and pushes off, biking back to town as fast as he can, over another bridge and back to the security of tacky gift shops and a diner meal.

"Stupid car. Stupid small town," he yells into the wind as he rides, but then he remembers the clue in his pocket and wonders who's actually in charge of his fate.

"Hopewell has a way of giving people what they need." That's what the tow truck guy said.

Rome stops at the 7-Eleven to buy mosquito repellent, itch cream, and on impulse, a tacky forest-green fishing T-shirt ("Show us your bass!") that he knows will crack up his best friend, Stella, who has an appetite for horrible kitsch. He loves having his credit card back. He rides back to the B&B, locks up the bike, and returns to his room to clean up. By the time he walks back to Main Street, his equanimity has returned. Hopewell is again a gracious spot on the northern map, and with his makeup reapplied, Rome feels like he is *representing* to its inhabitants.

"Do you have a vegan menu?" he asks the server at the Softshoe Diner.

"You could order a tuna salad."

He frowns. "Maybe I'll just get a burger and fries...or what do you recommend?"

"Everyone loves the grilled cheese with special condiments."

"Yeah, that. And orange juice and water. And...the wi-fi password?"

"It's shoeshoe87, all lowercase, no spaces."

It's only when his food arrives that Rome puts away his phone, takes the crumpled clue from his pocket, and puts it on the table. As he chews his grilled cheese, he glares at the front of the card, like turning it over would be admitting he's fine with whatever supernatural shit this is. But the card just sits there patiently, as if saying, "I've been in a basement for eighty-five years. I ain't getting all worked up over the likes of you." He turns it over:

Hiding in the smoke, armoured by the galvanized,
Peek inside and find Sir Prize.

A shiver moves through Rome. His vision blurs, and he feels like his head is moving in one direction and his chest another. It only lasts a second, and then he's fully back in the clatter and shine of the diner. And he's annoyed. Because he's already solved the riddle, and he wants more than anything to go back right away and see if he's right. But he is also tired and overwhelmed. His bubbie is sick, he's far from home, and he was just threatened by homophobes in the goddamned forest.

"Look, Hopewell," he complains. "I didn't sign up for this woo-woo."

The server, passing by with a tray full of beers and nachos, says, "Is there a problem with your order?"

He blushes. "No! It's really good. I have...other problems."

And it's true. The grilled cheese is excellent.

CHAPTER TWO

Discord Server: scavengers
#nitty-gritty_committee

betrayed_by_jo
We need you here. Costa is having anxiety attacks

rome_in_a_day
I'm leaving today! Don't panic. We got this!

Rome is seated at the desk by the open window, enveloped in the fluffy white bathrobe he found hanging in the closet. He sips coffee from the room's coffee maker out of a hand-thrown mug and listens to the birds sing. He luxuriates.

Last night, he crashed hard as soon as he returned from the diner and then woke up stupid-early this morning, disoriented, his phone under him, digging into his side. He took a long, hot shower and wiped the mirror to take wet hair selfies. He even took a nude or seven, but erased them immediately.

Rome sips his coffee and uploads the best of the SFW selfies. *Living the good life in Northern Ontario*, reads his caption.

His mom must have notifications on for his posts, because she immediately texts him. **Sleep well? Edith had a restless night, but we're okay. Don't worry.**

Rome frowns. At least Susan got the message that she shouldn't phone. But maybe he should phone her? No. Not until he gets back to

Toronto. This day is his, and he's going to enjoy it. His eyes wander back to the clue, lying curled and crumpled on the desk beside him. He reads it again, though he has it memorized. It's obviously about the guy he saw on the porch of the metal shed last night, vaping up a major cloud.

He could bike right over and see what's up. Maybe he'd find another clue and another beyond that. Rome feels the familiar tug of the hunt. Hopewell is pulling at him like a new puppy. But why him? Maybe those cream notes came to light after all these decades precisely because he was coming to town. *I'm special.*

But still, he doesn't want some random, northern town to think he's a pushover. "Look, I'm staying here at the B&B," he says out loud. "My car will be ready this afternoon. Until then, I'm just going to enjoy the room and the garden, and not play your stupid games." Outside the window in the buildings and the trees, Hopewell does not reply.

If he's honest with himself, he's scared of running into Xander and his thuggy buddies. On the other hand, he's damned if homophobic punks are going to make him hide like a child. Did his bubbie and zaidie and the rest of the Jews hide every night in their northern diaspora? No, they did not.

So yeah, he'll check out the clue and see where it leads. Still, a little caution never hurt. Rome combs his hair as flat as the curls will allow and puts in a minimum of product. He applies not a spot of makeup to his scrubbed face and dons the bass-fishing T-shirt to better fit in with local tastes. Luckily, his rose-coloured, 60s-cut shorts complement the shirt and bisect his thighs attractively. There's no reason rural can't mean stylish. He applies bug spray, sets his black backpack casually over one shoulder, and assesses himself in the room's full-length antique mirror. He is as incognito as he can go. But is this a betrayal of his values?

"Stop thinking so much," he says out loud and heads for the door.

Downstairs in the sitting room, he wolfs down the complimentary breakfast, filling a bowl with granola and raspberry yogurt, following it with an apple, an amazing cheese danish, and another cup of coffee, though he's already buzzing from the first.

"Check-out is at noon, Jerome," Candace reminds him as he passes through the foyer. She is sitting in a wingback chair, talking to two young people who must be the summer help getting oriented for their first day. The boy is beautiful, with flowing black curls and a brown, South Asian face that opens in a friendly smile at his approach.

"I know," Rome tells Candace. "I'll be back before then." He steps into the sunshine, realizing he had been so preoccupied with the beautiful boy, he has no idea what the girl even looked like. Why does being horny have to make him a misogynist?

He unlocks bike #4 and takes the time to adjust its seat to a better height. He could check if another of the small fleet might be better, but he feels loyalty to this bike. Good ol' #4 has already gotten him through danger and adventure, and adjusting its seat makes him feel like a knight greeting his steed at dawn, passing it the apple he pocketed on his way through the castle's kitchens.

It's another beautiful day as he as turns off Horace Road back onto Main Street. The antique clock in the square reads nine o'clock and Hopewell is just waking up. Sandwich boards open in front of stores, awnings in mauve and aqua crank into position. Rome does a circle of the square, not yet ready to commit to his quest, and stops in front of the real estate office. He dismounts and pops his bike up onto the sidewalk. There are six or seven properties for sale, from mock mansions to '70s ranch-style houses to empty lots. He's not quite sure what the point is of a sales picture of an unmowed field.

The ubiquitous cutesy bell tinkles as the real estate agent steps out. He's around thirty, with an unfortunate retro hairstyle, and he's wearing black pants and a baby blue blazer, like he's a cater waiter.

"Thinking of getting into the market?" the agent asks.

Is the guy making fun of him? Does he really think Rome is looking to buy a house? He decides to play along. "Yeah, I might. Just graduated from Cambrian College. Art and Design." He is stealing the life story from Stella's older brother, who was a queer mentor to Rome when he was just coming out.

"And ready to buy a home already. Impressive!" Maybe the guy is trying to pick him up. Some old creep who goes for teens. The idea makes him instantly self-conscious, but he also imagines the guy taking him out for dinner at the Italian place, giving him wine, and then driving him back to his apartment, where…stuff happens.

"Maybe I'll just rent."

"I'm not handling too many rentals at the moment." He points to the other side of the window display where the only picture is a squat brown apartment building under a sky that looks like permanent November. "One bedroom. North of the creek, but not too bad for someone at your stage of their life. Strip mall nearby, Sobey's Supermarket, not too close to the trailer park." Rome notes the snobbery in the man's voice.

He wants to test the guy, ask him about the local queer community, but that might just invite more creepy come-ons. As he stands there, pretending to look at the apartment listing, a brown Mercedes pulls up to the curb, and the agent drops him like they've never met.

"Mr. Milgrom! Glad to see you, sir. Come on in. My secretary has all the paperwork." The bell tinkles, and the two men disappear inside, the agent not even giving Rome a backward look. It's as if Hopewell is punking him for not getting on with his mission.

"Fine," he says, tightening his backpack straps and mounting his bike. He bumps off the sidewalk with his ass held high. The weather is changing as he rides east on Main. What was a still, blue early morning is turning breezy, the wind bringing in grey clouds from the north.

Soon Rome has veered off County Road 72 onto the road he followed back last night. Old Quarry Road, it's called. He stops on the bridge to watch the creek as it splashes below, then takes out the crumpled cream card and stares at the clue again. A visceral memory of Xander and his friends shakes Rome. In truth, nothing terrible happened. Maybe they would have hurt him, but maybe they were just messing around with the kid from the big city. Still, he can't help being reminded of an earlier time when his life was so bad, he sometimes wanted to end it.

Life is a heavy chain made of these wet links, slurping and slapping on the ground behind us as we drag ourselves forward. Scavenger hunts are also chains, but they extend into the future clue by clue, promising a prize for those who follow. Is he heading now for disaster or prize? Prize, says the clue. He rides on.

The morning sun is falling across the face of the shed as he rides up the short driveway. Shed isn't the right word. It's more substantial than that, but it's not quite a house either. A shack, maybe? It is somehow both DIY and professional. The wood frame construction with its walls of rippled blue steel is square and symmetrical, well built. But it has no windows, at least not on this side, so how could it be a home? Rome leans the bike against a tree and cautiously explores. The debris in the yard is made up of expected things like food wrappers, empty propane tanks, greasy rags, and a broken flip phone, and the more esoteric, such as a copy of J.D. Salinger's *Nine Stories* torn in half and a gaudy gold picture frame, with scraps of the former art still clinging to the corners.

Rome climbs three steps to the porch with as much stealth as he can manage. He stands and listens with all his sinews. Perceiving no movement in the shack, he carefully tries the doorknob of the heavy steel door. The knob won't turn, and besides, there's a sturdy deadbolt above it. Frustration overcoming caution, he hops down the steps and heads around to the back. The yard there is shaded by tall trees. The square of tamped earth in the centre, oil-stained a dark umber, is clearly a parking place. Surrounding it is industrial debris, but really *interesting* industrial debris—pieces of heavy machinery, some recognizable as truck engine parts, bits of what must be an old printing press with a big hand crank. Taken out of context, their curves are a dance of grace and sensuality, the shiny scratches in the gun-grey metal and wine-rich rust that read like hieroglyphs. The pieces echo the desecrated altarpiece in the woods.

While looking over his shoulder for the hundredth time, he notices that this side of the shack does indeed have a window, a single cyclopean eye of glass, high off the ground. If there was a ladder in the yard, he could climb up and peek inside. The window is just big enough for a skinny person to escape out of, which is, admittedly, a weird way to measure its size. But that's what this strange cabin out in the woods looks like: a serial killer's death house. Inside, corpses are piled five high. Or maybe there's a miniature maze lined with razor traps. He pictures a man with pointed metal teeth, a swastika tattooed on his forehead, rasping through a tracheostomy amplifier: "You have twelve minutes to solve the maze before I release the gas, Jew."

Is such a man looking at him even now through the dark window?

Rome lectures himself out loud again. "You're being an idiot, Rome Epstein." He'll just take some artistic pics of the industrial debris and post them to his Insta with a clever caption about accidental art. Except when he reaches for his phone, it isn't in his pocket. He pulls off his backpack and roots through its compartments, but he has forgotten the device, probably on the bathroom sink, just like yesterday. Without his phone, he has no way to call for help. He feels untethered, floating alone and helpless in the universe. Cursing loudly, then casting a nervous glance at the high window, Rome skulks back out to the front of the cabin.

He takes hold of the bike's handlebars and prepares to leave. But he's come this far… He marches up the steps and knocks loudly on the metal door, which thuds like a dull bell. Silence. Frustrated, he takes the clue card from the pocket of his backpack and checks it again, front and back, in case he's missed anything. He speaks the text out loud like it's a door-opening spell. Nothing.

"What else do you want me to do?" he shouts at the card, then up at the trees, to Hopewell itself. "*What?*"

The red pickup truck appears around the curve of the road so suddenly, he has no chance to vacate the porch and hide. Rome is not surprised when it pulls into the driveway and right up to him. The truck is dinged up, but clean, and it jerks to a stop in a little cloud of road dust. As the driver's window rolls down, Rome notices a faded sticker of Disney's Hunchback affixed to the side mirror.

The driver is a boy his own age—long face fringed by unruly dark brown hair that has just enough wave to make it bounce with the boy's movements. His pointy jaw is tight, and sparse islands of facial hair need shaving. The eyes above the ski slope nose, a brown so dark it's almost black, are angry.

"Who the hell are you?" the kid snaps in his gravelly voice.

Rome's head is full of excuses, transparent lies, and inappropriate confessions that mean nothing, so he just says, "I'm Rome."

"Rome?" Like he doesn't believe it. "You wait here." The kid pulls the truck into reverse and careens around the cabin to the parking area in the back. If only Rome had his phone, he could be standing by to 9-1-1 his way out of trouble. But he's a knight without a sword, protected only by the purity of his mission.

The kid returns, striding out from behind the cabin on his long legs in their skinny jeans. He stands in the middle of the yard, green eyes finding Rome and holding him where he is, like hypnosis or a magic lasso. Time comes to a halt.

"You're not from Hopewell," the kid finally says, stare unwavering. He bends and picks up two shiny rocks. Rome winces, but the kid just places the rocks on the ground with inscrutable deliberation.

"No, I live in Toronto."

The kid tears off a leafy branch from a bush which he flexes and then drops near the rocks, squatting to adjust the angle.

Rome has no idea what's going on. He starts to walk down the porch steps, and the kid snaps, "Stay where you are. Don't move. Tell me why you're poking around our property."

Rome isn't sure why he's obeying. It's not really fear, though the laser focus of the black eyes is unnerving. "I rode by last night, saw your shack—I mean cabin. I was curious."

"It's a workshop." With the toe of one worn red sneaker, he draws a curve below the rocks and the stick.

"Sorry, workshop." Rome watches him move. His actions are too abrupt to be called graceful, but they have control and a sense of style and intent that obliquely approaches dance. The play of sinewy arm muscle, the geometry of the long thin legs creates a palpable undercurrent of lust in Rome's unease.

The boy picks up a handful of gravel and shakes it so the dust sifts through his fingers. Dropping to one knee, he places clusters and lines of pebbles. "Yeah, I saw you. You looked different. More glamorous or something." His long arms reach around for more materials—sticks and stones and tiny flowers from the struggling ground cover—which he adds with precision to whatever it is he's making, turning back to stare at Rome every few seconds. Finally he stands up and walks slowly backward, surveying his work.

Rome, released from the grip of those eyes and driven by his curiosity, walks down the steps and crosses the yard until he's more or less beside the boy, though leaving a bubble of safety between them. At first he can't make it out. It's just an abstract assemblage, but then he sees the face, its particular outline. "It's me, isn't it?"

"It's nothing," the kid replies. "Just sketching." He walks over to the broken flip phone and places it beside the ear of the face he's constructed—Rome's face, and Rome grins at this final touch.

The eyes and lips are accentuated by the pebbles, by tiny purple flowers and fragments of blue glass. This portrait of him is wearing makeup, like the kid must have seen him last night, face caught in a shaft of summer evening sun. He wishes he had his phone to capture this weird, magical moment. Rome looks up at the kid, who is deliberately looking away, a thousand mile stare into the forest. *He's shy.*

"What kind of workshop?" Rome asks.

"My dad used to have a welding business. Now I…make stuff. It's not a big deal." He walks past Rome to the porch, and with his back still turned says, "Want to see?"

"Okay." Rome joins him at the door where he's unlocking the knob and deadbolt. "What's your name?"

Before the boy can answer, a badly muffled roar fills the air, and with a screech of tires, a battered old Ford sedan brakes and skids into the yard, obliterating the sketch of Rome's face. The car is desperately in need of a wash, and the ladder on its roof, a blue bandana tied to the last rung, doesn't look to be well secured. Without turning off the engine, which smokes and growls like a tiger in a nightclub, the driver throws open the rusting door and steps out. Rome recognizes Xander, and his stomach drops out from under him.

"Yo, Darcy!" Xander shouts, like he's much farther away than he really is. He has exchanged his baseball cap for a dirty fedora. A bored girl with peroxide-blond hair is sitting in the passenger seat, looking out the window and not at anyone, occasionally typing one-word texts into her phone. "I see you've met the little gay tourist from Toronto. You look all ordinary, Influencer. What's wrong? Run out of lipstick?"

The boy beside Rome says nothing, just crosses his arms on his chest and glares back. Rome wants to step behind this boy he now knows is Darcy, to hide from Xander, but he stands his ground and tries to stop himself from shaking.

Xander raises finger guns in the air and does a little dance. "Fuh-fuh-fagaroonie from Torontoonie!"

Darcy says, "What do you want, Xander?"

"Yeah, I need those headphones back you borrowed off me. Gonna sell them to a guy."

"You mean the ones you gave me instead of the fifty bucks you owed? I think you even called them a late birthday present."

Xander spits in the dirt. "Why the fuck would I buy you three-hundred-dollar headphones for your birthday?"

"Oh, I doubt you bought them."

Xander marches forward, kicking up a cloud of dust, and Rome presses himself against the workshop's metal wall, heart pounding.

"I'm no thief!" Xander yells. "You take that back."

Darcy leans forward, gripping the porch railing, glaring down at Xander. "Get the fuck off our property, lowlife!"

The car horn sounds, long and strident, echoing through the forest. Everyone stares. The girl sticks her head out the window and screams, "Xander! I'm gonna be late for work, damn it."

"I'm doing business here, Laila!" he screams back. But he starts to back away, finger pointed at Darcy. "This ain't over. I need my stuff back."

Darcy stands tall again. "You know what's yours? The shit in your ass. Get lost!"

Only when the roar of the car finally vanishes back down the road does Rome fall apart. His legs go wobbly, and he drops into a squat, hugging himself and shaking.

He hears Darcy saying, "What a fucking clown," but then he sees movement through his tear-filled eyes, and Darcy is there, kneeling in front of him. "Hey, what happened? You okay?"

"I...I'm...c-can't..." He squeezes his eyes shut.

"Fuck, breathe. You're gonna be okay. I'm gonna touch you, don't freak." Rome feels Darcy's long, cool fingers slip around the back of his neck. The touch is intimate but firm, and Rome wants to pull away, but he breathes deep and allows himself to be comforted.

They stay like that for probably a minute or two before Rome can speak. "I'm okay, I'm okay, sorry." He starts to get up, and Darcy grabs his hand and pulls him the rest of the way.

"My mom," Darcy says. "She used to do the hand on the neck thing when I was little and I got scared. It always worked."

Embarrassment washes over Rome. "I'm sorry, I'm an idiot. That guy, Xander, and his friends, I met them last night in the forest. I just didn't expect to see him here. Hey, you probably have a lot to do. I'll go. Thanks for helping. And the sketch. It was cool. Bye."

Rome, his face hot, scuttles down the steps and over to #4, but before he can jump on and ride the hell away, Darcy calls, "Don't you want to see the workshop? I make, you know, art stuff. Or...forget it if you have to go."

Rome turns back, and their eyes lock again. He puts the bike back against the tree and follows Darcy through the door.

The air inside is stale and a bit too warm. When Darcy closes the door behind them, they are in darkness, alleviated only by the weak glow from that single high window in the back. The darkness swallows Darcy as he navigates deeper into the room, and Rome tenses, like he's been led into the killer's maze after all. But then the room comes alive in a complex glow of lamps, spots, and string lights. Darcy is kneeling against the far wall, where he has just plugged in a heavy-duty extension cord.

"The overhead fluorescents are really ugly. This is better."

The workshop is all purposeful chaos: two large worktables with a lane between, the table to the right covered in tools large and small, the left one full of what must be works in progress. Rome sees machine parts like the ones littering the yard, strings of Christmas lights, and scatterings of toy cars and figurines, from LEGO minifigs to antique matchbox soldiers. Some of these objects are strewn haphazardly, pushed to the back of the table, and some are assembled into neat lines. On the wall are drawings and reference photographs of anime cityscapes and leaping herds of gazelle. Lengths of coloured crepe streamers hang limply from the ceiling, as if left over from a birthday party years ago.

Rome feels Darcy's eyes on him as he walks around, investigating the artwork. A machine housing with old telephone dials and plastic sunflowers glued to it. A black metal orb with a garden of steel bolts welded to the side, toy soldiers half melted on the top in great globs of solder. One piece—a toaster covered in miniature graffiti tags, with lines of plastic bugs climbing out of the toast holes—makes Rome laugh, and he checks to see if his reaction offends Darcy. No, the boy's face is quirked in a half-smile.

Rome gets a whiff of rank sweat under his arms from his panic attack, feels ashamed that he was so pathetic in front of this stranger. He can also feel the ghost of Darcy's hand as if it has left a subtle but permanent mark on his neck.

"They're beautiful," Rome says.

Darcy shrugs. "I used to just draw and paint, but then Dad taught me how to weld...Making tactile stuff is just, I don't know, more satisfying." Darcy picks up a long pole leaning in one corner and uses it to unlatch the high window. A strong breeze makes the streamers on the ceiling dance. "Nice breeze today. It gets wicked hot here in the summer. By July, I gotta work naked."

Rome files that mental image. "You made the altarpiece in the woods."

Darcy turns and stares at him from the half-light. With the long pole in his hand, he looks like a wizard with a staff. "You saw that?"

"Yesterday. That's where, uh, Xander and his friends—"

"How did you know it was an altar? I never told anyone that."

"It just reminded me of one?" Embarrassed by the boy's focus, Rome wraps his arms around himself and walks along the table to another sculpture, an unadorned cube of dull gray metal with a large round hole. "I'm sorry it got messed up. That sucks."

Darcy puts the pole back in the corner, all but vanishing in the shadows. His disembodied voice is heavy and flat. "I should have expected it."

Rome hates that the boy is so sad. In a bright voice, he says, "We could fix it up! Clean the altar and the clearing."

Darcy emerges from the darkness and leans against the other table. "No. It's dead now." They stand in silence for a minute before he speaks again. "Hey, you see that power cord? The green one beside you? Plug it in."

Rome fumbles the cord, feels like a dork, gets it back in his grip and plugs it in. He had thought the dull grey cube was an unfinished piece, but suddenly it is aglow with micro-lights. They are sparsely scattered across the surface, like fireflies in a meadow, but they lead the eye to the large round hole, like a cave in a cliff face, that descends down into the sculpture. Rome is immediately caught up in the play of light and space. Something shifts in him, a change in perspective like when he was a child kneeling in the grass with a tiny toy dinosaur, utterly convinced it was real, gigantic, and hurtling through a forest of towering green blades. The sculpture might be a hundred metres high and Rome a tiny bug hovering before it.

"I'm starting to work with light," Darcy says.

"It's amazing," Rome whispers, as his spirit tumbles into Darcy's work along the path of spiralling lights that vanish into the piece's heart. Toy dogs are glued inside, figurines of smaller and smaller scale the farther in they are placed, enhancing the illusion of depth. One is a boxer, one is a corgi...

"Can I ask you," Darcy says, and then goes silent. Rome would ask *what* if he weren't caught in the sculpture's hypnotic grip. "What was that about? Outside, I mean, after that clown Xander left?"

"Panic attack. It doesn't matter," Rome says. His voice feels far away. "He triggered...reminded me of something that happened a long time ago. You must think I'm an idiot."

"I don't think you're an idiot. You don't know what I think."

Rome has never told anyone the whole story. And this guy is a total stranger, so why does Rome suddenly decide to tell him everything? Because Rome isn't really here, standing in a metal cabin in Hopewell. No, he's a bug flying down a spiral, dog-guarded path into a magical world where the only other figure is a wizard with a patchy beard.

"There was this guy at school," Rome begins. "I was in grade seven and he was in eight. I thought...I thought he liked me." He's forgetting to breathe; he has to keep breathing. He locks all his focus on the void within the sculpture. "I thought he liked me, and that was the reason he was always circling around me in the cafeteria. I mean, he was doing dumb shit like knocking my books off the table, or spilling my juice. But I figured maybe that was how you flirted."

Rome hears the stool scrape as Darcy sits down near him, but he doesn't look over, just continues his tale. "It was the end of the school day—just a Tuesday or something—and he sticks his head out of the equipment room beside the gym as I'm walking by. 'Hey, Jerome! Come in, I want to show you something.' So I go in, and he's there with three of his friends. He kicks out my legs from under me, and I go down. Then he's..." Breath, breathe. "He's pushing my head into the pile of volleyballs, all tethered in a mesh bag, saying, 'Lick the balls, you know you want to.' I can taste the rubber, feel my nose getting all crushed, and I can't get any air, and I can't escape. I guess I'm fighting because he smacks me in the head and keeps crushing me while the other guys laugh. I stop fighting."

"Did you tell anyone what happened?" Darcy says after a long silence, and it's a surprise he's really there, that Rome's confession has taken place in the real world, in real time.

"No, you're the first one I ever told."

"I don't get it. Couldn't you go to the principal? Your mom?"

"No. I didn't dare. Because I thought it was my fault. I dropped my guard, let him see what I was."

"Gay."

Rome frowns, and wants to say, *obviously*. "So after that, my whole life became about not letting it happen again, not being caught alone, not dropping my guard ever. For all these years. Do you know how…" He gasps in a breath he's needed for the last half minute. "How exhausting that is?"

"Then why are you telling me now? I mean, it's okay, I don't mind."

Rome struggles not to cry. He wishes he could reveal his secret but not feel the shame. "Because you asked. Because…Because your sculpture hypnotized me." He makes a choking, phlegmy laugh. "I guess I thought you'd understand. Since Xander did that to your altar."

"Might have been Xander. Might have been anybody. It doesn't really matter."

"Bullies are all the same, aren't they? Mine, yours."

"I don't know. I guess. It's so fucked up, because when me and dad moved to Hopewell, we never told people my mom was Indigenous, but they found out, and they thought they were pretty fucking funny with their stupid racist jokes. Then they messed up the altar, like they own the woods and I'm the trespasser."

"That sucks."

"Who cares? Fuck them all, they don't get to see any more of my work."

Rome finds a crumpled napkin from the diner stuffed in his pocket and blows his nose with it. A weight has been lifted off his chest. He has told the story and survived the experience. Then he notices what Darcy said. "Was? You said your mom 'was'?"

"Yeah, she died when I was eight."

"I'm sorry. My dad left, too. When I was like four."

"My mom didn't leave. It was fucking cancer."

"Sorry."

"Me too. About your dad, and what that asshole did to you. I'm glad you told me."

"You knew I was queer, right?"

"Yeah, I guess I did."

Something makes Rome ask, "Are you?"

It's Darcy's turn to frown. "No. I don't know. I mean, I have sex with guys, but they're all straight. I don't call myself anything."

"Uh-huh," Rome responds, automatically falling into support mode, but suddenly everything feels different. The touch on his neck, the invitation to see the workshop. The calm he has found in telling his story is now blown. Everything is suddenly tinted the colour of sex.

"I'm glad you like my light sculpture."

"Are there any more like it?"

Darcy licks his upper lip, and his toes flex in the red canvas sneakers. "Yeah, there's one…" Something falls outside with a clang of metal on metal as the ceiling streamers thrash chaotically. "Fuck, that wind is getting serious. Um, okay, I'll show you. Hold on." He kneels and sticks his head under the tool table, giving Rome a view of his slim hips and firm ass. He hears the sound of a clasp unlocking, and then Darcy slowly extricates himself with something under his arm.

He has a dust bunny in his hair as he stands again and places the object in front of Rome. The sculpture is egg-shaped, about the size of a human head, its pocked and faceted surface all rust and chrome. "No one's seen this one yet," he says. "Not even my dad."

He plugs it in, and the sculpture comes to life. The soft lights are all hidden in the crevices and holes, making the egg glow like its alive.

"Look inside," Darcy says, and Rome can hear the tightness in his voice. He's nervous. Rome bends down and peers into the openings. Inside are pictures. They are old and blurry, dreamlike, especially with the lights illuminating them from behind.

"Is that your mom?" Rome asks, and Darcy grunts an affirmative. She's young, caught in moments of a life lost, laughing, serious, hair obscuring her face or pulled back defiantly. One picture is blurred almost to abstraction, until Rome makes out a tiny hand rising from the blanket in her arms, fingers splayed to touch her face. The smile she has for the tiny creature is a sharp centre of radiance.

Peering into these intimate moments of this dead woman's life feels like a violation but also like an act of reverence. There is so much love here and so much loss. The roughness of the damaged casing, the softness of the indistinct images—the sculpture is a doomed attempt to hold on to a past already slipped away.

"It's beautiful," Rome whispers. And in that instant, he knows he's found the prize for his scavenger hunt. He has to take a picture, send it right off to the discord server. He reaches into his pocket for his phone…and remembers again he doesn't have it.

"Shit. Hey, listen…" Rome says, afraid he'll put it wrong and lose the opportunity. "Have you ever, um, sold your art to anyone?"

"No. I'm just messing around. No one would be interested."

His excitement mounting, Rome moves closer to Darcy. "You're wrong. Everybody will love this. I mean, I guess not everyone, art is a personal thing, but I'm telling you. Listen, listen. I want to buy this from you. I mean my committee does."

"Your committee? What the fuck is that?"

He tells Darcy about SciCon, about the scavenger hunt and his role in it, his failure to find a worthy grand prize. "But this is it. This is perfect! I think…I think Hopewell led me here." *Peek inside and find Sir Prize.*

"What the fuck are you talking about?"

"Never mind, that doesn't matter."

"You want me to give you my sculpture?"

"Of course not. We would pay. We have budget for that."

"But this isn't just…I'm not fooling around here. It's personal."

"Artists sell their work, Darcy. You're an artist."

"I'm a guy fooling around in a shed."

"But…"

"Stop pushing me."

Rome bites a knuckle. "I'm sorry," he says. He's gone too far. He's arrogant and doesn't know when to back off. "Do you want me to go?"

Darcy exhales loudly. "Are you hungry? I have a ton of leftover lasagna at our apartment."

Rome's heart beats faster. It's not just the possibility he might still get the sculpture that excites him, it's the unspoken tension in the air, all those mysterious "straight" boys in Darcy's past. So he says, "I like lasagna."

Darcy is quick. He unplugs the sculptures and the workshop lights and hurries them out the door, securing both locks before striding around the building to get the truck. Rome thinks he should have followed him instead of standing on the porch, waiting to be picked up like a girl on her way to prom.

The red truck pulls up in front of him, growling low. Through the open window, Darcy calls, "Throw your bike in the back."

They turn left, driving away from Main Street and the Hopewell Rome knows. With one hand on the wheel, elbow sticking out the open driver's window, Darcy looks confident and sexy in a way Rome wishes he could. After a couple of minutes, they leave the forested area, and now they are driving along a stretch of businesses, each one proudly taking up its square of the earth. He sees car and truck dealerships, a garden centre with a huge menagerie of concrete animals, boat repairs and sales, and then the trailer park. Beyond an overhead sign reading "The Garden of Edna," the park is smaller than he expected, with maybe thirty trailers in neat rows.

"That's where me and Dad lived when we moved here. Just after my mother died."

"How bad was it living here?" Rome thinks how bereft the boy must have been.

"Oh, I loved it. Maybe the last time I really had friends. My gang were little terrors, but folks were pretty patient."

Rome checks the disappearing park in the side mirror, checks his assumptions. And then there are landmarks he knows from his brief excursion into local real estate—the strip mall, the Sobey's, the squat brown apartment building. Darcy hangs a right into its parking lot.

They enter the building through a side entrance off the lot, the electronic lock on the metal door clunking open when Darcy puts his wallet against the sensor pad. Inside, the light is weak and yellow, the corridor smelling of cooking oil and garbage.

"Apartment's on the third floor," Darcy says. "We can take the elevator, but I usually walk."

"Stairs are fine."

Darcy doesn't walk, he gallops, and Rome, who is unsure if he should have come, gets to the third floor half a minute behind him. They walk down the hall, past notices from management about a broken washing machine in the laundry room and scheduled elevator maintenance in July. A cardboard eye is taped to the exact middle of Darcy's apartment door, surrealistically painted in watercolour, its edges curling.

"Should I take off my shoes?"

"Don't worry about it."

Inside, it's neat and masculine, the colours muted, the front hall shelves handmade, unpainted. But on top of this restraint are signs of a brighter mind, an imagination not content to live within drab confines—a papier-mâché dinosaur on the television stand, a diorama that looks like a hybrid of a zen garden and a race track, the cars in the sand competing against ostriches and zebras.

"Is your dad at work?"

"He's on the road till Monday. He's a trucker. Got his license after the welding business went bust."

And there he is, Darcy's dad, in a huge, messy oil painting, framed in gold and given place of honour above the sofa. The painter, though obviously a beginner, has captured something essential about him. He's a man who takes up space, who radiates strength, and yet has a gentle smile. Long auburn bangs peek out from under a black baseball cap. The man's big arm is around another figure who is clearly the artist—a skinny young scrawl of colour that must be Darcy a few years ago. His face is a blur, the personality as obscured as his father's is vivid.

Darcy appears at Rome's side, handing him a can of Coke. "Don't look at that. It's embarrassing."

Rome peers around the room, seeing no other art on the wall other than a few framed photos. "It's kind of hard to avoid."

"I was maybe thirteen when I painted it. I keep asking Dad to take it down, and he's like, 'Never! I love it.'" He throws himself onto the couch. "Lasagna's in the oven. It'll be ready soon. Sit down if you want."

Rome takes one corner of the long sofa, and Darcy takes the other, pushing off his shoes and bringing his feet up onto the cushions so that Rome is contemplating the long feet in their white socks, soles the permanent grey of many washes. The arrangement is weirdly relaxed and intimate, as if there was already some history between them.

He needs to break the silence before he explodes. "Are you still in high school?" he asks, "I just finished grade eleven."

Darcy isn't nervous like him, or at least he can hide it. "Just finished last week. I'm out of that prison forever. Dad wants me to go to the Ontario College of Art and Design in Toronto."

"OCAD is a great school. Did they accept you?"

"I didn't apply. Not yet. I still can for winter term. But I told him I'm not a real artist. I just fool around with stuff."

"But isn't that why you go to school? To learn how to be an artist?"

"Look at me. I don't belong in Toronto. It's full of hipsters. They all talk in bullshit Twitter *discourse* about *identities.*"

"You mean people like me."

Darcy blows out an exasperated breath. "Like, the way you call yourself 'queer,' and I'm supposed to be impressed by the layers of meaning, by the way you wear makeup in public, and I should know what pronouns to use."

"You could ask. It was they for a while, but now it's he/him."

Darcy gives him a hard look. "Not wearing any makeup today, are you? After you almost got your ass kicked. Welcome to the boonies."

"It's not easy in Toronto either! I get called the f-word sometimes. But you have to fight back. My boyfriend and I walk down Yonge Street holding hands, because screw the haters."

Darcy looks down, fingering a little hole in the upholstery. "You have a boyfriend?"

Rome remembers he doesn't anymore. "Uh, not really."

There is a ding from the kitchen, and Darcy jumps up to take care of it. Rome looks at his abandoned red runners, pyramided on the floor beside the couch.

They eat lasagna at the kitchen table with some baby carrots on the side that Darcy dumps out of a bag. "It would be better if we had some red wine, but my dad doesn't like me to drink if he's not here. Unless you want some?"

Rome, who doesn't really like alcohol, says, "Maybe not. I have to drive later."

"The thing is," Darcy says, picking up the discussion as if there hadn't been a twenty-minute pause, "I never thought about what I do as art until I was fourteen. My dad signed me up for a summer art program with this artist named Maud Moreau. Did you see the tree stump sculptures on Main Street?"

"The chainsaw things? They're wild."

"Yeah. She scared the shit out of me at first. She's a big lady with a deep voice, always telling us about passion and instinct, the courage to express yourself. I'd be painting with all these careful little strokes, and she'd come up behind me shouting, "No! Put that line down strong, no hesitation. You're an artist! Use your body, use your breath. Let me see what's inside you.""

He's lost in the vividness of the memory, saying all this with his fork suspended in the air, a chunk of lasagna hanging off it.

Rome, who is embarrassed to have finished his food so much faster than Darcy, says, "That sounds inspiring."

"Anyway, on the last day, I'm waiting out front of the community centre for my dad to come pick me up. I have all these paintings and pieces of sculpture around me—everything I made in those six weeks. And Maud comes and sits beside me. Not too close. She gives me space. That's one of the things about her, she gives you space.

"She says, 'You could be an artist, if you work hard enough. It's not easy to find your voice, and the work never ends. But you can use that voice to explore your heritage. Your Métis heritage.'"

Darcy puts the dangling lasagna in his mouth, chews thoughtfully, swallows. "I didn't say anything. Did she know my mother? Or did my dad tell her? That would surprise me. It's not something he ever talked about, as if my native part died with my mom."

Rome says, "Maybe that's one of the reasons he signed you up for her course. He doesn't know how to talk to you about that part of your heritage."

Darcy doesn't answer.

"I guess here in Hopewell it's easier for you to just pass for white and straight," Rome says. "I understand."

"Oh, you *understand*. How's it feel to be telepathic?"

Rome's face goes hot. "Sorry, I said that badly. I just mean in Toronto, you could explore it all. The art, the native stuff, the queer stuff." His heart is beating hard, and the beating redoubles when Darcy reaches out and wipes the skin beside Rome's mouth, his finger coming away with a spot of tomato sauce.

He licks it off his finger. "Do you want to come to my room?"

Darcy stands, and Rome does the same, knocking his chair off balance so he has to spin around and grab it. Darcy enters the small bedroom first, peeling off his T-shirt and dropping onto the bed in just socks and tight jeans while Rome lingers at the door, one hand gripping the frame like it's the only thing holding him up. He looks around the room. Clothes and pop bottles litter the floor, but it's not a disaster zone. A bookshelf mostly filled with art books and graphic novels. Pictures on the wall torn out of magazines or printed from Google searches. The wall beside the open closet is covered in architectural pictures—heavy concrete buildings that look like something from a video game about some future war.

"I'm getting into Brutalism," Darcy tells him. "You know it?"

"I saw an exhibit at the AGO." Rome can barely breathe. Darcy gets up on his knees so his head is now more or less at the same level as Rome's. He reaches out a hand, which Rome takes. The gap between them closes. Darcy's lips are soft and teasing, then insistent. Rome is aware of the soreness where he bit his lip last night. Their tongues find each other, and Rome feels dizzy, his dick crazy-hard. He's not sure if Darcy pulls them down on the bed or if he falls and is caught in the boy's long arms.

The heat, the mindless transcendence is like nothing he's felt before, but then Darcy is undoing his belt, pushing his hands down into Rome's underwear. Rome says, "No!" and pulls back—not out of Darcy's arms altogether, but far enough to stop their forward progress.

"What's wrong?" Darcy asks, panting, voice thick with desire.

"This is too fast. I never..."

"You never what?"

"This. Had sex. I mean, I made out with, um, three guys but we haven't...I didn't..." Burning shame replaces the burning of lust, and Rome wants to run out of the apartment, down the stairs, and out into the hot, windy day.

"But I thought...Aren't you the one who has the boyfriend? You hold hands on Yonge Street or whatever."

"I do, I mean we did. But I never had sex before. Not any of it. I-I want to, okay? It just...never felt safe enough."

Darcy touches Rome's tousled, sweaty hair, caresses his head. "Okay."

The caress feels so good, breaks through the cycle of shame. "I want to, I really do! But maybe not yet?"

"That's what you said, yeah. Don't let anyone make you until you're ready, Rome. It's your body."

Rome knows he's crying, but maybe that's okay, too. "Why is it so easy for you?"

"I don't know. Maybe because it doesn't matter. I'm not...I'm no one in Hopewell. I'm just this weird ghost who doesn't have friends, who hangs out with his dad or by himself in the woods. Sex is just this thing that happens. It feels good, but it doesn't cost me anything."

"You're not no one, Darcy."

"Whatever."

"You're not." They kiss more, and they're careful with each other, not letting the passion mount so far they'll have no choice.

Later, when Darcy's shirt is back on, they sit on the bed. Rome has his feet on the floor, and Darcy is leaning against the headboard, sketching him in pencil on a small, ring-bound pad. They are silent, giving each other space, but still connected.

After a while, Darcy puts down the pad and says, "Okay, I'll do it."

"What?"

"The sculpture. Your scavenger committee or whatever, they can buy it off me. But I want to be there. That's part of the deal."

"In Toronto? This weekend?"

"Yeah. I want to be onstage when you present it to the winners. That is, if you can find me a place to stay."

"Yeah, of course. I'll have to ask my mom, but I'm sure you can stay at our place."

"I bet you got some big house in the suburbs."

"No, just an apartment downtown. Oh my God, I can't wait to tell the committee. They're going to love it!"

"Okay, we'll go pick up the sculpture, get your car from the garage, and hit the road."

"What are you going to wear to the presentation ceremony? Show me your wardrobe!"

They try on a bunch of things and end up stealing a jacket with a dark check from his dad's closet which they accessorize with old watch faces Darcy has turned into pendants. He admires himself in the mirror, his shyness dissolving into enthusiasm and silly laughter. Happiness swells in Rome, like all the weird pieces of his life which usually stick out at contradictory, mutually sabotaging angles have magically lined up for once. He reaches over and hugs Darcy hard.

But when they get back to the workshop, the sculpture is gone.

CHAPTER THREE

"God fuck it! What the hell?" Darcy screams as he stands in the middle of the metal cabin. He spins around on his axis, eyes wild, like the sculpture might be playing hide and seek. "I didn't put it away, did I?"

"No, I don't think so."

But Darcy drops to the floor, scrambles under the table and swears again when it's not down there. He sits up and smacks his head with the heel of his hand.

Rome notices the streamers on the ceiling dancing in the breeze. "Darcy, the window. You...we left it open." Darcy is out the door in a second, and Rome chases him around to the back where they see a ladder against the wall, its peak resting on the window frame.

"Look at that blue bandana on the ladder," Rome says. "It's Xander."

"I know it's fucking Xander. *Fuck!* What does he think? It's a Van Gogh? Does he think some art dealer is going to buy it?"

"I can't believe he robs you and then leaves his ladder behind."

"The guy is stupid as rocks."

Rome wants to put a hand on Darcy's back, but he has a feeling Darcy doesn't want to be touched. "What if you just give him the headphones back?"

Darcy kicks a wooden fruit crate into the air, and it smashes against the old printing press. "I gave them to my dad for his birthday. And I don't need to bribe that little jerk. I just need to know where he is."

Darcy marches back around the building and inside, Rome right on his heels like a loyal dog. "Does Xander live with parents or what?"

"He won't be home. He's scared of me. He'll go to ground for a few days. Could be anywhere…in a friend's basement, at his uncle's place in Abitibi…"

They are both glancing around the workshop, like it could still be a terrible mistake, like the beautiful, glowing egg, heavy and light with the ghost of Darcy's mother, might just materialize in a shower of magical sparks. Instead, what Rome sees is a cream-coloured card, prominently propped against the drill press.

"Oh my God."

"What is that? How did it get here?"

"It's the next clue." He doesn't explain, just turns the card over and reads.

Don't let the bastards grind you down
The river of Hope keeps on turning

Darcy is giving him an absolutely sulphurous stink-eye. "Are you going to explain this bullshit to me?"

"I wish I could. It doesn't matter. I have an idea where Xander is. 'Grind you down.' 'River of Hope.' Hopewell must have been a mill town at the start, right?"

"I don't know. I guess."

"No, it was. Milton Horace cutting down all the trees. What happened to his old mill? Is it a museum or something?"

"Not even. Just an abandoned site. One of the buildings used to be this real party place. People dragged in couches and shit. Lots of drugs and sex and smashing shit up."

"That's where he is. Let's go."

Darcy secures the window this time. He ties Darcy's ladder on the roof of his truck, and they hit the road. They circle around Hopewell, coming off another county road onto Mill Street, which runs parallel to the river for a while before veering east. Darcy leaves the paved road for a rutted dirt track, and coming around a corner, they reach a battered metal gate in a worn chain-link fence.

"Open it," he tells Rome, who hops down from the cab and lifts the corner of the gate from the dirt so he can swing it open on its rusty hinges. The wind is blowing relentlessly, a low rushing sound, and Rome has to squint against the dust the gate has thrown up. They drive slowly down the winding road, protected from view by thick, haphazard vegetation.

There is no room to pull off the road, so Darcy just stops the truck and switches it off. He takes down the ladder, holding one end and offering the other to Rome. "We'll walk from here, surprise them."

"Hold on," Rome says. He goes for his backpack and takes out his makeup kit. A couple of minutes later, he joins Darcy by the truck's warm hood, lips drawn cold and geometric, black eyeliner extending out into wings, like a raptor on the hunt. "Ready," he says. Darcy gives a single, approving nod, and they head down the road single file, carrying Xander's ladder.

They come around the corner into a wide clearing. The world is roaring—the rush of the river to their left, the wind shaking the leaves of the tall Norway maples like a beaded rattle, the blood pounding in Rome's ears. The main mill building is crumbling, fenced off with warning signs, but there is a second building in front of it, smaller, still structurally sound, its broken windows covered in plastic sheeting. They are all there. In the foreground, Rome sees Xander and his two buddies from the forest clearing, and farther back, Laila, sheltering in the lee of the building, seated on an old truck bench, scrolling through her phone with a permanent scowl.

"They've got guns!" Rome whispers anxiously.

"Just old air rifles. They won't kill you."

Xander's buddies have their backs turned to the new arrivals. They're firing at a line of beer bottles propped on a fence, the guns going pop-pop. The one who wore the Megadeth shirt yesterday has changed it for a Black Sabbath one. He yells, "Can't hit shit in this wind!"

"You gotta make yourself one with the elements," says his friend with the long blond hair. He takes a drag off his joint, lines up the shot, and misses. "Shit!"

Xander ignores their sport. He is unarmed, sitting on a tree stump, trying to look casual as Darcy and Rome put down his ladder and approach.

"Hey, it's team freak," he says. "Didn't expect you to show your faces here."

Now, with some ten feet between them, Darcy stops. "You mean, how did we find you? That was Rome. You're not as clever as you think."

Metalhead and Blondie have turned. Darcy promised the air rifles aren't really dangerous, but Rome doesn't want to test the theory.

Xander says, "So anyway, this is a private party. You should leave."

Darcy hasn't looked anywhere except at Xander's eyes. "We have no interest in your White Trash Olympics. Give it back, and then we'll leave."

"Give what back?" Xander says, not even pretending to act surprised.

"My sculpture."

Xander scoffs. "Sculpture! Listen to the ar-teest!"

Metalhead laughs a whooping stoned guffaw. "The artist and his supermodel girlfriend." Rome's heart is pounding, but he *does* feel like a supermodel. His makeup is armour, and he will not back down.

"I'm an honest citizen, boys, and this guy keeps accusing me of being a thief."

"You left your ladder against the building, you idiot," Rome yells.

Xander glares at him, then says to Darcy, "Then give me the headphones, and you can have it back."

"No."

Xander laughs. "So, what are you gonna do? Call the cops? I could tell them a story or two about the weed you were selling at school. My uncle's a cop, and they don't really like Indians. Not that I approve of racism. Anyway, have a nice day, sign the guest book on your way out." He turns and starts walking toward Laila.

"Come on, Rome," Darcy says. Uneasily, Rome follows him as he walks deliberately between Metalhead and Blondie, not even acknowledging their presence. "Xander! Let's negotiate."

Xander stops, crosses his arms over his chest. When they reach him, he's grinning like he's already won. "What have you got to offer? Better be good or that sculpture ends up in the river."

Rome looks to see how Darcy will respond and is confused when his face softens, eyes squinting, mouth dropping open with tongue lolling.

"Ohhh, yeah…" Darcy moans, throwing his head back, running his tongue over his upper lip. "Don't stop. Do it harder. *Harder!*"

Xander looks alarmed, takes a step back like something radioactive is happening. "What are you doing?"

Darcy's voice is pitched so only the three of them can hear, but his theatrics are full on. "Oh, God, gonna fuckin' nut. *Fuh-fuh-FUCKALOOOOOOOO!*"

"You shut the hell up!" Xander hisses, going red.

Darcy turns to Rome, grinning. "Every time this fool cums—every single time—it's the same thing: *fuh-fuh-fukaloooooo!* It's dopey, I know, but kinda cute."

"Wait," Rome says, incredulous. "Him? You did it with *him?*"

Darcy shrugs. Xander grabs the front of Darcy's T-shirt, cocks a fist at his face.

"I'm telling you, shut up!" They're all watching now—the boys with the air rifles, Laila over by the building.

Darcy smirks. "Why? Because Laila knows your little orgasm song? Of course she does. Should I go tell her we've both ridden the Xander train before? I bet she'd *love* to have that information."

Xander lets go of Darcy's shirt, shakes out his fist, and stomps around in a tight, furious circle. "Fuck you!" he growls.

"Give me my sculpture, Xander, and me and Rome leave without saying a single word."

"Shit, fine." He spins on his heel, and they follow him to the building.

"What's going on?" Laila asks, annoyed, like Xander is doing something just to mess with her.

"Nothing!" he barks, marching into the building. The sheet of plywood blocking the door from just this kind of invasion lies discarded to one side of the moldy front room. Old, destroyed furniture, some of it half-burned, is piled in one corner, and a disgusting mattress that Rome wouldn't touch on a dare lies in another. Cigarette butts, condoms, broken glass, and crack pipes litter the floor.

Bolted into one wall is a rusty metal ladder that leads to a trapdoor in the ceiling. Xander jumps up on the ladder, which protests with a whine, brick dust drifting from some of the bolt points. Darcy stays by the door, on guard, but Rome enters, because someone better keep an eye on Xander. At the top of the ladder, Xander pushes open the square door and feels around until he has hold of something. He pulls it out—an object the size of a head, wrapped in moldy, old cloth.

"See? Safe and sound?" he says, immediately fumbling the package. Rome sees it fly through the air and moves without thinking, crossing the room like the football player he never was, and catching Darcy's sculpture against his chest.

Rome can't believe what he's just done. He turns wide-eyed to Darcy, who looks like his heart might have stopped. The three boys remain frozen in this tableau for a moment before Darcy says, "Let's get the hell out of here."

"Yeah, you better go!" Metalhead yells after them as they walk back toward the road. They ignore him until an air rifle pellet ricochets off a rock to their right. They freeze.

"Faggots!" Metalhead screams, his voice twisting in the wind. Rome's whole body is begging him to run, but he is waiting for a cue from Darcy. He hears Darcy let out a slow breath, and then he reaches out his hand and takes Rome's. It is sweaty and warm and holds him with firm sincerity. Without looking back once, they leave the yard hand in hand, only breaking into a run when they have turned the corner, out of sight.

❖

Rome cradles Darcy's sculpture in his lap as they drive back through town. They are silent but content. Rome smiles as the comforting sights of Main Street roll past his open window.

"Take a right here," he says.

They pull into the parking lot of the Honeyrose B&B, and Rome wheels #4 around back to lock up. "Thanks, noble steed," he whispers to the bike. Back in front, he tells Darcy, "I just have to pack up and check out. I'll be fast!"

Candace and the cute summer help boy are putting up a framed painting of a moose on the wall behind the front desk. The moose is posing proudly, dressed in Elizabethan finery—a green velvet tunic with a big ruffled collar. Candace is up a stepladder with her back turned, but she still knows it's Rome.

"Check-out," she says, "was at noon. That's almost three hours ago."

"Sorry!" Rome replies, not stopping. "I'll get out of there fast!"

"I could charge you for another night, young man!" she calls after him.

The first thing he does when he enters the room is to get his hands on his phone. He wants to kiss it. In fact, he does. The messages are myriad, and his fear of disappointing everyone passes through him as a mini panic attack. But first things first.

"Hey, Susan."

"I've been leaving messages all day. I'm not happy you didn't call back."

"I forgot my phone."

"All day?"

"Mom, seriously crazy times."

A pause. "Are you okay?"

"Yeah, it all worked out. Listen, can a friend come stay at our place this weekend? He wants to go to SciCon."

"This is someone you know and trust?"

A very small pause. "Oh yeah, for sure. How's Bubbie?"

"Here, talk to her."

"Je...rome. H-how's my b...bab-y?"

He puts the phone on speaker, leaves it on the dresser as he packs his bag. "Busy. I feel bad that I didn't stay longer with you. Are you going to be okay now?"

A deep, rattling sigh. "W...ould have beeee...n easi-er if I died."

"Don't say that, Bubbie! Listen, I'll come and visit soon, I promise."

She makes a noncommittal noise. "Re...mmber the song? C-car song we sang?"

"You mean 'Little Boxes'?"

"No..."

She goes silent for many seconds, until Rome finally says, "Bubbie? You there?"

She's humming. Then some lyrics tumble out. "...Je-rome t'eat his ca...carrots."

It hits him like a hammer, the memory emerging from the void. He is in the back seat of the old brown Honda, wearing shorts on a hot summer day, his legs sticking to the seat, squelching every time he lifts them. His bubbie is in the front passenger seat, a bright light of joy and comfort. His zaidie, at the wheel, is less vivid in the memory—noble and distant, though still representing safety. Rome, fully inside this moment, can suddenly sing the whole song, which he does:

Mommy wants Jerome to eat his carrots
Zaidie wants Jerome to grow up tall
Bubbie wants Jerome to squawk at parrots
Jerome-y doesn't need a dad at all

He is, frankly, appalled. What a fucked-up song to make up for a little kid! But he kind of gets it. His dad was just gone. *Poof.* Little boy Jerome must have been terrified, confused. Did he think it was his fault? It's all a blank to seventeen-year-old Rome. He no more remembers his emotions than he remembers the man himself. His father is just a hazy figure looming in the smoke. But did that song really make it better? What if he did still need his father? His family just cast the man and any memory of him into the fire. *Poof.*

His bubbie sighs again. "You were a...good b-boy. S...aad boy."

"I'm not sad now, Bubbie," he says, though he's not sure this is true.

Down in the lobby, he hands the phone to Candace, who talks to his mom so they can smooth out the late check-out. Through the window, he can see Darcy's truck, but no Darcy.

"Yes," Candace is saying, "you're so right. At that age they don't think their behaviour affects others."

Rome scowls, a scowl for both women and the way adults always make a big deal out of nothing. Still, he apologizes on his way out and gives her his best smile. Candace, appeased, says she hopes he'll come back and stay again, and she gives him a business card.

He notices her stack of the old cream-coloured cards has been dumped into the recycling bin beside the front desk. "You don't want them anymore?" he asks.

"Too old-fashioned. Hopewell needs to project a modern image."

"Can I take a few?" Rome asks. As he leaves the building, he turns one over, half-expecting to find a final message—farewell, congratulations, maybe sex and relationship advice—but it's blank. He puts the cards in his jacket pocket.

The truck is locked, the wrapped sculpture on the floor of the passenger side. Rome wanders up to Main Street and finds Darcy looking at the tree stump sculptures. They look different under the overcast sky than they did in yesterday's sunshine. The animal forms are imbued with a darker purpose and a grave wisdom. The wind, rushing through the branches, is their voice.

The boys stand side by side in silence until Darcy says, "I hate when people tell you what you should do with your life."

"I know. They think they're being helpful, but they don't really know."

"Right? And we didn't ask for help. We got this."

"We totally got this."

The garage phones to say the car is ready, and they drive right over. Darcy asks the owner some technical questions Rome can't follow.

"Careful out on the highway," she tells them. "Weather app says the wind is gusting up to ninety kilometres per hour. Won't stop until tomorrow. Wouldn't be surprised if we lose power. Maybe lose some more old trees."

"We'll be fine," Darcy tells her, but Rome is nervous.

Rome follows Darcy's truck back to his apartment, where they grab his suitcase from upstairs with the clothes they picked out. Rome sets the GPS, though the route couldn't be simpler.

He drives with both hands on the wheel, afraid a gust of wind will blow them off the road. "I hate this wind. And I hate that it's this late. I don't like driving at night, especially on the highway."

"No problem. I'll take over at sunset."

"Really? That would be great. Then I can answer all these messages for the scavenger hunt. Tell them I found the grand prize!"

Rome imagines walking into their apartment with Darcy, Darcy moving around in his space, looking at his books, touching his stuff, stumbling upon his secrets. He could give Darcy his bed while he sleeps in his mom's. Or one of them could take the living room couch. Or they could both sleep in his bed…

His phone rings again, startling him.

"Hey, Mom. We're on the road."

"How was Hopewell?"

"Not bad as small towns go. Nice people, mostly."

"I looked it up online. There was an article in *Xtra* called 'Queers of the North.' Did you know Hopewell has a queer mayor? Pan, I think."

When the call is done, he repeats the question to Darcy.

"What's pan?"

"It's kind of like bi, but instead of—"

"I didn't even know the mayor was a woman."

"How can you not know who your mayor is?"

"I bet you don't know the captain of your school hockey team."

He's right, but Rome won't admit it. "Don't you need to tell your dad you're going to Toronto?"

"He always phones around nine. I'll tell him then. We operate on a system of mutual trust."

"Ha, sounds nice. My mom is totally up in my business about everything."

They are leaving Hopewell. "Come again! You're one of the family!" says the cheesy departure sign. Darcy suddenly undoes his seat belt. Kneeling on the seat, he opens the window and sticks his head out, looking back down the highway as his hometown recedes.

Rome is scared he's going to jump out, like a frightened dog. "Everything okay?"

Darcy sits again and puts his seat belt back on, staring at the road unfolding ahead of them. "Yeah, it's fine," he says. "It's good."

Hope Echoes

'Nathan Burgoine

CHAPTER ONE

"So, the town name. What do we think? Total overcompensation, or meant to be ironic?" Fielding nodded at the sign up ahead. "Because I'm putting my money on overcompensation."

Hopewell 10.

He glanced at the passenger seat, but Tate stared out the windscreen, not so much as glancing his way.

"Ouch," Fielding said, smiling. "This is some of my best material, you know."

He checked his phone but nothing had changed. Held in place with a holder clipped to the air vent, it showed him a map with one long road the same way it had done for the whole morning. Highway 11 was nothing if not consistent.

Consistently boring, to be specific.

So far the most fascinating thing had been passing a town with a fake UFO—Moonbeam, honest to God, a town called *Moonbeam*—but on his way to SciCon in Toronto, Hopewell was up next in endless parade of blink-and-you'll-miss-it towns he'd encounter.

Sort of like Fielding himself. Fielding totally existed in a year-long blink-and-miss-it right now. Out of sight, out of mind. Barely existing.

Crap.

His mood soured, and not for the first time since he'd started off at the crack of dawn from home. A two-lane highway, hills, trees, and occasional slices through the layered rock of the Canadian Shield didn't offer a lot to distract him from the reality of the last twelve months.

Wake up, eat, go to work, eat, work some more, come home, eat, shower, sleep. Repeat. Not even hanging out with friends now and then to keep it interesting. Anup and Kristin and everyone else he'd even marginally be interested in talking to from high school went off to university, and he went off to stack cat food.

And dog food.

All the animal foods.

For months. For a year, almost.

As years went, the last one would already have been a top-five contender for the worst, but if you added in the reasons—his uncle's heart attack, his mom's sudden reduction in classes and take-home pay—it landed its place as number one with a bullet. And his mom's job and his uncle's health and Fielding pretty much taking over for his uncle at the pet store wasn't even all of it. It was just icing on the bullet cake.

He smirked. Kristin and Anup would love that. Bullet cake icing. He made a mental note to share that one. They could add it to their weird personal lexicons of indecipherable anti-cool.

God, he couldn't wait to see them. Anup and Kristin and SciCon? It was going to be so welcome. Hell, seeing *anyone* he wasn't related to would be a welcome change. He glanced at his phone again, saw the trip timer, and cringed.

Eight and a half more hours to go.

Tate's Mustang started a long, low slope down toward a river and a two-lane bridge, the wind shoving the classic car, making it rock. Fielding gripped the wheel tighter. He'd already stopped once for gas, so right now the tank was okay. Didn't have to feed the beast again. Yet. Sucking gas was definitely one of the downsides of driving the Mustang, but this trip was worth it, and for once, he wasn't going to think about money. He didn't need the bathroom, either. And Lord knew his mother had piled enough snacks into the bag on the back seat.

No, he had no reason to stop. He'd breeze on through. It wasn't like he didn't have an entire day of driving ahead of him. He should save his breaks for when he needed to get gas. Multiple birds with one stone.

Cresting the hill, Fielding saw a sign up ahead, beside the bridge. *Welcome to Hopewell. Well North, Well-being.*

"Wow," Fielding muttered. "You think anyone ever believes that?" He eyed Tate, who happened to be smiling at him. Fielding couldn't help but return it, even though it was just a coincidence. He turned back to the road, ignoring the tightness in his throat. The times Tate appeared in the passenger seat always made him feel better, even if this Tate was just a memory, replaying a day from a few years ago. No one else would see Tate, and though his mouth was moving, clearly giving Fielding some advice, this version of his cousin was completely silent. Still, having even an echo of Tate here was better than being alone.

They passed the sign. Fielding shivered and something inside him—something he did his best not to really think about—*shifted*. It reminded him of the time he'd come off the only plane flight he'd ever taken, when his ears had been plugged for so long he'd gotten used to it, then they finally popped.

Something just *changed*, and he wasn't sure it was for the better. He gripped the steering wheel, fighting off the sudden rush of unease, and checked the rear-view. Nothing there.

What was the saying? Like someone walking over your grave? Like that, to the nth.

"Not now," he said.

Fielding shivered again, and then a third time finally dismissed the odd chill. He should be used to it, but it wasn't the kind of thing he imagined he'd ever get used to, if he was honest. And as much as he didn't want to know, he kept an eye out. Nothing seemed out of place.

At least, not yet.

Another blast of wind lashed at the car, and he clenched his jaw until he was off the bridge. It wasn't raining, and the sky was mostly clear, but the wind was kicking up a fuss.

"So far, Hopewell? Really not a fan," Fielding said.

Yeah, he was definitely blowing right through this place.

Fielding was definitely not blowing right through Hopewell.

Or, more to the point, he had a feeling defeat was about to be snatched out of the jaws of victory. After offering barely a glance at what was charitably called Main Street, the highway veered off south from the town almost immediately. Fielding's phone announced first a simple "stay to the right" and then a "continue" followed by a discouraging number of kilometres. He'd seen a single traffic light, and while he was certain he'd driven by some buildings and maybe some people, he'd let them wash by without paying much attention. But *someone* there had been behind the shiver he felt. The wind, to his surprise, was even worse on this side of the river, and more than once he'd muttered a few swears while keeping the car moving in a straight line.

But after the "stay to the right" announcement, he'd pulled away from Hopewell and returned to the monotonous two-lane highway, the view giving way to trees on either side of the road and some rocky bits. Then he came across an ever-thickening clump of cars. He'd had to slow down, and then stop.

A single police car with its roof lights and hazards going was parked in front of a very large tree which lay across the entirety of the highway and then some. It had smashed into one of the four main legs of the Hydro pylon on the other side. The whole tower had twisted, leaning from the impact. Though it didn't look like it was about to fall, and none of the wires seemed to have snapped, they were pulled taut on one side while the others hung way lower than usual.

It all looked precarious. And there was no way around it.

"Continue on Highway 11," his phone said. He put the Mustang in park, becoming the fifth or sixth in a line otherwise made up of entirely of pickups.

"Would love to," Fielding said. "But I think that's not gonna happen." He eyed Tate, who was looking out the window again.

"How about I check on this?" Fielding said with a cheer he didn't feel. "You stay there, eh?"

He made sure there were no cars coming and got out of the Mustang. The wind whipped at his hoodie. He shoved his hands in his pockets to hold it down and zipped it up over his Catadora T-shirt to stop it flapping about. It wasn't a long walk to the OPP car. The police officer stood chatting with two other adults, a stocky Indigenous man in a denim jacket, and a grey-haired white woman in a sleeveless black shirt.

"How long we talking, Mick?" the woman said.

"Hydro's on its way," the officer said. "Coming down from Abitibi. Need them to check out the pylon before we do anything."

"Abitibi?" The man laughed. "Guess I'll go home, then?"

"Won't be quick," the officer said with a smile.

That didn't sound good. The man pulled out a phone and walked off to the side to call someone. The woman said a friendly see-you-later to Mick and headed back to her car.

Fielding swallowed. "Excuse me. Do you know when the road will be clear?"

The cop looked at him, and Fielding tried not to look away. "Sorry, son. We need the Hydro folks before we even think of moving the tree. You're not from town." It wasn't a question, as though the man had everyone who could be local memorized. Maybe he did. Hopewell looked smaller than home. Definitely possible to memorize everyone. "Where you headed?"

"Toronto." Fielding looked past the tree. A lot of branches had shattered when it hit the road, and every time the wind gusted, little bits of wood were flung about. No cars on the far side of the tree though, not yet. Apparently, no one was coming to Hopewell from the other direction.

How very unsurprising.

"You could head back the way you came." The officer blew out a breath, considering. Fielding could imagine him looking at mental maps and drawing much the same conclusion his phone had drawn for him when he'd planned this trip. "Cut through Nagamisis, get to Highway 17. Hit the Soo and Sudbury." He rubbed his chin. "Maybe get there tomorrow, a couple of hours from now, if you don't stop."

Fielding closed his eyes. *Oh, God.*

"Probably best to wait here, then," the officer said, and Fielding opened his eyes again. The man gave him a little shrug and a smile.

"Right." Fielding tried not to be mad at him. It wasn't this guy's fault. Also, getting mad at cops didn't end well for anyone who wasn't a cop.

"That your car?" the man said, nodding at the Mustang.

"My cousin's."

The cop whistled. "'65 Fastback?"

Here we go, Fielding thought. "Yeah. My cousin and my uncle restored it together." He hoped the man didn't have any car-guy questions. Fielding was not a car guy. If asked, Tate could—and would—answer questions all day about things like pistons and rims and other things that weren't pistons or rims. Fielding pretty much tapped out at "Yes, it's a 1965 Mustang" and "Except for the white stripes, it's red."

"How do you feel about grilled cheese?"

"I'm sorry?" What did grilled cheese have to do with 1965 Mustangs?

"The diner does a mean grilled cheese sandwich."

Fielding blinked, not following.

"While you wait. Might as well eat something. Get the ketchup."

"Oh," Fielding said. *Get the ketchup?* "Right. Okay." He bit his lip and eyed where he'd left his car. He could eat. And he had his sketchbook.

"You going to be okay? You traveling alone?" the officer said.

"Yeah. It's just me."

"Well, I promise the grilled cheese is good company. You got a smartphone?"

"Yeah." Of course he had a smartphone.

"Keep an eye on the Hopewell social media. As soon as this is cleared, they'll tell everyone."

"Oh. Right. Thank you." Fielding trudged back to the Mustang and slid inside, then pulled on his seat belt. Before he started the car, he turned to check, but the passenger seat was empty now.

Of course.

"Don't mind me, I'll be fine. *Alone.* In the middle of goddamn nowhere."

Fielding checked over his shoulder to make sure he was clear to turn around. Three of the four pickups had already left, and no one else was behind him.

"Recalculating," his phone said.

He stabbed at it with one finger, turning it off.

"Okay, Hopewell," Fielding said. "It's just you and me. Let's see what you've got to offer."

He turned left.

CHAPTER TWO

Finding a parking spot on Main Street wasn't difficult. Fielding wondered if that was a bad omen or because it was still the morning. He checked the passenger seat again, but Tate was still gone.

He'd come back. Sometimes it could take a while.

The wind tried to yank the car door from his hand, and closing it took effort. The sound of the wind whipping through the Manitoba maples lining the street was almost as loud as rain. Fielding glanced up and down the street. It could have been his hometown. It was no effort at all to imagine his uncle's pet shop and shelter in place of one of these buildings. Hopewell wasn't home, but Middle of Nowhere, Ontario definitely had its own look: faded, broken, and tired.

A glance or two later, though, and Fielding had to reassess. While the storefronts of Hopewell might not be brand new, they weren't faded or broken or even tired. Most of them looked pretty spry. Nicely painted, though the store options included a decided lack in the Starbucks department. Not even a Second Cup.

Hell, he'd settle for a Timmies at this point.

He gazed at the signs, and two stores down from where he'd parked, one caught his eye.

One Man's Treasure. Beneath that: Glassware, Kitchenware, Clothes, Toys, and Books.

An A-frame sign outside the shop declared it open.

Anup would love this. She always wanted to check out antique stores and second-hand shops. In high school, her bedroom had reaped the rewards, too. She had the coolest stuff, and she usually restored most of it herself, following YouTube how-to videos. Her biggest project had been to unstring and redesign a massive chandelier. She'd turned it into a wall of hanging lights behind her bed, and her video had gotten thousands of hits.

She'd slowed down on the videos since she went to university, but the ones she had done showed the Toronto apartment she and Kristin shared slowly transforming into something amazing and cool.

An amazing and cool apartment he was supposed to have shared with them.

He sighed.

If Anup were here, she'd totally drag him inside.

But she was in Toronto. Like Kristin. Like a significant portion of his graduating class. Definitely all the ones who could string a coherent sentence together.

He pulled out his phone and took a picture of the store. He got as far as opening their group conversation but then realized he'd sent Anup and Kristin four messages now without any replies from either of them. Admittedly, his were all sent very late last night and were just letting them know what time he'd be hitting the road, sure, but…

He turned off his phone and put it away. He could send her the picture of the Hopewell second-hand store after she replied, maybe.

He eyed the store again. Without Anup, would it even be fun to go in there? She was the one with vision—he snorted, the irony of that particular thought not lost on him—but he was not completely without skill at finding cool things. He'd been the one to spot the chandelier, after all.

Okay, maybe he'd noticed a cat sleeping near the chandelier, but it still counted.

Fielding rolled his eyes. He was stuck in Hopewell anyway. It wasn't like he had a lot to do. Why not check out the store?

❖

One Man's Treasure was apparently run by a middle-aged white woman, something he was sure Kristin would find both amusing and worthy of a heated discussion of the perceived inherent value of gender or something.

"Hello," the woman said. She had cool earrings, mostly white squares with black lines crossing them and touches of red and yellow. He'd studied the artist last year. Mondo-something?

"Hi," he said.

"Looking for anything in particular?"

"Not really. I just like second-hand stores."

She smiled, and waved one hand. "Enjoy."

Fielding passed between a shelf of glasses and pots and pans and a shelf of plates and cutlery in short vases, spotting a couple of bookshelves against the corner. Jackpot. He'd only taken another two steps toward the books when a girl appeared.

Oh no.

She wove together in twists of light at first, as though where she stood was drenched in sunlight, and it made the girl brighter than the world around her. The real world.

Fielding shivered, holding his breath against the little knot he sometimes caught when this happened.

Dark eyed, with a little dent in her chin, the girl looked to be about his age, though her haircut seemed old-fashioned, and her outfit was definitely from another time. More striking than that, though, was how clearly upset the girl seemed. She swiped angrily at a tear on her cheek, and then she looked up at the ceiling, blinking rapidly as she held a book open in front of her. She looked to be trying to get herself under control. Finally, she pulled a small envelope from her blouse pocket and put it into the book. She closed the book, and then turned sharply, as though someone had called her name.

She held the book to her chest for a moment, and then she reached out to put it somewhere. The book vanished the moment she let go, and a second after that, with another shimmer of out-of-place sunlight, the girl followed suit.

Fielding let out his breath, alone again.

Okay. He'd been expecting something like this since feeling the pressure change on the bridge, and here it was. Over and done with.

He rubbed his eyes and glanced around the store. He stood there a few more seconds, then forced himself to keep going to the bookshelf. The book the girl held was a small hardcover with a faded orange dust jacket. He scanned the books, which were more or less in alphabetical order, not that that helped. Still, it didn't take too long. He found it right near the top. *Sense and Sensibility.* He reached for it, hesitating a second before touching it, then pulled it off the shelf.

He looked around, but the girl didn't reappear. Sometimes it was like that. She might come back right away, or she might not come back for weeks, if at all.

But the book felt right. It had a *pressure* to it.

He bit his lip, considering putting it back without checking for the envelope, but then he remembered how upset the girl seemed, and the tears she'd been angrily fighting off. Fielding could relate. Angry crying was the worst, and he did it too. It was so humiliating, and people didn't understand you were frustrated, not sad, and you weren't crying because you needed a hug, you were crying because they weren't listening, and…

He flipped through the book. The envelope was still there, tucked between the final few pages.

He turned it over. There was no address, only the name Elinor L. Kelly, in carefully written cursive. He flipped it over again and checked the seal. The glue had pretty much given up the ghost, barely sticking. It looked old.

He closed the book on the letter and brought it to the cash. The woman with the cool earrings checked the little tag on the back, and told him it was two dollars, plus tax.

He dug a toonie and some change out of his pocket. She rang him through, and when she handed him his change, Fielding tried to sound casual. "Hey, do you know an Elinor Kelly?"

The woman shook her head. "I'm afraid not."

"Thanks anyway."

"Enjoy your book."

He held it up. "Will do. Is there a coffee shop around here?" He wouldn't hate a cup of coffee, and he needed a place to sit to figure out exactly what he should do with the envelope now that he had it. It had meant something to that girl.

"The café in the business tower won't be open until noon. The gas station has a Tims if you're looking for something to go, but I hear there's a tree blocking the highway, and there's nowhere to sit at the gas station."

"The tree is why I'm here," Fielding said.

"Wild wind out today, eh?"

"Yeah."

"Well, you should try the Softshoe Diner." She smiled. "How do you feel about grilled cheese sandwiches?"

Outside the shop, Fielding took a few seconds to regain his balance from seeing the girl from the past. It wasn't the first time that had happened in a second-hand shop, so he shouldn't be surprised. He snorted. Right. Like he was ever not going to be surprised. At least it tended to be pretty rare. And the last one had been, what, two months ago? The library. He and his mother and his uncle were getting their library cards renewed, and an old man had popped up in the mystery section on the large chair they kept there. It hadn't happened before, but Fielding wasn't sure he'd ever been in the mystery section before that.

Either way, Fielding hadn't gone back to the library since. He did most of his borrowing and reading on his phone and his e-reader anyway.

Remembering the library brought his attention back to the book. *Sense and Sensibility*. He'd never read it. And he probably never would. He flipped it over, but it was an old book and didn't have anything written on the back. It didn't even have a barcode on the faded orange dust jacket.

Fielding considered going back to his car, but armed with the knowledge of coffee at the diner—terrible coffee, he assumed, but even terrible coffee was coffee—he looked left, then right.

Where the hell was the diner?

He pulled up the map on his phone. It was still trying to tell him how to get to Anup and Kristin's place in Toronto. He undid the trip with a resigned sigh, then hit the restaurant icon. The diner was one of a whopping three hits in the whole town of Hopewell. It was farther down Main Street, on the opposite side, just after one of the side roads that led to the highway.

He got back in the Mustang, putting the book on the back seat. The passenger seat was still empty. Fielding closed his eyes, took a steadying breath, and opened them again. Still empty.

God, he wished Anup was here. Or Kristin. Or anyone.

At least there'd be people at the diner. There had to be, right?

He buckled up, checked his rear-view, and pulled out onto Main Street. The drive to the diner took no time at all, and there were, indeed, a few cars in the parking lot.

The building itself wasn't much to look at. A squat, brick building fronted mostly with glass windows, the most interesting thing about it was the neon sign above the doorway proclaiming its name in red letters. To one side, a spread of four picnic tables waited, though no one was using them.

Everything about the Softshoe Diner said small-town, and not in a quirky, fun way.

"What am I even doing?" Fielding said. He grabbed his phone again and did a quick search for Hopewell, then narrowed the search down to Hopewell, Ontario—because *of course* this place wasn't even on the first page of hits—and found the official town website. It didn't load particularly well on his phone, but after some awkward navigating, he found the links to the town's social media, which was only Twitter and Facebook. Not even Instagram. He groaned and tapped the little blue bird.

The last tweet from the city was a picture of the massive fallen tree and the dented pylon.

"Highway 11 is currently impassable at the south end of town due to a downed tree from the windstorm. Trucks on their way from Abitibi. Watch here for updates."

Still no texts from Anup or Kristin.

Fielding tapped his thumbs against the steering wheel.

A man appeared, walking by the front of the Mustang. Taller white guy, floppy dark hair, maybe twenty-six? Buff, too. Blue shirt and shorts. Fielding barely had time to catch an admiring glimpse of his calves as he took two or three steps, and then he was gone, twisting apart into the same nothing he'd come from.

"What. The. *Hell*." Fielding stared, but the man didn't reappear. Twice in one day? That had never happened. Never.

He grabbed the book and got out of the car. He was done being by himself. Small-town or not, he was going to the diner. He'd even try the damned grilled cheese.

CHAPTER THREE

At first glance, the Softshoe Diner lived down to Fielding's expectations. It leaned into the whole diner thing, with a long Formica bar and a series of actual stools down the opposite wall from the entrance, with booths and tables making up the rest of the space. But the longer Fielding looked, the more he had to grudgingly admit it wasn't as bad as he expected. The chrome and deep blue colour scheme avoided being over-the-top the way a traditional bubblegum pink or cherry red would have and the artwork on the walls seemed to be a mix of abstracts, carved pieces, and other paintings, rather than the expected kitsch. In fact, the whole place avoided being hopelessly dated and came in somewhere closer to retro-cool.

Score one for Hopewell.

It wasn't packed, but neither was it empty. Most of the people looked like the drivers he'd seen at the downed tree, frankly: jeans, jackets, and work boots. Fielding aimed himself at an empty booth at one end, one hundred percent sure he was standing out in his bright red hoodie.

He put the book down on the table, went to slide into the seat, and came face-to-face with a smiling boy drinking a milkshake from a large glass.

Fielding managed not to yelp. Barely.

The echo of the boy was there and gone before Fielding could even really get a good look, but that didn't stop his heart from jackhammering around inside his ribcage.

"For fuck's sake, what is wrong with this town?" Fielding said, taking a few seconds to breathe. Three times in the same day? Crying girls, hot guys, smiling boys—all he needed was some creepy dude in a mirror's reflection and today could give him the heart attack it seemed determined to deliver.

"Not up to your standards?"

"Jesus!" Fielding jumped again and turned. Behind him, a tall white guy about his age had approached without him noticing, which wasn't surprising. The guy wore a T-shirt with the Softshoe Diner logo across his chest, jeans, and a little apron-pocket thing around his waist. Also? He was cute. Like, really cute. Broad shoulders, arms clearly capable of lifting heavy things, and wavy dark hair.

"Sorry," Cute Diner Boy said, without a trace of apology in his voice at all.

"Warn a guy," Fielding said, sitting down. Cute Diner Boy smiled, revealing he also had nice teeth. Either the guy had won the tooth lottery, or he'd successfully completed braces. Oh, and he had a name tag. Cute Diner Boy's name was Joshua.

Joshua's smile was twitching a bit, like he was holding off on laughing.

"You snuck up on me on purpose," Fielding said.

"Guilty," Joshua said. "But you hate my town, so it's only fair."

"I hate your…" Fielding didn't follow. "What?"

"So you *don't* hate my town? Because you were pretty clear just now."

"Oh! Oh, no. Your town is fine. Really." *It just seems to be full of insistent history and jump scares.* Fielding bit his lip. "I didn't expect to be here, is all."

"Unexpected?" Joshua leaned against the bench on the other side of Fielding's booth, in a move both casual and cool. "Now, that sounds like a story."

Fielding shrugged. "A tree fell on Highway 11."

"Okay, so a short story, then. I heard about that. Can I get you some coffee?" Joshua handed him the menu. A single laminated page, one side was completely devoted to breakfast, which it declared was available all day. As were the grilled cheese sandwiches, which took up a whole quarter of the page and came with two complimentary choices from six "secret recipe" condiments.

Unreal.

"I'd love some coffee," Fielding said. Something moved out of the corner of his eye, and he flinched. Oh good. The boy and his milkshake were back.

"Everything okay?" Joshua said.

"Is it all right if I move to that booth?" Fielding pointed.

"Knock yourself out." Joshua did a little flourish with one hand, pushing off from where he leaned. "I'll bring your coffee over. Take your time with the menu. From what I'm told, the Hydro folks are coming from Abitibi, so…" He raised his eyebrows.

"Yeah, that's what the cop told me," Fielding said, resolutely ignoring the movement beside him. Whoever that kid was, he freaking loved his milkshakes. Fielding slid out of the booth and moved, putting his back to the memory of milkshake kid. He—it—could do whatever the hell it wanted. Fielding didn't have to watch.

"Be right back."

Joshua the Cute Diner Boy also had a nice butt.

Fielding glanced down, catching himself. Open ogling was likely not a good idea. He pulled out his phone and refreshed the Twitter page. The same tweet as before was the most recent from the Hopewell account. Downed tree. Pylon. Wait for updates.

Great.

All things considered, he'd rather be stacking cans of cat food, and if that didn't sum up the day, nothing could.

God, he hoped the coffee was good.

❖

One cup of admittedly decent coffee in hand, which Joshua the Cute Diner Boy had dropped off with another one of those nice-teeth smiles, Fielding had ordered the grilled cheese—how could he not?—and settled in to wait. Out of the wind, he unzipped his hoodie.

He picked up the book again and flipped open the front cover. The writing on the inside of the dust jacket made it clear *Sense and Sensibility* was a classic, which was not a plus, then declared it also a romance, which was. But Fielding only got a few paragraphs in before he decided his first instinct had been right. He wasn't going to read this book. Who had time for books about straight people?

Flipping to the middle of the book, he checked the envelope. The name, Elinor L. Kelly, in impossibly perfect penmanship meant nothing to him, but the memory of the girl's tears imbued it with something far too familiar.

Heartbreak, maybe. But definitely loneliness.

He blew out a breath and gave the envelope a good long stare, but nothing happened. Annoyed with himself, he flipped it over.

The flap came open. Fielding pressed it with one finger to see if it would reseal itself.

It came open again.

"At this point, it would be shirking my duty not to read you," Fielding said.

It didn't reply.

Despite his completely founded and objectively reasonable responsibility to read what was inside, Fielding couldn't help himself from checking the diner to make sure no one was looking at him, not that he was doing anything wrong, then he undid the flap all the way and pulled out the paper.

It was one piece, folded into thirds, with no writing on the outside.

He unfolded it and stared.

16-3-13, 16-4-35, 16-4-67… Most of the page was full, but it was all the same: a series of handwritten numbers.

"What the hell?"

He smoothed out the page and scanned up and down the lines of numbers, but nothing changed. It was a piece of paper covered in numbers grouped in sets of three.

Why would this make the girl cry?

"Math homework?"

Fielding jumped again, trying not to glare at Joshua the Cute Diner Boy. "Oh my God, please stop doing that."

"You're too easy," Joshua said. The guy had zero guilt on display. It should be annoying, but it wasn't, which in itself was annoying. He held up the plated grilled cheese and smiled. "Here you go."

Fielding moved the book and letter. The numbers caught his eye again. "It's not math homework," he said. He was sure of that. For one thing, it didn't make sense as math homework. Sixteen minus three minus thirteen? No one needed that much practice at subtraction.

"What is it, then?" Joshua leaned over Fielding a bit to see the letter, and Fielding tried not to react to how close the guy was. Who knew the smell of coffee and toast could be attractive?

"I actually don't know," Fielding said. Then he remembered the envelope. "Hey, have you ever heard of an Elinor Kelly?"

Joshua shook his head. "No. Sorry."

Fielding exhaled. "That's okay."

"Well, enjoy. You said I should pick your condiments, and they are both our own special recipes. I recommend dipping into the sweet and spicy ketchup between bites. The dill mustard mayo is also a popular choice, but less of a town favourite." Joshua took a step back. "I'm going to walk away now. I'll try and stomp my feet and whistle when I come back."

"Oh, you're funny."

"That's what my boyfriend tells me," Joshua said. "Enjoy decoding your whatever-that-is." A moment later, he was gone.

Fielding sat there, napkin in hand, processing for a second. Did he just…? Boyfriend. Huh. Conflicting feelings battled briefly in Fielding's stomach. Joshua the Cute Diner Boy was gay or bi, or pan! Hurray! And also had a boyfriend. Boo. Why had he mentioned it to Fielding? Fielding had crappy gaydar, but he also didn't think he projected gay boy out into the world. Nerd, yes. Gay boy, no. How had Joshua known he could mention his boyfriend to him?

Or did he do that with everyone?

Fielding tried to imagine that being the case. Places like Hopewell? Not likely. Heck, even when places like this were actively trying to be decent, Fielding couldn't imagine it. Never mind decent, it'd have to be amazing. But outing yourself to random strangers? He tried to imagine doing that back home at the pet store. There was that guy who worked at the Second Cup. Would Fielding ever casually drop a hint to him while he was getting his coffee?

Probably not.

No. Joshua the Cute Diner Boy must have great gaydar. It probably came as a package deal with nice smiles and dented chins or something.

Still, it was nice to be included, even in such a small way. He hadn't felt included in much of anything this year.

He picked up the first triangle of grilled cheese, which honestly smelled pretty good. It was crispy and gooey all at the same time. He took a bite, then had to stop because holy flying crap, the sandwich was amazing. He chewed and swallowed while his eyebrows rose to the stratosphere, and couldn't help but shake his head. Grilled cheese. Who knew? He looked down at his plate and eyed the two little silver cups, then gave in and dipped the sandwich into the whatever-it-was ketchup. The second bite was even better.

By the time he'd finished the first triangle, Fielding agreed with Joshua's take. The mayo was also tasty, but the whatever it was in the ketchup was the best thing that ever happened to a tomato. He took a second to wipe his hands. He hadn't been particularly hungry when he sat down, but he was totally going to destroy the other half.

Fielding noticed the letter again, off to the side where he'd left it.

Good luck decoding your whatever-that-is.

Decoding.

He pulled out his phone. The Hopewell social media was still telling him to wait for updates, but he closed it and opened a search window.

He typed in "three number codes" and then picked up the other half of his grilled cheese while the results loaded.

At first, it looked pretty hopeless. Three-number codes were plentiful, but none of the ones that showed up on the first few pages of his search seemed to be the key to the letter. He tried a few different combinations and earned a few more failures, but when he remembered the way the crying girl had tucked the envelope into the book with such purpose, Fielding tried a search for "three number code" and "novel." With that, he hit the jackpot.

Book ciphers.

Two similar book-related methods of encryption, book ciphers and book codes, have been used often in history and continue to be of considerable strength as a method of encrypted communication. Both require both the sender and the receiver to have copies of not only the same book, but the same printed edition, and both use numbers to point the reader to specific words (book ciphers) or letters (book codes).

The simpler version, the book cipher, involves locating a particular word one at a time in the text, and is therefore limited to the vocabulary included in the original book itself. A starting position can be encoded in a number of ways, or the book can be used as a whole. In the latter case, this often means the use of three numbers: a page, a line (or alternatively, a paragraph or sentence), and then a particular word. In this case, 3-3-9 would be the third page, third paragraph, and ninth word.

Fielding turned to the letter and eyed the numbers. The first number of the various sets of three tended to go up and up, though not always, and started at sixteen. Could the girl have tucked the letter in the book it was coded with? He picked up the book, eyed the first trio of numbers, and turned to page sixteen.

16-3-13 was "I."
16-4-35 was "do."
16-4-67 was "not."
17-7-4 was "wish."
16-2-14 was "to."
17-2-5 was "be."
17-3-29 was "parted."

Fielding stopped, staring at the letter, then eyeing what he'd tapped out on his phone as he went. He wished he'd brought his sketchbook inside with him. Counting out sixty-seven words was tedious, and the screen kept going dark in between words.

I do not wish to be parted.

Tell me about it, book girl.

"You doing okay?"

Fielding turned to see Joshua there, holding up the glass jug of coffee and offering the same bright smile. At least this time he hadn't scared the crap out of him.

"I am," Fielding said, though he had to clear his throat. What were the damn chances? He looked down at the letter, which still had quite a bit more to go, and then his phone, which had gone dark again. He should have brought his sketchbook. "Hey, could I maybe borrow a pen and a piece of paper?"

"Sure," Joshua said. "More coffee?"

"Yeah, thanks."

"Good book?" Joshua asked as he poured.

"Not really my thing." Fielding closed it to show him the cover.

"*Sense and Sensibility* isn't your thing? But it's a classic," Joshua said.

Fielding stared at him.

"Okay, fine." Joshua laughed. "I've never read it. But I've seen the movies."

"Would you believe it's not a book at all, but a key?"

"Sorry?"

"You were right," Fielding tapped the letter. "It's a code."

"Huh." Joshua tilted his head. "Check me out. I'm a genius. Your plate is bare, so I'm assuming the grilled cheese was okay?"

"Life-changing."

"See? I don't lead you astray. I'll be right back with the pen and paper."

Fielding watched him go—not openly ogling, what with Joshua having a boyfriend, but a glance was still nice—and caught another glimpse of the milkshake kid. He watched the boy laugh silently, nod in agreement to someone who hadn't been there in years, most likely, and then take another long pull on his straw. The kid looked happy. It was a strong echo, and kept repeating.

I do not wish to be parted.

Such a formal turn of phrase, but like the website said, you had to use the words in whatever book you had. He wondered why the person the girl was writing to had to go or if it was the girl herself who was leaving. But for some reason it wouldn't take his therapist long to point out, he was sure the crying girl was being left behind.

Joshua returned with the pen and a kids' paper place mat. A cartoon grilled cheese triangle needed help getting through a maze. Fielding blinked at it until Joshua turned it over to the blank side.

"When you're done, I can bring you crayons so you can colour."

"Thanks," Fielding said, voice heavy with sarcasm.

Joshua laughed as he left, but Fielding turned his attention back to the letter and got to work.

Chapter Four

Fielding got as far as the picnic benches outside the diner before he stopped walking.

Where, exactly, was he going? There was no point getting back in Tate's Mustang.

He'd checked his phone again after paying the bill, which Joshua the Cute Diner Boy had dropped off in between chatting with a trio he assumed were his friends and dealing with other tables, all of which were starting to fill up. Apparently, the Hydro people from Abitibi had been reached and would be coming, which was good, but it would still be a while.

He'd eaten. He'd had coffee. He'd used the bathroom. After he'd finished with the letter, he'd felt foolish sitting in the booth by himself, so he left a solid tip that had nothing to do with how cute Joshua was.

Okay, well, more to do with how nice he'd been. If in a teasing sort of way. Someone to talk to after the worst year ever was definitely worth a few extra toonies.

Especially since Anup still hadn't written back. Neither had Kristin. He considered letting his mother know he was stuck, but tossed that idea almost immediately. Better to let her know about the delay once he was back on track, and she couldn't ask him to give up, turn around, and come home.

The last place he wanted to be was back home.

And besides that, if he talked to her or texted her, there'd be an update. Even if the update was no news.

Or maybe worse news.

He looked at the texts he'd last sent Anup and Kristin and blew out a breath before turning off his screen.

I do not wish to be parted. The first sentence of the decoded letter set the tone for the rest, and was all too familiar. *We have no choice. It is not up to us. I wish you to remain here with me. I do not know how I will survive. My love for you is as precious as air.*

Fielding closed his eyes, turning his face to the sun and letting the gusting wind blow past him. It wasn't blasting anywhere nearly as strong as earlier, which he decided at random to consider a good omen.

When he opened his eyes again, the hot guy in shorts and the tight blue shirt faded into sight at the corner of the intersection, took a few steps, waved at someone, and faded back out. The guy was dedicated to his waving, that was for sure. But this time Fielding noticed more than his calves, though they still stole the show. It wasn't just blue shorts and a shirt, but some kind of uniform. And the man sported a tattoo around his left biceps.

As echoes went, at least it was fun to look at. Had he ever had hot beefcake replaying before? He didn't think so. He'd call it another win, even if it was unnerving to have so many in one day.

The door to the diner opened again, and Fielding caught a glimpse of Joshua the Cute Diner Guy holding the door open for one of the people he'd been so chatty with. He was a skinny white guy, who, now that Fielding could see his front, had the whole nerd-boy-hot thing going for him, complete with the ability to check his phone even when his hands were full with two big to-go containers and coffee stacked on top. Fielding had to give him credit, though. He had the walk-and-text down, using chin power to keep the coffee in place.

Fielding glanced at the Mustang, figuring he could grab his sketchbook. Do some drawing. Maybe outline the girl from the second-hand store, rough the image onto paper while it was still fresh in his memory.

A loud yelp interrupted his thoughts, and Fielding whipped around, keys in hand, then winced at the view.

So much for chin power. Mr. Nerd Hot was on the ground, and it didn't look like a single container had been spared in the fall. Someone else was standing across from him, one arm held out to the side and clutching a phone, now wearing the contents of the various containers in question. Fielding was already dead from second-hand embarrassment.

Fielding waited, tense, but the bigger guy didn't yell or throw a punch, so he exhaled. After a conversation he couldn't hear, Mr. Nerd Hot was back on his feet and the other guy was walking off, his gait as awkward as expected for someone covered in food, coffee, and condiments.

Not wanting the remaining guy to notice him staring, Fielding grabbed his sketchbook and pencils from the Mustang, and by the time he'd arranged his pencils just so at one of the picnic tables, Mr. Nerd Hot had picked up all the worst of the detritus from the sidewalk, gotten another order, and left with his attention firmly placed on the space ahead of him.

Fielding roughed out a pose of the girl in the second-hand store, trying to capture her facial expressions. She'd had dark eyes and a little dent in her chin, like Joshua the Cute Diner Boy.

He paused, looking up while he tried to remember exactly what her blouse and skirt had looked like, catching the sight of someone else approaching the diner.

He frowned. It was just a man in jeans, work boots, a heavy-duty plaid work shirt, and a trucker hat, but Fielding hadn't seen him pass by the picnic table he was working at. While he could sometimes get a little lost in the drawing zone, he hadn't even noticed the man's car pull in, and—

The man in plaid vanished at the door.

Another one. Fielding took a few seconds to get his breathing under control, letting the jolt of shock pass him by.

Draw. Just draw. It wasn't the first time he'd distracted himself by drawing, and it wouldn't be the last. He put his attention back to the girl's skirt and blouse, doing his level best to remember, wondering if she'd appear to him again. In the shop, the book and letter had that strange sense of weight in his hand, but there was no telling when, or if, it would trigger her appearance again.

He easily lost another hour in the lines and shading, and started an inset drawing of the girl's face, trying to capture her features without tears, imagining what she would look like were she not upset. On an impulse, he did an even quicker sketch of the girl wearing glasses.

Once he had the three drawings, he tried his phone again. Nothing new. He pulled the envelope out of the book again and sighed.

Elinor L. Kelly.

The door to the diner opened. Fielding glanced up and found himself making accidental eye contact with Joshua, who was pulling on a light blue jacket over his diner T-shirt. To Fielding's surprise, he walked over to his picnic table.

"You didn't get far," Joshua said. "Have you been sitting here all this time?"

"There's still a tree across the road," Fielding said, closing his sketchbook. "There's nowhere to go."

"Are you insulting my town again?" Joshua paused, tilting his head and narrowing his eyes.

"I already admitted I was wrong about the grilled cheese." Fielding raised his hands in surrender. "What more do you want?"

Joshua crossed his arms. "Are you really just going to sit there until the road is clear?"

Fielding shrugged. He felt foolish admitting that had, indeed, been his plan.

"You draw?" Joshua said.

Fielding eyed his sketchbook. "I draw."

Joshua was about to say something else, but then his pocket buzzed. He reached in and pulled out his phone and grinned, turning around and yelling "Pervert!"

Fielding blinked, then saw a guy walking up from around the corner of the diner. Slender, with sandy-blond hair, he sported a black T-shirt that made his white skin appear all the paler, and really cool-looking glasses, the frames of which were entirely white on the exterior, but black on the interior of the arms. He held his hands out to the side, aimed a lingering look at Joshua's butt, then said, "I call it how I see it."

Joshua pulled the guy into a hug, then kissed him.

Ah, Fielding thought. The boyfriend.

"Logan," Joshua said, spinning the guy slightly so he was facing where Fielding sat. "This is…" He frowned. "Wait. What's your name?"

"Fielding."

"Logan, this is Fielding. Fielding, this is Logan."

"Hi," Logan said, amiably enough.

"Hey." Fielding's attention caught on Logan's right eyebrow, which was pierced with a little silver hoop. Compared to the small-town jock vibe Fielding got from Joshua, Logan felt more familiar. He imagined he and Anup would get along. They had a similar creativity in the way they presented. Even Logan's belt was neat. It was made out of a seat belt, right down to the buckle being the seat belt clip.

Joshua turned to Logan. "Fielding was driving through town, and had no intention of stopping here ever in his entire life—"

"Hey," Fielding said.

"But had no choice, because tree."

"I heard," Logan said. "Where were you headed?"

"Toronto. I'm going to SciCon and to see friends."

"Cool," Logan said. "Except for the tree part."

"Except," Fielding said.

"I thought maybe we could give him the town tour," Joshua said. "Show him how badly he misjudged his situation."

"What?" Fielding said, but Logan laughed.

"He's not misjudging, Josh," Logan said.

"He was maligning our town when I met him."

"Ooh, 'maligning.' Good word." Logan shoved Joshua's arm, and Joshua grinned and swooped in for another quick kiss to Logan's cheek.

Fielding grinned. Okay, it was early, but he was going to say he liked Joshua and Logan. They were adorable.

"Seriously, though," Joshua said, turning back to Fielding. "Town tour. You in?"

"Well, I'll have to check my schedule," Fielding said, but he got up from the picnic table. He glanced at the diner. "Are you on a break, or…?"

"I work the breakfast and lunch rushes," Joshua said. "I am now free for the day. We shall show you all the sights, doubter of Hopewell."

"Don't worry. It won't take very long," Logan said.

Fielding laughed. "Let me put these in the car." He held up his sketchbook, pencils, and the novel. Which reminded him. "Hey, do you know an Elinor Kelly?" he asked Logan.

Logan shook his head. "No, sorry."

Fielding nodded, not particularly surprised, and pulled out his keys. When he slid the key into the lock of the passenger side of the Mustang, Joshua made a loud, strangled noise, and Fielding turned, alarmed.

"What?"

"That's your car?" He looked back and forth between Fielding and the Mustang like a metronome, his mouth open.

Ah. That.

"It's my cousin's car, and my uncle's before that, but he lets me take care of it while he's overseas," Fielding said. "He taught me to drive in it."

"It's a '65?"

"Yes. And before you ask, that's everything I know about this car."

"It's gorgeous," Joshua said. "Oh my God, the upholstery." He'd tented his hands over his eyes to look through the windows. Logan, for his part, was smiling and shaking his head. Clearly, this outburst was not unusual. Joshua did seem to have one setting: genuine outbursts.

"Thanks," Fielding said, opening the door to toss the book and his stuff onto the passenger seat.

"Wait!" Joshua said, and Fielding jumped.

"What? What's wrong?"

"Nothing," Joshua said. "But…could we sit in it? And take a picture?"

"He wants to make Lyn jealous," Logan said.

"Lyn?"

"A guy we know," Logan said. "Cars are one of his things."

Fielding glanced back into the car. The passenger seat was still empty. "Sure. Okay."

"Oh my God, you're the best," Fielding said, going around to the driver's side.

"Oh, so I get shotgun, do I?" Logan said.

"Let me have this," Joshua said. He held his hands together like he was begging.

Logan laughed and slipped past Fielding into the passenger seat. He leaned across to unlock the driver's side door for Joshua, and Fielding had a visceral memory of Tate.

"The best thing about a classic car is the date test."

"The what now?"

"No automatic locks. So, I unlock the door for a date, they climb in, and I walk around to the driver's side. If they lean over and unlock the door before I get there? Quality date."

"How do people even know they have to do that, though?"

"That's the thing, Fielding. Quality dates figure it out."

"Can you get the shot?" Joshua was leaning across Logan, offering his phone.

Fielding forced the memory back, swallowing past the sudden ache. "Sorry. Yes."

He stepped back and Logan closed the door. Fielding took a few shots of the guys through the windshield, then got them to roll down the windows for a couple of side shots. Then Joshua ran his hands over the steering wheel almost reverently while Logan laughed at him. Fielding snapped a candid of the moment, grinning when he saw their faces.

"Here," he said, passing the phone back once they'd climbed out again.

"He is going to be so jealous," Joshua said, tapping on the phone.

"He means 'thank you,'" Logan said.

Fielding smiled. "It's fine." He'd gotten used to the effect of driving around in the Mustang. Back home, guys would often drift over and ask questions whenever he was parked somewhere. None of them had been like Joshua and Logan, though. Certainly, none of them had been dating each other.

"Okay," Joshua said, his phone making the telltale swoosh sound of a sent text. "Now we owe you the full five-star tour."

"Sure," Fielding said. Why not? These guys were fun, and he had nothing else he could be doing. "Do we start with the well?"

"Pardon?" Joshua shook his head.

"The well. Where is it?"

"Oh, I get you." Joshua shook his head. "There's no well."

"But the town's called Hopewell," Fielding said. "How can you name a town Hopewell if there's no well?"

"Maybe people cared more about hope," Joshua said.

"Wow." Fielding stared. The guy even looked like he meant it.

"He's got this relentless optimism thing," Logan said. "It's jarring at first, but I promise you get used to it."

"It beats the alternative." Joshua wrapped an arm around Logan, who leaned into it. "I just happen to think this place is special."

Behind them, Fielding saw the hot guy in blue fade in, take a few steps across the far side of the intersection, wave at someone, then fade out again. He focused his attention back to Joshua and Logan. "I can't argue with that."

CHAPTER FIVE

Joshua promised the Mustang would be fine in the Softshoe Diner's parking lot, suggesting they start on foot doing what he called "the loop." They headed up to Main Street. Joshua, unsurprisingly, was doing most of the talking.

The guy seemed to have endless enthusiasm for, well, everything.

"Okay, so, this is cool. Hopewell Tour nugget—see all those carvings?"

Along their side of the street, there were indeed a series of carvings randomly spaced among trees lining this side of Main Street. They were mostly animals, polished up to a shine, and... Fielding tilted his head. Unless he was mistaken, they were carved out of tree stumps that still had roots in the ground.

"Were those trees?" he said.

"Score one for the new guy. Yep." Joshua ticked off a point on an imaginary score-board with one finger. "It used to be Main Street had trees all down this side. There are still a bunch of them, obviously, but there were way more. Manitoba maples."

Sure enough, the pattern of carved tree stumps wasn't as random if you included the trees. They were evenly spaced.

"Ice storm," Logan said, answering Fielding's next question before he could ask it. "Back in the nineties. My mom said the whole town lost a tonne of trees. Instead of replanting the ones here along Main Street, they had our local famous artist carve whatever was left in the ground."

Fielding had to admit the result was pretty cool. They stopped at a particularly tall carving of three forearm-length salmon jumping out of a swirl of water. Beyond being sealed and polished, it looked like the colour remained the natural grain of the wood beneath. He knelt down to check the edge where the artist had stopped carving the splashing water and left the original tree stump and bark, creating a kind of platform for the piece. The whole thing felt clever to him. Using something leftover to make art? He snapped a photo and considered sending it to Anup, but tucked his phone away. He glanced back up—and nearly screamed at the broadly built black-haired woman with a chainsaw looming over him.

She vanished.

Fielding swallowed hard, then rose shakily.

"All good?" Joshua said. He shared a quick glance with Logan.

"Head rush." Fielding managed a weak nod and a wan smile. "Great workmanship. She uses a chainsaw?"

Joshua tilted his head. "Another point for the new guy. Yeah, they're all carved with a chainsaw to start with."

"You can tell?" Logan sounded impressed. "Just by looking?"

"Just by looking," Fielding said. He focused on breathing, trying to get his heart rate to go back down to something normal. Chainsaws. It couldn't have been a little old man with a whittling knife or something. Oh no, not in Hopewell. Large women wielding chainsaws or nothing.

He tried not to look too closely at the rest of the carvings they passed, which was admittedly made easier by the fact the hot guy in blue shorts was still popping in and out of view on the other side of Main Street, waving and showing off his legs and biceps. It looked like he was calling to people, too, though whoever he'd been talking to didn't show up with him.

Joshua pointed something else out, and Logan forced himself to pay attention.

Hot guy appeared again, waving. So distracting.

This town had it in for him.

"Did you just get out of school?" Logan said.

"I deferred," Fielding said, and when both of the guys looked at him, he found himself explaining. "I was supposed to go to Ryerson, but basically everything fell apart. My uncle had a heart attack, and my mother's hours got cut at work, so I stuck around. My uncle owns a pet store and shelter, and I covered him." He gave them a half-shrug, not feeling up to eloquence. "It hasn't been the best year."

"I'm sorry about your uncle," Joshua said. He looked it, too.

"It was fixable," Fielding said. "He had no idea he had a defective heart until it happened, but he got a pacemaker. And he's going to be okay, so it worked out."

"Still, that sounds scary. And hard. I mean, it wouldn't be what you want to do, but it's not like you can complain about it, right?" Joshua said. "Because people would think you were centering yourself."

Wow. Okay. Joshua really did just sort of *say* stuff. Fielding nodded, awkwardly embarrassed by the accuracy.

"What are you going to study?" Logan said. It wasn't a subtle change of subject, but Fielding appreciated it regardless.

"Art. Graphic design is the end goal," Fielding said. "That's been one plus to this whole year of stacking cat food—my portfolio is bigger."

"Oh cool. Digital, or paint, or…" Logan waved a hand.

"Digital and drawing. I like to sketch first."

"He's a photographer," Joshua said, tugging Logan against him affectionately. "I cannot even draw a stick man."

"Is that what you're studying?" Fielding said.

Logan shook his head. "Hobby. I'm in psychology right now."

"He's going to be a psychiatrist," Joshua said, practically beaming with pride.

"Or a therapist," Logan said. "I haven't decided yet, but psych felt like a way to see if I like the path without, y'know, doing a whole medical degree first."

"Oh! Speaking of paths, the Hopewell Tour continues with the greenbelt footpath. Maybe we'll even find one of the mystery artist's art bombs," Joshua said.

"Okay, the what?" Fielding shook his head.

"Someone's been leaving these cool metal sculptures around town," Logan said.

"By all means," Fielding said.

Art bombs. How was that even a thing?

❖

"Okay, what's wrong?" Joshua said. They hadn't found any art bombs, but the greenbelt footpath had still been a nice way to pass some time. It was a sort of nature walk that followed an arc where Hopewell hadn't built up at all, though they could hear occasional traffic in the distance. On the other side, they'd come out near a large, boxy brick building Joshua had been waxing poetic about, a community centre, complete with a curling rink and hockey arena. Hopewell's claim to fame included not one, but *two* former NHL players, for which Fielding attempted to conjure admiration, but then the hot guy in blue shorts had appeared directly in front of Fielding, and Fielding had jumped back.

He wouldn't have actually bumped into the hot guy. But it still didn't stop him from reflexively tripping himself up trying to avoid a non-collision with the wide man who wasn't actually there.

He did get a good look at the strange bag he was wearing, though, and the penny finally dropped about why he was seeing the hot guy all over Hopewell, but the end result of his admittedly awkward dance was Joshua finally stopping his walk-and-talk.

"What's happening?" Joshua said. As blunt and direct as always, Joshua didn't appear to be ready to accept anything other than an explanation. Logan aimed a similarly concerned glance his way.

Crap.

"Pardon?" Fielding knew he wasn't fooling anyone. He was so not a bluffer.

"You keep jumping," Joshua said. "You nearly tripped. Your eyes are like…" He mimicked looking around, turning his head with little jerky motions. It might have been comical had it not meant to be an impression of Fielding.

"Josh," Logan said.

"I do *not* look like that." At least, Fielding hoped that was true. He'd been trying his best not to overreact. And doing a not-so-stellar job, apparently.

Joshua crossed his arms.

"Well, not as bad as that," Fielding said.

"Spill."

"Josh," Logan said, a little sharper this time. "It's possible he doesn't want to share."

"Why not?" Joshua looked so obviously confused by that possibility, Fielding let out a little snort of laughter. Which made them both turn back to him.

"What?"

"Sorry," Fielding said. "You're just, like…so…" Fielding remembered what Logan had said. "Optimistic."

"You say that like it's a bad thing." Now he was pouting. Who knew it was possible to pout adorably? Then the pout shifted closer to hurt, and Fielding felt bad. Then Joshua's face smoothed and his eyebrows rose. "Oh! I'm doing it again, aren't I?"

"A little bit," Logan said gently. Clearly they had some sort of shorthand for whatever this was. Logan turned to Fielding. "You don't have to talk about whatever's up if you don't want to."

"But if you want to—"

Logan elbowed him.

"He might want to," Joshua said, hands spread, not remotely deterred.

"Thanks," Fielding said. "But I don't really talk about…it."

"It." Joshua's gaze locked on his. "So there *is* an it."

"Yes." He sighed. Why had he even said that? "Look, it's just… people freak out. Or could freak out. I mean, theoretically."

"Fielding." Joshua's eyebrows rose. "You can't do that. This is not making me want to know what's going on less."

"Me neither," Logan said. Joshua grinned at him, and Logan rolled his eyes. "What? I'm human."

"I…You'll think I'm delusional or something." That was certainly how it had played out with Tate.

"So?" Logan said. "You met me, what, an hour and a half ago? You'll never see us again after today. Who cares what we think of you?"

Fielding blinked. "Wow."

"I do optimism, he does realism," Joshua said. "It's why we're so good together. Also he's cute as fuck, and he tells me when I'm hyperfocusing or missing social cues."

Logan rolled his eyes, but then bumped shoulders with Joshua, who leaned over and kissed his head.

Yeah, Fielding definitely stanned these two.

I'll never see them again after today. That was true, wasn't it? Fielding considered the odd sort of freedom at play, but then the usual voice piped up, telling him not to speak. The voice itemized the list: how worried Tate had been, the disbelief, the anger. The voice reminded him how long it had taken Tate to look at him normally again, how he still wasn't sure if Tate actually believed him, how strained it had been before Tate left for his posting, and how awful it had left things.

I'll never see them again after today.

He glanced back up at Joshua's friendly smile and the way his arm was casually flung around Logan and Fielding decided the voice could, just this once maybe, shut the hell up.

"I can see things." Fielding waved a hand. "Everywhere."

"Things." Joshua leaned forward.

Right. Things wasn't very specific, was it? Fielding pointed to where he'd nearly tripped avoiding the man who wasn't really there. "Okay, so…well…there was a guy. Right there."

"Ooh, a guy," Joshua said with a grin. "Of course it's a guy. Is he hot?"

"Do you want to hear this or not?" Fielding said, aiming for stern but missing by miles. His face burned with embarrassment.

Joshua mimed sealing his lips.

Fielding blew out a little breath. "I keep seeing him at different corners. Intersections. Dark hair, a little long, but yeah, okay, he's cute."

"Cute," Logan said, his tone skeptical at best.

"Fine, he's hot."

"I knew it!" Joshua crowed. "Details. Make with them."

Logan rolled his eyes, but he nodded when Fielding looked at him. "Okay…Uh, he's buff. Like, wide. Really nice arms. Great calves." The two other boys frowned, and Fielding added, "He's in shorts."

They stared at him.

"Okay, forget the hot guy for now. It's not about the hot guy. That's not all it is. There was a kid with a milkshake in the diner at the first table I sat at—that's why I wanted to move—and there was this girl in the second-hand store, That's how I found the letter."

Joshua nodded slowly at him.

"Oh! It's also how I knew about the chainsaw," Fielding said, eyeing Logan. "When I was checking it out, I looked up and saw the artist for a second. With a chainsaw. At least, I assume it was her."

"Yeah." Logan blinked. "That's right. You said *she*."

"She's big. Burly. Like, if I had to guess, I'd say that's what a lady lumberjack looks like. She looked strong." He closed his eyes, trying to remember more details from the brief glance. "Long black hair in a ponytail or a braid or something. I think maybe she was Indigenous?"

"She's Métis," Logan said, speaking quietly but evenly. He didn't seem freaked out, but Fielding imagined Logan was cool enough to hide any tells.

"So you see people. Like the artist," Joshua said. Fielding could tell he wasn't quite sold, but he wasn't dismissing him. That was something, right? "Can we go back to the hot guy? You said you keep seeing him. Does that mean he's following us?"

"He's not following us. Wherever we go, he's already been there." He wasn't explaining this right. "It's not a *now* thing. They're not here *now*."

"So, he's not after us," Logan said, his voice dry. "This hot guy with great legs."

Fielding frowned. "You don't believe me."

Logan didn't reply right away, and Fielding turned to Joshua. "I guess you don't, either?"

"Hey, I don't judge. Hot guys to look at, at will? Sounds pretty cool. But why would a ghost follow us?"

"*It's not ghosts!*" It came out sharper than he intended. "I don't see ghosts."

Joshua and Logan glanced at each other. Fielding wanted to swear. Yeah, they thought he was delusional.

"I know it's not ghosts," Fielding said, bringing his voice back to something closer to normal, "because I've seen people like this before. People I know are still alive."

"I'm sorry. I don't think I get it," Joshua said. His voice had gotten all soft and placating, like he was trying to talk Fielding down or something.

The gentle sympathy brought tears to Fielding's eyes, which was the absolute last thing he wanted. He shook his head. "It's like a replay of emotions. Or important moments. I think places or things can sort of remember when something happened, or maybe when people really feel something strongly, something gets left behind. Like birthday parties or weddings, or even everyday things like teaching someone how to drive." Fielding choked and cleared his throat. "They repeat.

They echo. And sometimes I see it. Them. The echoes." His throat grew raw, and he knew he was a few moments away from tears.

God, he hated being a frustrated crier. *Hated* it.

"Hey," Joshua said. "It's okay." He and Logan exchanged another meaningful look.

"See?" Fielding snapped. "This is why I don't tell anyone. But no, I don't think the hot buff guy is following us. He's not following anyone." He remembered his last glimpse, and the bag the man carried. "He's delivering mail."

"What?" Logan said, eyes widening.

"He's a mailman. Blue uniform. Shorts. Really nice legs. If I had my sketch pad I could draw him for you. Oh! Barbed wire tattoo, right there." Fielding tapped his arm. "Which is tacky, but hey, if I had biceps like that—"

"Oh my God," Joshua said. "Are you sure?" He shuddered, shaking his hands out like they were wet. "Ew. Oh my God. *Ew ew ew.*"

Fielding stared at the two of them. "What's wrong? What's happening?"

Logan didn't reply at first, tapping at his phone. After a few seconds, he showed it to Fielding. "Is this the hot guy?"

"Stop *calling* him that!" Joshua said.

Fielding looked at the screen. The photo was of Logan and Joshua and two older adults, a man and a woman. They were all sitting at a dining room table, with whoever was taking the picture standing at one end of it. Joshua was at the head of the table, a birthday cake in front of him, candles lit. Logan was to one side of him. The woman laughing on the other side had the same dark curly hair as Joshua. Fielding would put money on her being Joshua's mother. The man had his arm around her. Fielding could see the barbed wire tattoo, much like one on the man he'd been catching glimpses of throughout Hopewell.

Was it the same one?

He looked closer. The man had some grey at the temples now, and he'd cut his hair much shorter than it used to be, but his face seemed right—same square chin, same smile. And he was definitely a big guy, though he'd put on some weight.

"I think so. Yeah, that's him," Fielding said. The longer he looked, the more he was sure of it.

"Your dad used to be a mailman," Logan said, turning to Joshua.

"Oh," Fielding said, finally getting it. "Hot guy is your dad."

"This is so gross," Joshua said. "So. Gross."

After Joshua calmed down a bit, Logan found a picture of the chainsaw artist online, and Fielding confirmed she'd been who he'd seen. They had no ideas about the milkshake kid in the diner, though.

"Do they ever stop?" Logan said, putting his phone away.

Fielding looked at him. "Pardon?"

"The…I keep wanting to call them ghosts, sorry."

"I call them echoes," Fielding said.

"Echoes, then. Do they ever stop?"

Fielding blew out a breath. "Sometimes I think they do. I mean, I'm not sure. There've been a couple I only saw once and I never saw again, but maybe they're still happening and I'm not there to see them? But I *have* made them stop. I can sort of push at them, and they fade away. I've only done that twice, though. But then for sure I never saw them again. I try not to do that, though."

"Only twice?" Joshua said.

"Just twice." Fielding looked down. "First time was by accident, because the echo scared me. It just sort of happened. I was walking home from the pet shop and then this guy was running right at me on the sidewalk, and it scared the crap out of me. Like, one second I'm alone, and the next there's a guy bearing down on me. And I could feel it, in here." He tapped his forehead. "It's like a pressure. Anyway. It was a shock, and I kind of shoved at it, and the guy broke apart into these little twists of mist."

"That doesn't sound less scary," Joshua said.

Fielding laughed. "I guess not. But I could feel it go. I *knew* it wouldn't be back. It's hard to explain."

"And the second time?" Logan said.

"The second time was different." He let the words drift off. "There's this kid at my school, and he got in a bad car accident about a year ago. This other man hit him in an intersection. Turned out the man had been drinking. I kept seeing him at the side of the road, crying. And I pushed at it to make it go away. But like I said, I try not to do that."

Logan frowned. "Why not? Why him and not others?"

"Well, part of it is that guy is still alive. I know him. We're not friends or anything, but he works at a coffee shop now and he seems okay. The drunk driver was at fault, not him, and I thought he got through it, so maybe he'd want that echo gone. So, I pushed that one away. But if I pushed an echo away, and it turned out the person isn't alive anymore…I mean, what if that's it? What if that's the last thing left of somebody?" He choked, annoyed all over again at the way he welled up so easily. "I don't want to do that."

When Fielding finally forced himself to look back up, Logan and Joshua were looking at him with thoughtful expressions. Logan had a little line between his eyebrows, like maybe he was trying to work something out, but neither of them pressed the issue.

"So," Joshua said. "Are you still up for the tour, or did you maybe want to just do something else?"

Fielding's chest relaxed, filling with warmth. He was pretty sure he'd never been so grateful to someone in his life.

"I'm okay," Fielding said, sounding convincing even to his own ears. "I'm not used to it happening so much. Usually it's every other month or so between echoes, but there've been, like, *five* already here today. It's like this whole town is dialed up to eleven."

"I wonder why," Logan said, that little line back between his eyebrows.

They believed him. They both believed him. He supposed the thing with Joshua's dad had sealed the deal, but a second rush of gratefulness flooded Fielding.

Joshua turned his head, looking up and down the street like maybe he could catch a glimpse of what Fielding saw. Fielding almost wished he could.

Logan reached out and took Joshua's hand, squeezing. Joshua turned back to him and offered the soppiest smile Fielding had ever seen.

You did that. He's smiling like that because you told him about his dad. The voice in Fielding's head sounded suspiciously like Tate. He swallowed.

"I kinda feel like showing you the water tower is going to be a letdown in comparison now," Joshua said.

"Yeah, I'm not sure anything is going to top Art Lady and her chainsaw," Fielding said, miming holding a chainsaw and swinging it through the air.

"Fair." Logan laughed.

Fielding took a moment to check the Hopewell feed again. No change. He put his phone back in his pocket. The three stood together on the road in what felt like an amiable silence. It reminded him of being with Anup and Kristin, and he smiled to himself.

"What?" Joshua said.

"Just thinking of my friends." Then he asked what he'd wanted to know since the diner. "How did you know I was gay?"

Joshua tilted his head. "What?"

"At the diner. You told me you had a boyfriend. No hesitation. How did you know I'd be okay with you having a boyfriend?"

"You're wearing a Catadora T-shirt." Joshua pointed. "I figured you could handle me being bi if you were a Catadora fan."

Fielding looked down at his chest. Sure enough, his favourite cat girl and princess were right there, snuggling on his chest. "I guess that's probably smarter than relying on gaydar."

"Oh, I could tell. But the T-shirt sealed the deal," Joshua said.

"Right." Fielding wasn't so sure he wanted to know more.

"So if we're not heading to the water tower," Logan said, in what felt like another rescue via not-so-subtle subject change, "what do we want to do instead?"

"Drive down to the river?" Joshua suggested.

Fielding bit his bottom lip.

"What?" Joshua said.

"It's…" Fielding paused, feeling kind of pathetic. Whether or not they believed him was one thing. Whether they'd want to do something as potentially pointless as what he had in mind was another. "Never mind."

"Say it," Logan said. "You'll never see us again, who cares, etcetera etcetera."

Fielding laughed. "Okay. Well. The girl with the letter I found in the book at the second-hand place was so sad. And she looked old— well, not old, she looked our age in the echo, but her outfit, her hair? They make me think she's from a while back. I keep thinking about how that letter never got to the person it was for, and it's a goodbye letter. Whoever this Elinor was, the girl didn't want to say goodbye to her, but she didn't have a chance to give her this letter."

"Okay," Joshua said.

"She was crushed," Fielding said. "She wrote this letter in code for someone, so she couldn't risk anyone else seeing it, right? I can't help but think it was maybe someone like us? Maybe she loved Elinor? And so I thought…" Fielding took a second, bracing for resistance. "What if we delivered it?"

"That," Joshua said, "is the best idea ever."

Chapter Six

"What was the name on the letter again?" Logan said.

"Elinor Kelly." Fielding had it memorized now. "Elinor L. Kelly."

"And it was in code?"

"Yeah. Numbers tell you which page, which paragraph, and which word." Fielding had the place mat from the diner in his back pocket. He pulled it out and read it. "*I do not wish to be parted. We have no choice. It is not up to us. I wish you to remain here with me. I do not know how I will survive. My love for you is as precious as air.*" When he glanced at the guys, both were staring at him. Logan's eyes were wide. Joshua's mouth hung open. Fielding shrugged. "You have to work with the words in the book, so it's maybe a bit dramatic."

"Poor Elinor's friend," Joshua said. "That sounds awful."

"Right?" Fielding said.

Logan held out his hand, and Fielding handed him the place mat. He read it again, to himself, then nodded. The little line between his eyebrows was back. "Yeah. Okay. We deliver this."

"Neither of you know who she is, though, right?" Fielding said.

"Or was," Logan said.

Fielding frowned but didn't argue. He preferred to assume otherwise until… Well. Until.

"Let me try my phone," Logan said.

Fielding let him, figuring he'd have a better idea of what to use to narrow things down to Hopewell, but after a few moments, he'd hit the same wall Fielding had. "It's too common a name."

"Yeah, I tried in the diner," Fielding said.

"Mailman," Joshua said.

They both looked at him.

"Maybe that's why you kept seeing my dad," Joshua said.

Fielding didn't follow. It must have showed on his face.

"My dad delivered the mail. So he knew where everyone lived. I mean, right up until I was a little kid and he changed jobs at least. But he might know her."

Fielding grinned. "Oh, wow. Yeah. Okay."

"He'll be at work," Joshua said. "But we can totally drop in."

"He's a lawyer," Logan said. "His building is just off the loop."

"I can drive if you want," Fielding said, not sure how far they'd gotten from Main Street.

"Okay!" Joshua said at the same time Logan said, "We can walk."

They looked at each other.

"It's not very far," Logan said.

Joshua pressed his hands together, begging again.

"A ride would be nice," Logan said, rolling his eyes.

A couple of men were standing by the Mustang when they got back to it, and Fielding gratefully let Joshua take the lead in answering some of their questions about "four-bolt mains." It gave Fielding time to check the passenger seat. Still empty except for the book and letter. A slick little knot of anxiety tightened in his stomach. He'd never had anyone other than Tate in the passenger seat while he drove.

"Do you want the chauffeur experience?" Fielding said, once the car questions were answered and the men had moved on. He unlocked the driver's side and gestured to the back seat.

"It's too much to ask if I can drive, isn't it?" Joshua said.

"It is." Logan held up a hand. "Don't even think about it, Fielding. Seriously. Get in the back, Josh."

"But—"

"Get in the back." Logan crossed his arms. For a skinny kid, he could look pretty stern.

Joshua got in the back.

❖

Joshua's dad's office building was one of the few modern-looking places in town. Newer than the rest of the buildings around it, three storeys tall, the sign proclaimed it the "Hopewell Business Centre."

The café the woman at One Man's Treasure had mentioned took up half the ground floor and was full of people now.

They went up to the second floor, and Joshua led them down the hall to a door marked Derek Bilodeau and opened the door without knocking. Beyond was a small waiting room with four chairs and an assistant at a desk, a white lady about Fielding's mom's age, only her hair was way cooler, sort of short and spiky, and was he seeing some blue undertones in there?

She greeted Joshua with a smile.

"Hey, Josh. Your dad should be done in fifteen minutes or so," she said. She had a little name plate on her desk that said "K.T." beside which stood a small collection of little LEGO people.

"We okay to wait?"

"Of course," she said. "You work today?"

The two chatted while they waited, and after about ten minutes, the door to the office opened and two men stepped out.

"Thanks again, Derek," the first said, a fit white guy with a shaved head and a neatly trimmed brown beard, shaking hands with the second man, who was absolutely hot shorts guy from the echoes, only older now. Fielding had to work hard not to stare. Joshua was one hundred percent right. It was really, really weird. Being in front of him was jarring, like watching a movie and crushing out on a super-hot actor only to do a search after and finding out it was an old nineties movie and the actor was now fifty or something. But when Joshua's father smiled, it was exactly the same.

Yeah. Weird.

"Any time, Evan."

The two parted, and Joshua's father turned to smile at the boys. "Hey, bud, what's up?"

"Do you have time?" Joshua said.

He turned to the assistant. "When is Marie due?"

"You've got an hour," she said.

"Come on through," Joshua's dad said, and Fielding followed Logan and Joshua into the office. Much like the building itself, the office gave off a more modern vibe, if maybe a bit plain, with comfortable grey leather chairs, a sleek-looking desk with a pretty large monitor on it, and a bookcase full of large, boring-looking books with ten-word titles.

"So what brings you by?" Joshua's father asked, leaning against the front of his desk.

"This is Fielding," Joshua said, pointing to him.

"Hi, Fielding." Joshua's father offered his hand, and Fielding shook it.

"Nice to meet you."

Joshua's dad did a manly-man shake, and he tried to match it. Fielding couldn't help but remember the man's calves, and this was so, so weird.

"Fielding got trapped here because of the tree on the highway, so we've been entertaining him," Joshua said, and Fielding brought his concentration back to the conversation. "But something came up, and he was wondering if we could pick your brain about your mailman days."

There it was again. The same smile Fielding had seen all day in the echoes. "I loved that job," Joshua's dad said. He raised one finger and took a breath.

And Joshua jumped in. "It was his *first real job*, taught him the *meaning of hard work*, *everyone loved him*, he *loved being outside*, even in the bad weather..." Joshua said, not quite affecting sarcasm, but definitely delivering a list he'd heard enough times to know by heart.

"You mock me, child of mine, but I was a local fixture. And it was also the job where I had the singular best day of my life."

"What?" That made Joshua stop. "The best day of your life?"

The way Joshua's dad smiled at his son made Fielding grin himself. Total "Dad With Upper Hand" smile. His uncle used the same one on Tate, usually before delivering some sort of verbal smackdown, albeit a gentle one.

Fielding's good mood faltered a little at the memory. He hadn't seen Uncle Brandon and Tate talk like that since Uncle Brandon's heart attack. And now with Tate gone...

"Let's see. We need to go back..." Joshua's dad paused, which caught Fielding's attention again. "Wait, how old are you now?"

"I'm eighteen." Joshua rolled his eyes.

"Right. I knew that, just testing you. So let's go back eighteen years and seven months, give or take." He waved his hand vaguely in the air, and Fielding caught a glimpse of the tattoo at the edge of his shirt sleeve. Same tattoo, same biceps, same man he'd been seeing all around Hopewell. Albeit eighteen years later, at least.

"Wait, what?" Joshua said. "Why seven months?"

"Picture it. A beautiful summer day, and the town's most beloved mailman is out and about, spreading joy to every citizen." Joshua's father waved his arm like a regent would, with a little twist at his wrist. Fielding grinned. He happened to know with absolute certainty that was not how Joshua's dad had waved at all. He'd thrown his whole self into it.

"Oh my God, Dad." Joshua shook his head.

"Don't interrupt," Joshua's dad said, grabbing him around the neck and yanking him in for a head rub. "I'm talking."

Fielding slid his hands into his hoodie pockets and looked away, second-hand embarrassment getting the better of him.

Logan, for his part, looked like he was barely holding in laughter. He bit his bottom lip and kept glancing at Fielding, eyes bright.

"The best day, as it would become known in the Bilodeau Family Legends, was the very day I learned about you." He squeezed Joshua, who he hadn't let go. Joshua squirmed, but it made his dad rub his head again, messing his dark hair. "I told everyone. Handed them their mail, told them I was gonna be a dad. Saw them on the other side of the street? Waved and yelled across to them that your mom and I were expecting. I covered my whole route in half the usual time. I was walking on air." He grinned, then looked down as if only now remembering he had the child in question in a headlock. He let go. "I mean, if I'd known then what I know now..." He shrugged.

Joshua, breaking free, straightened his hair and his shirt, looking at his dad with a mix of annoyance and something else. Pride, maybe? His dad was calling finding out about him the best day of his life. It had to be pretty awesome. "Really?"

"Yeah. It was a big deal." Joshua's dad leaned on his desk. "See, the thing is, son, your dad has defective loins."

"What?" Joshua's voice rose a half-octave. Logan made a spluttering noise. Fielding's eyes widened, but he couldn't look away.

"Turned out I mostly fire blanks. Your mom and I had been trying for a while and no luck, so we got ourselves tested. She was fine. Me?

Well, let's just say you'll probably need to get yourself checked out at some point. I mean, if you want to make kids the old-fashioned way."

"Oh my God." Joshua stared at his father in horror. "Why are you telling me this?"

"I'm explaining the context of the best day of work I ever had," Joshua's dad said, clearly having the time of his life. "And you're older now, and it's important not to feel shame about things like this. Infertility is a lot more common than you think, and I don't want you to wrap your self-confidence up in some outdated notion valuing men as virile creators of children." He shrugged. "You might have a perfectly fine sperm count, but maybe not." He tilted his head and eyed Logan, winking at him. "Then again, maybe Logan can handle that part. He's cuter than you anyway."

Logan made a second choking noise.

"Dad, stop. I'm begging you," Josh said.

Apparently deciding he'd humiliated both boys enough, Joshua's dad leaned back on his desk again and smiled at Fielding. "So what can I do for you?"

"Uh." Fielding had to clear his throat to make his voice work. *Defective loins?* Holy flying crap. "We...I mean I...I found a letter. But there's no address. It looks kind of old. I thought maybe I could deliver it to the person it was for, since it never got there. It's addressed to Elinor Kelly. Do you know that name?"

Joshua's father frowned, thinking. "No, I'm sorry." He took a few more seconds with it, then shook his head. "No, I'm pretty sure I never delivered anything to a Kelly."

Fielding sighed. "Thanks anyway."

The three said their good-byes, Joshua's father inviting Logan and his parents over for dinner on Saturday for a barbecue, and then hit the sidewalk.

"So," Logan said, once they were outside. "That was—"

"Don't," Joshua said.

"I mean—"

"Just. Don't."

A few seconds passed.

"Plus side? Now we know why you're an only child," Logan said.

"Begging. I'm *begging* you." Joshua turned to him. "We never speak of this again."

"The best day of his life," Fielding said.

The other two turned to him.

"Oh God, not you, too," Joshua said.

Fielding looked out at the streets of Hopewell. The way the hot guy—*Fielding's dad*, he corrected himself—was always smiling and waving? That's what he saw, A man having the best day of his life. The next time he saw him, he was going to try and hang on to the image. It was a nice one. His fingertips itched for his pencil. Yeah. He wanted to draw it. Maybe he could even draw it for Joshua. It was a really cool moment, after all.

Well, except for all the sperm stuff.

Logan shook his head. "Dead end."

"Just means the letter is more than eighteen years old," Joshua said.

"And seven months," Logan added.

Joshua pointed one finger at him. Logan pretended to button his lips.

Fielding tried not to laugh.

"We could try the library," Joshua said.

"I was thinking about that," Logan said. "But like you said, the letter is older, right?"

Fielding nodded.

"Well, you know what we've got right here in town?" Logan said.

"A water tower but no well?" Fielding said.

"Yes." Logan laughed. "But we also have the font of endless knowledge."

"We already tried online," Fielding said.

"I'm not talking about the internet. We've got something better. You want to know anything that happened years ago in Hopewell? There's one place to go." Logan grinned, clearly pleased with himself.

Fielding glanced at Joshua. Joshua shrugged. "Care to share?"

"Light of Grace."

Fielding shook his head. "Which is…?"

"A retirement and care community."

"Old people!" Joshua said. "You're a genius."

"Old people. And specifically? My great-grandmother, Abigail," Logan said to Fielding. Then he smiled at Joshua. "And yes. I am a genius. Also, I'm cuter."

"Only according to my dad," Joshua said.

"Well," Fielding said. "Your dad is hot guy."

"Oh my God," Joshua groaned.

Logan high-fived Fielding.

CHAPTER SEVEN

Fielding drove, not checking the passenger seat too often. To keep himself busy, he pointed out every appearance of Joshua's father's echo, and what he was doing.

"Other side of that intersection. He's waving."

"This is wild," Joshua said, turning that way. "It must be so cool."

Fielding caught himself smiling. That had never been a word he'd chosen for it. Weird, maybe. Strange. Abnormal. Freakish. Freakish was a good word. But maybe today, after hearing Joshua's father's voice and the way he'd described learning he was going to be a dad? Fielding could agree with "cool."

"How many times has it happened before today?" Logan asked, in a much more sedate tone than Joshua's energetic take. "The echoes, I mean."

Fielding took a second to think, though he knew the number. He could say eleven or admit it was twelve. It depended on whether or not he wanted to talk about the twelfth. Despite only knowing Logan for a few hours, he definitely seemed the type to ask follow-up questions, which made it a non-decision, really.

"Eleven," he said, glancing in the rear-view long enough to catch Logan's gaze.

"Every other month or so," Logan said, reminding Fielding he'd asked him how often it happened earlier. "So it's been happening for two years?"

"Roughly," Fielding said. Yeah, Logan was smart.

"Do you think today is unusual, or do you think you're…I'm not sure how to put it. Picking up speed or something? Getting better at it?"

"I…" Fielding swallowed. Well, there was a terrifying thought. Like he didn't have enough on his plate, what with his deferment, the ongoing silence of Anup and Kristin, his uncle's shop, his mother's job, and everything going on with Tate. If seeing every strong memory people had left behind became an hourly event, he'd never be able to handle it. Joshua and Logan had noticed him going all squirrelly in one morning. How could he spend his entire first year of university like this? "I don't know."

"It's the next right," Joshua said.

They'd been on the move for less than ten minutes. It shouldn't have surprised Fielding. Small towns were, by definition, small, but still.

The next right brought the Light of Grace into view, and Fielding had to school his reaction yet again. It looked more like a pretty hotel than a retirement home, with nicely tended gardens and trees out front, beneath which were shaded tables with benches. No umbrellas were up, probably because of the wind, but people were sitting outside regardless.

"If you park over there," Logan said, pointing, "your car will be visible from the main activity room. That way our arrival will be noticed. By a lot of the men, at least."

"Oh, you're good," Fielding said, ignoring the closer empty spots and following Logan's lead. He felt oddly nervous once he'd parked, turning off the engine and glancing once more at the passenger seat.

Still empty.

"Who are you looking for?" Logan said.

Crap. He aimed a guilty smile Logan's way. "Pardon?"

"Really?" Logan's smirk made it perfectly clear what he thought of Fielding's attempt at deflection.

"I'll tell you later," Fielding said, getting out of the car and letting the other two follow suit. If he was clever, maybe later wouldn't happen. After locking up, another glance at Logan disabused him of that notion. He had that little line between his eyebrows again. Maybe Joshua could rein in Logan.

"Are we allowed to just walk in?" he said, hoping to change the subject.

Logan waved a hand. "Technically we need to sign in as visitors to a particular guest, but if my guess is right, that won't be a problem." He nodded at the door.

Fielding turned. Three old men were already walking right toward the parking lot. Between them, they had three canes and a walker. Fielding wondered if they should meet them halfway and offer some help.

"Whose car?" one of the men called.

"It's his." Joshua pointed at Fielding.

"My cousin's," Fielding said weakly, not loud enough for them to hear, then raised his hand and his voice. "Hi."

"You are such a genius," Joshua said to Logan.

"And cuter." Logan smiled.

❖

Their names were Mr. Gidney, Mr. Jeffers, and Mr. Vance. Logan did a quick round of introductions, and Fielding tried to keep up. Mr. Gidney, a Black man whose short hair had more salt than pepper, was a former high school principal, though from before Logan and Joshua's time. He used one cane. Mr. Jeffers, the completely bald and incredibly pale white man who used the walker, was a former mechanic. Mr. Vance, a burlier white man, walked with two canes. He had a full grey beard but seemed the heartiest of the trio. He'd mentored Joshua's father and passed his law practice on to him. They'd offered hands to shake and then turned their attention completely to the Mustang.

Fielding passed the car baton to Joshua, who knew the answer to "Is this a '65 or a '64-and-a-half?", which was a new one for Fielding, and he stepped back to watch the magic happen.

Then he saw the others.

A child ran down across the narrow field beside the parking lot, a kite in tow that flickered in and out of view before vanishing entirely and taking the child with it. An older couple whispered into being on the bench on the path running alongside the field, gone between blinks.

He looked back to the large trees and the tables that sat beneath them, except now one of them had an umbrella up and in place, untouched by the day's wind. A group of four people played some sort of card game. He could see them laughing.

At the entrance, two bundled-up women were holding out their hands and catching snowflakes in their palms, a sphere of winter appearing around them like a snow globe come to life.

They were replaced by a man and a woman side by side in wheelchairs, holding binoculars and pointing at something Fielding couldn't see.

Everywhere he looked, moments were blooming, replaying, and then wilting away in front of him. It was incredible.

And terrifying.

"You okay?" Logan said.

"I think so. Add five more." He managed a reassuring nod that made the little line between Logan's eyebrows disappear, turning his attention back to the men, the Mustang, and Joshua.

"Mine ran sub-eleven seconds in the quarter," one of the men was saying.

Joshua whistled.

Fielding checked his phone again while they talked. The Hopewell social media had issued an update of sorts. The Hydro people from Abitibi had arrived. That was it. No word on what they were doing or how long it would take for them to do it. Which meant there was still no rush. Which meant he really didn't need to interrupt the Mustang love-fest happening right now.

Still, he held the paper in one hand.

"Give it another minute," Logan said.

"It's fine," Fielding said.

"And that's what she's got in her." With what looked more than a little bit of reluctance, Joshua finally lowered the hood. He turned back to Logan and Fielding, a bashful glance on his face, as though it was sinking in how long they'd all been standing there.

"So what brings you to visit?" Mr. Vance said, as though it had only just occurred to him three teenage boys might not have dropped by to let them ogle a car. He eyed Logan. "Here to put a good word in for me with Abigail?"

Logan crossed his arms. "You're not good enough for her."

The men all laughed, and even Logan cracked a small smile.

"His great-grandmother," Joshua said to Fielding.

"Right."

"Actually, we're hoping you can help us with something," Logan said, glancing at Fielding. Fielding's face started to burn, but he cleared his throat and took a breath.

"I'm looking for Elinor Kelly," he said, holding up the envelope. "I found this letter, and I wanted to bring it to her. But I'm pretty sure it's from a while back." No need to go into reasons why.

"Anyone?" Mr. Gidney said, eyeing his two compatriots.

"I barely remember my own damn name," Mr. Vance said.

"No Elinors. I think I knew a Kelly but…" Mr. Jeffers shook his head. "You should ask Abigail, though. She always knows everybody's business."

Mr. Vance scowled at him.

"I mean it in the best way," Mr. Jeffers protested.

"How is there a damn best way for that?"

"Okay," Logan said. "Thank you so much." He nodded meaningfully toward the building. Fielding looked, and two more men were on their way out the door. Wait, no, a third was joining them. He took a second to confirm they were real people, not echoes, and holy crap that wasn't something he'd ever had to consider before, was it?

"Did you want to stay out here?" Fielding asked Joshua. He held out the car keys. "No rides, but if they want to sit and check out the inside or take pictures…"

Joshua took the keys with a grin. "You're a saint, Fielding."

"Hardly."

Logan and Fielding passed the new arrivals on their way.

"It's a '65," one said.

"'64," another said.

"He's right." Fielding paused long enough to offer the information. "It's a '65."

"I told you, Hank."

"Need new glasses is all."

"Bradley Vance can't drive. They took his license away. Why is that fool boy letting him get behind the damn wheel?"

Logan opened the door and waved Fielding through.

❖

The entrance of the Light of Grace was wide and welcoming, with a little check-in counter, three separate benches, and a high ceiling with a hanging chandelier. Two archways led off to the left and right, and elevators faced them.

"How are you holding up?" Logan said, once they were out of the wind.

Fielding turned. "You know, I have friends I've known my entire life who don't read me as easily as you do."

Logan shrugged. "You should get sunglasses."

"Pardon?"

"It's your eyes. You keep looking at things when there's nothing there." He shook his head. "Well. Nothing I can see. You know what I mean. You said five just now. That's a lot."

"Pretty much everywhere," Fielding said. "It's never been like this. I'm kind of freaking out." As he said the words, he could hear the shake in his voice. "What if it doesn't…" He hesitated, then forced himself to complete the thought. "What if this doesn't stop?"

Logan looked at him for a few seconds, his lips twisting up on one side like he was tasting something and trying to decide if it was sweet or sour. He could have said something flippant or calming, but it looked like he was really trying to consider what to say.

Not for the first time, Fielding decided Joshua was a lucky guy.

"It started when you got to Hopewell, right? Or started getting more frequent?"

Fielding nodded. "The second I went across the bridge." He remembered the deep shiver and the sense of change. Looking back, it had been like crossing through a curtain of something different.

"Well, this is the oldest part of town. The old town hall used to be across the street, and the first church is half a block to the right. I think the whole 'there's something weird about Hopewell' theory still makes the most sense. And it's not the first time I've heard the sentiment. Our friend Lyn? The one you took photos of us for? His mother says Hopewell has a way of making people stop and look around at things. Maybe in your case, that's even more true. Once you put us behind you, I think it's safe to say you'll go back to normal." He offered a little smile with the proclamation.

Fielding exhaled. "Right."

"How is it in here?" Logan asked, scanning the fairly empty entrance as though he'd be able to see what Fielding could.

Fielding looked. A woman behind the counter was trying not to be too obvious while she watched them talk, and voices came from the archway to the left, but other than that, Fielding didn't see any echoes.

"All clear," he said, feeling a little foolish. "But this place seems really new, so I guess I shouldn't be surprised. It's usually older places. Though outside…"

"After the pulp and paper place closed, this was the next big business to open in Hopewell," Logan said. "A residence was here before, only way smaller. They knocked it down and built this place."

Fielding took a breath. "I wonder if that meant any echoes from inside would háve been lost."

"Let's go sign in. I'm sure my great-gran is up by now. If anyone knows Elinor Kelly, it'll be her. She knows everyone."

Fielding smiled and nodded, and they went to the counter together.

The large room they entered had an entire wall of windows that overlooked the parking lot where Logan had suggested Fielding park. He'd been right, the Mustang was front and centre and highly visible. Joshua had the hood up again, pointing animatedly at something inside. The group of men were nodding.

"There she is," Logan said.

Two old women sat together by the windows. The first, an Asian woman with steel-grey hair, was settled comfortably in one of the plush chairs, talking to a white woman who knitted in a wheelchair beside her.

"The knitter?" The white-haired woman didn't remind him of Logan in any obvious way, but she was the smaller of the two, and had a sharp look to her. Smart. Or witty, maybe. She was nodding at whatever the other woman was saying, and it looked like she was truly listening.

"That's her," Logan said, smiling. "Come on. I'll introduce you."

They left a wake of mild interest as they passed by the other seniors in the room. Some of the staff, all women as far as Fielding could see, gave them polite nods or little smiles. Especially Logan. They clearly knew him. Fielding kept his attention as much on Logan's great-grandmother as he could. He didn't really want to see if anything might be echoing around in the room.

"Hi, Nan," Logan said once he was close enough.

She turned and her whole face lit up. "Logan," she said. She put her knitting into her lap while he leaned over for a kiss, and then turned to the other woman. "Logan is here with a friend," she said.

Fielding glanced at the other woman, who turned in their direction and blinked but didn't meet their gaze. She was blind, he realized.

"Hello, Logan," the woman said, her English faintly accented. Her voice, much like Logan's great-grandmother's, was stronger than Fielding would have assumed.

"Hi, Aunt Rose," Logan said. Then he turned. "Nan, this is my friend, Fielding. Fielding, this is my great-grandmother, Abigail, and my great-grandaunt, Rose."

Fielding blinked. A great what-now?

"It's a small town," Abigail said. "Rose married my brother."

"Oh," Fielding said. "Nice to meet you."

"I didn't know you were coming today, Logan," Abigail said, picking up her knitting. She nodded at two nearby chairs. "Sit, sit."

They pulled the chairs a bit closer and sat.

"It wasn't the plan," Logan said. "But we bumped into kind of a mystery, I guess, and I thought you could maybe help us."

Rose's smile was wide. "Oh, I do love a mystery."

"She's listened to every mystery audiobook she can get her hands on," Abigail said to Fielding. "And watching a mystery show with her is an exercise in futility. She always figures out who did it."

"Well," Fielding said. "This isn't a murder. It's more like a missing person, I guess." He pulled out the envelope. "I found a letter in a book at the second-hand store. There was no address, only a name. Elinor Kelly." He took a breath. "I guess I wanted to get it where it was going, finally. Even if it's been hidden for a long time."

"In a book?" Abigail sounded delighted.

It gave Fielding hope. "Yes. *Sense and Sensibility.*"

"Well, that explains the Elinor."

"I'm sorry?"

"Elinor. That's the heroine of the book." Abigail paused her needles, looking at him.

Fielding opened the book and re-read the inside flap. Sure enough. It was right there.

"Oh." He deflated. If the name on the letter wasn't real, then this was all for nothing. "So much for Elinor L. Kelly."

"Oh, L. Kelly? Her I know."

Fielding exchanged a glance with Logan, hope bubbling back up in his chest. "You do?"

"Well, I knew an L. Kelly. Linda Kelly. She lived here when I was a girl. The Elinor could be a reference to *Sense and Sensibility*." Abigail's knitting needles practically flew while she spoke. "I'm not sure why, but she's the only L. Kelly I can think of."

"Oh my God. It's the key," Fielding said, realizing. He grinned. There was still a chance. "The Elinor is the key. The L. Kelly was for her, but the Elinor is the key!"

"Key?" Logan said.

"The code." He realized the two women had no idea what he was talking about, and backtracked. "The letter was written in a book cipher." Fielding paused, realizing that was no better. "Sorry. That's a—"

"Code based on a particular book," Rose said. "You use notations to direct to pages, lines, and words or letters. Next to impossible to break unless you've got the same book. The same print edition of the same book, even." She nodded sagely. "It's an excellent choice for clandestine communication."

"Right," Fielding said. "So maybe putting Elinor on the envelope was the writer's way of telling Linda Kelly which book to use. Because Elinor is from *Sense and Sensibility*."

"But you found the letter in the book," Logan said. "Isn't that overkill?"

Fielding remembered the crying girl, the misery in her eyes, and the way she quickly tucked the book aside somewhere. "I don't think the letter was supposed to stay with her copy of the book. It was supposed to go to someone else, but she didn't get her chance to address or deliver it. To Linda Kelly."

"Well, if it was for her, you could ask her granddaughter," Abigail said.

Fielding frowned. *Granddaughter? Oh. Oh no.*

"Who's that?" Logan said.

"Rachel Ryan. Linda Kelly married Brian Landry and had two

boys. The eldest, Justin, married the Hurtubise girl, Stephanie, and they only had the one daughter, Rachel. She and her husband took over the Landry farm. I can't recall when, but I feel like Linda Landry lived with them for a while before she passed on."

Every word Abigail spoke struck against Fielding's chest like little fists of stone, crushing the hope that had rekindled there moments ago. Linda Kelly got married. Linda Kelly had children. And Linda Kelly died.

"Oh. I know the Ryans," Logan said. "I mean, they had kids at my school."

"Mystery solved," Rose said. They all turned to Fielding, expectant.

"Yes." Fielding forced himself to reply. "I guess so."

"You don't sound happy about it," Rose said.

"Sorry." Fielding winced. "I'm sorry. No, of course it's good news. I am happy. If the letter was for Linda Kelly, or I guess Linda Landry, that's good, we can get it to…to her granddaughter. Thank you." He did his best to inject some cheer into his voice.

Abigail was peering at him. She had the same "I can see right through you" gaze as her great-grandson. Spooky.

"Sorry," Fielding apologized again. "I mean it. Thank you." He wanted to get out of there, but he couldn't just get up and walk away. He made eye contact with Logan, who gave him a little nod. Fielding closed the book again, gripping it with his hands.

His chest hurt.

"Any time," Abigail said. Then she glanced out the window. The men were still all gathered around the Mustang, and Joshua was taking pictures of two of the men, who were now sitting inside. "I take it I won't get to say hello to your fellow? He seems busy." She said it with a sly little smile, though.

"Given how popular you two usually are, I thought the car might chase the boys away so we could talk," Logan said, getting up.

Fielding all but jumped to his feet. He figured Rose likely had no idea what they were talking about. "I'm driving a classic car. It's my cousin's. Logan said I should park it where people in here could see it."

"Oh, believe me," Rose said, "I heard the excitement when you pulled in."

"Tell me." Abigail eyed the car for a few seconds. "Is it a '65?"

"Yes," Fielding managed. He was sucking in breaths between each sentence. Why was it getting hard to breathe? "It's a '65. Thank you again."

He started walking the second Logan finished hugging the two older women.

❖

Outside the Light of Grace, Fielding glanced at the parking lot, saw the men were still gathered around the Mustang, and stumbled off in the opposite direction.

"Fielding?"

"N-need some air," he said. His voice sounded strangled even to him. He figured he wasn't fooling Logan, but he didn't turn back. He walked down the slight incline of the grass, coming to a low fence that separated the side lawn of the Light of Grace from the river. On the other side of the river, he saw two people sitting together by a tree leaning on each other.

Were they real or an echo? He didn't know.

Fielding gripped the copy of *Sense and Sensibility* in his hand and closed his eyes. The girl who'd written the letter had been so sad. Heartbroken. And the words she'd chosen from the book: *I do not wish to be parted.*

He struggled for a breath. And then another. It didn't help. His chest grew tighter and tighter, and his hand started aching from gripping the book. He was panting, like he'd been running or something, but it felt like he couldn't breathe at all.

I do not wish to be parted.

He unzipped his hoodie, then tugged his T-shirt out of his jeans, desperate to let some of the air cool his skin. Why was it suddenly so hot?

"Fielding?"

He turned. Joshua and Logan both stood a few steps behind him. Well. That explained why Logan hadn't followed right away. He'd gone to get Joshua.

"Hey." Fielding nearly croaked the word and had to gulp in air. He shoved a smile in place, and nodded. "Sorry." He resisted the urge to tug at the neck of his T-shirt. They continued to watch him, almost pityingly, and that was too much. To give himself something to do, he pulled out his phone, determined to refresh the Hopewell social media page.

He nearly dropped it, his hands shook so much.

"Fielding?" Joshua said.

Fielding managed to unlock the screen.

The social media feed had been updated again. Thank God.

"The tree is almost dealt with," he said. "I should be able to go soon." He looked back up, cheeks sore with the false smile now, and eyed Logan. "If I gave you the letter, you'd give it to those kids you know, right? The Ryans?" His heart hammered away in his chest. He'd started sweating. It trickled at his temples. Why was he sweating?

Logan glanced at Joshua, then faced him again. "Their farm is about twenty minutes north. You don't want to drop it off before you go?"

"I—" Fielding choked. Swallowed. "It's okay. I need to get going." A gasped inhale. "I can drop you guys off wherever."

"Fielding," Joshua said. "It wouldn't take long."

Fielding couldn't reply. He stared at the ground.

"Is this because she died?" Logan's voice was tentative.

"N-no," Fielding said. "It's…" He shook his head. "I just…" He clenched his jaw.

"Are you okay?" Joshua said. "You're shaking."

Fielding laughed. Or he meant to laugh, but he more or less *barked*. "I don't know why…I'm surprised. It didn't work…out for me. Of course it didn't. It never…works out for me." He had to suck in breaths between the words.

"What doesn't?" Joshua took a half-step toward him, and Fielding backed away.

Joshua stopped moving. It could have been comic if it wasn't so pathetic.

"Anything. Something. All of it," Fielding said. "I'm supposed to be in Toronto. I'm supposed to be having a life. I'm supposed to be like you guys—I'm supposed to have a Cute fucking Diner Boy of my own. I should already be in university with my friends, not stacking bags of dog food and cleaning out litter boxes. But I'm not. I can't. I'm…" He ground out the words. "I'm needed and I'm helping and I'm not…I can't…" His fists were shaking visibly. It was so hot. Why weren't they hot? How could they *stand* it?

He ran out of words. Or there were none. Either way, he couldn't find any, and he *needed* to make noise.

Fielding yelled.

The sound that came out of him had been building for a year, but it had been bouncing back and forth in his ribcage, growing louder and louder, and now that it was out, he couldn't pull it back. So Fielding bellowed, shutting his eyes as tears followed. He used up every bit of breath he'd managed to gasp into his lungs, and when that ran out, no matter how much he wanted to still be angry, what followed was more like a sob.

He took a single, shaky breath, opening his eyes. Tears spilled freely down his cheeks.

Joshua closed the distance and grabbed him in a bear hug before he could react. Fielding buried his face in Joshua's shoulder, and a second later he felt another pair of arms wrap around him from behind. Logan.

They both hung on to him, squeezing him.

"He could be dead," Fielding said. It was the first time he'd ever said it out loud, and it was muffled by Joshua's shoulder, but it was clear enough and he couldn't take it back now. He'd said it. He knew they heard him. "Tate could be dead like my dad and I'm so tired."

They didn't let him go. If anything, Joshua tightened his hug. Logan shifted his grip a bit, putting his hands over Fielding's and closing his grip over Fielding's fingers.

"I'm so tired."

CHAPTER EIGHT

On a scale of one to completely humiliating, realizing he'd been sobbing while two strangers hugged him turned out to be not that bad, really. A three. Maybe a four. Once he got the last of the immediate shudders out of his system and spent some time getting his breathing back under control, dealing with the whole sob-related snot-bubbles thing, he just sort of sat there for a bit, wedged between Logan and Joshua.

Joshua squeezed him every few seconds, like he was reminding him he was there. Logan was more of a consistent pressure sort of hugger.

Both were nice.

"Okay," Fielding said. "I'm okay." His hands had stopped shaking, and his skin didn't feel like it was burning any more. "Sorry. I'm…I'm sorry."

The two guys pulled back, settling onto their knees. Fielding realized at some point they'd all sort of sunk to the ground, which he didn't remember exactly, though he definitely recalled feeling like he had zero strength left in his whole body.

I'm tired.

"Panic attack?" Logan said.

Fielding turned to him, opening his mouth to reflexively disagree. Instead, he said, "I don't know. That hasn't happened before." His shirt felt gross. He'd sweat through it in places.

"It looked like one," Joshua said, surprising the heck out of Fielding. "I get them."

"You do?"

"All part of the neurodivergent package," Joshua said. "Which is a more fun way of saying my brain likes to misfire when everything gets to be too much." He smiled. "But I'm an eternal optimist, too."

"So does that mean you've got a bright side about panic attacks?" Fielding said, joking. He pressed his palm against the grass beside him. The grass felt real and comforting in a way he couldn't put words to.

"Sure." Joshua put his hand on Fielding's shoulder. "It means you're overwhelmed, and maybe there's some stuff you should talk about with someone, and oh, look!" He pointed at himself and Logan. "Two someones! How lucky is that?"

Fielding laughed. "Of course it is."

"Only if you want to," Logan added. "But he's not wrong. Also—"

"Never going to see us again," Fielding said with him, more or less in tandem with Logan's now familiar refrain.

"Yeah, that," Logan said.

Fielding shifted into sitting cross-legged, and after a second, the other guys followed suit. The wind blew past them, and it felt cool and soothing against his skin. Fielding took a second to figure out where to start, but there was really only one place. "My dad died when I was young. I don't really remember him."

"I'm sorry," Joshua said.

"It's okay." Fielding shook his head. "I mean, it wasn't great or anything, and there are definitely still times where it sucks, but my Uncle Brandon was always around, and he was basically like a dad. He's single, too, widowed—I never met my Aunt Jess, my mom's older sister, she died before I was born. Cancer. That left Uncle Brandon alone with my cousin, Tate, who I mentioned before." Fielding glanced at the two. They nodded. "Okay. My Uncle Brandon sort of threw in with my parents before my father died, and then he stuck by my mom and me after. My dad was in the military. Special forces. Like, I remember he had to have a bag ready to go at any time. He'd get a call at any moment, and he'd be out the door."

"Wow," Logan said.

"Right?" Fielding smiled. "I basically thought I had an action hero for a father. Until he didn't come back. That's honestly all I really know about it. I don't know if my mother or my Uncle Brandon know the details—I mean, I assume they do—but I've never asked, and since I don't really remember much about him, it seemed cruel to ask questions, I guess."

"That's really empathetic," Joshua said.

"Thanks," Fielding said. Sometimes he wondered if it was more cowardice than empathy, but it was a nice thought. "Tate is older than me, and he loved my dad. Tate told me pretty much everything I know about him. I grew up with Tate being more like a big brother than a cousin."

"He's the one that taught you to drive the Mustang," Joshua said.

"Right. And he's also the person I keep looking for in the passenger seat," Fielding said to Logan. "Sometimes he echoes there. Ever since he taught me to drive."

Logan nodded.

"Anyway." Fielding pulled out his phone and scrolled backward past his photos of Hopewell and skimmed along until he found the picture he was looking for. Tate, in a black shirt and uniform pants, grinning at the camera. He had mud all over him, thanks to some obstacle course or something, but you could practically see triumph coming off him in waves. Fielding held up the phone.

"He's a soldier," Logan said.

"And really jacked," Joshua said. When Logan and Fielding stared at him, he held up one hand. "If I can survive my dad being the hot guy, you two can handle this objectively attractive muddy soldier."

"Fair enough," Fielding said.

"So he joined the military, too?" Logan said.

"Yep. And we haven't heard from him in a while," Fielding said. "He's overseas. It's not completely out of the ordinary to lose touch when he's deployed, but I know my uncle is worried. And I know both he and my mom have reached out through the family services people. But there's been no word, and it's been almost a month."

Logan and Joshua said nothing, and that was better than anything they could say. Fielding couldn't have handled a platitude.

"We kind of argued before he shipped out," Fielding said. "I thought he should stay. My uncle wasn't well—I think I told you that? He had a heart attack?"

"Yeah," Logan said.

"Things were already off between us, because I'd told Tate about the echoes." Fielding waved a hand in front of his eyes. "He was worried and definitely didn't believe me, at least not at first. I'm not even sure if he believes me now. When we were arguing about whether or not he should ask for leave to help take care of my uncle and the store, he told me I needed to accept that some things in life were real and some things weren't, and no amount of wishing would change that. It felt like he was telling me to grow up and stop pretending, admitting he didn't believe me. I was so mad. I walked out."

Fielding was understating how painful their argument had been, but he figured the guys could probably see it clearly enough. There'd been no walking. He'd *run* out, feeling completely betrayed by the only person he'd always trusted to have his back, and he'd avoided Tate like a humiliated coward for the last four days before he shipped out. His mother had forced an awkward farewell before driving Tate to the airport, and that's when Tate handed him the keys to the Mustang.

"Take her when you visit your friends," he'd said.

As apologies or olive branches went, it was the best he could have imagined he might ever get from his cousin, who didn't really do feelings well.

And it had shamed the crap out of him.

"Be careful," was the best Fielding could come up with in return. And then Tate was gone. They'd texted once or twice, and Tate had managed a single video call with Uncle Brandon, but then everything had gone silent.

As far as he knew, Tate hadn't even found out Uncle Brandon had gotten the all-clear about his heart.

The three sat quietly for a bit, letting the wind blow by them. Finally, Joshua said, "And the letter?"

Fielding pulled out the children's place mat, unfolding it again.

"The letter," he said. "I guess I thought getting the letter to Linda Kelly or Linda Landry or whatever would, I don't know, remind me it was possible things could work out, even if it took a while." His face burned. "It sounds kind of pathetic when I say it out loud."

"It's not pathetic," Logan said.

"Well, in this case knowing turned out to be worse than not knowing." He sighed. "Whoever the girl was who wrote this, it didn't get to Linda Kelly. Landry. Whatever. And she cried over nothing." He stared at his own writing. *I do not wish to be parted*. He thought about

Tate. And Anup, and Kristin, and Toronto, and university. All the things that were *supposed* to be happening, but weren't. All the people he was supposed to be with, but wasn't. "I wish I'd never found this," he said.

"We need to deliver it," Joshua said.

Fielding frowned. "What?"

"The letter. The girl's letter. We need to deliver it." He stood up, batting grass off his knees. "Come on."

"Josh," Logan said, rising himself. "If Fielding doesn't want to—"

"I don't care. Sorry. That wasn't specific. I *do* care about you, Fielding. I think you're pretty great, and I'm glad we met. But if we don't deliver it, we're letting that girl down. You said it yourself." Joshua looked at Fielding. "You think this was something important between them. You think this was a love thing. And, okay, maybe it's sad to deliver it now, but it's sadder not to let anyone know it happened. You're the only person who could see it, and you did. If we don't try, it'd be like erasing it. Enough queer stuff gets erased as it is."

Fielding stared up at the two guys. "You think her granddaughter would be okay about it?" That was the real thing stopping him. He didn't want to deliver the letter and face down some homophobic small-town crap. That definitely wouldn't make him feel better. No, it would make everything about today, everything about that crying girl, everything they'd managed to figure out feel so…

Pointless.

"The Kellys are cool," Logan said. "We don't move in the same circles or anything, but they've always been nice to us. And I think their mom worked on the mayor's campaign."

Fielding stood. It was too hard to keep looking up at them. "The mayor's…?" He shook his head. What did the mayor of Hopewell have to do with anything?

"The mayor and her wife," Logan said. "Two terms so far."

Oh. Fielding took a breath, then looked across the water again. So many echoes of people milled about, fading in and out in turn along both sides of the river. It had been scaring the hell out of him all day long, but right now they weren't scary. Maybe it was the crying, or maybe it was the group hug. Or maybe it was what Joshua had said. These echoes were memories. Just memories. They couldn't hurt him. For the first time in his life, watching people fade in and out along the water was calming. He had no idea what was important about any of them, but it didn't matter. It was important to them at some point, and they seemed happy enough.

But he knew what had been important to the girl in the second-hand store. And she hadn't been happy.

Joshua was right. That girl he could help. So what if it was too late? He could make sure something was said, rather than left unsaid. Maybe that could be enough. It would have to be enough. He looked across the water again and noticed the two people he'd seen earlier were still there, leaning on each other against a tree. They weren't fading in and out. And unless he was wildly mistaken, it looked to him like they were two guys.

Fielding turned back to Joshua and Logan.

"You said their farm wasn't far?" he said.

Joshua whooped.

CHAPTER NINE

Fielding was starting to assume things in Hopewell wouldn't turn out to be what he expected, and the Ryan family farm was no different. He'd pictured fields of wheat, but this was Hopewell, and apparently in Hopewell you farmed something else.

Trees.

Rows and rows of little trees filled the area beside the road where Joshua told him to turn.

"A tree farm?"

"The Ryans started a small cedar farm after the pulp mill closed down," Logan said. "I think it's used for landscaping, but don't quote me on that. They also have cattle and sheep, I think. They grow corn in the other fields, but it's not the corn you eat. It's for livestock."

"Silage," Joshua said.

As the long driveway continued, the rows of trees stopped abruptly and two large open fields appeared. Sure enough, Fielding saw corn. And from the smell of things, somewhere nearby there were either cows or their inevitable by-product.

The house itself was simple, more or less a square block with a pitched roof, though it did have a lovely front porch, complete with a pretty wooden porch swing with faded cushions and a canopy. The garage was separate, and he also saw a large barn and a silo much farther off to the left.

Fielding pulled the Mustang over and turned off the engine.

They all sat there for a few seconds in silence.

"Remember ten minutes ago when this didn't seem like something really, really weird to do?" Fielding said.

"What? You've never walked up to someone and delivered a long-lost lesbian love letter to their grandmother before?" Logan said.

They laughed. The noise of it filled the car and some of the empty bits Fielding could feel in his chest. He pulled out the book and the envelope and held them up. "Ready?"

"Hell yes!" Joshua said.

A pickup and an SUV were parked in the garage, so Fielding assumed someone was home. They could be out in the fields doing whatever people did for non-edible corn or cedar trees or cattle or sheep, he supposed, but he didn't see anyone at the large barn in the distance. Or maybe they were inside.

The three of them went to the front door. Fielding was biting his lip, but when Logan nodded at him, he reached out and pressed the doorbell. It chimed.

Well, no turning back now.

The door opened, and the woman standing there looked to be about Fielding's mom's age, though she was taller and broader across the shoulders. Her fair skin had picked up some sunburn already, and while she smiled at the three of them welcomingly enough, she frowned a bit when she looked at Fielding. He knew that look. It was a polite small-town I-don't-think-I-know-you look.

"Logan," she said, warmly. That was something. Fielding tried not to fidget. "What can I do for you?"

"Hi, Mrs. Ryan," Logan took the lead. "I'm sorry to drop by without texting or anything, but, um…" He turned to Fielding. "This is our friend, Fielding. He found something."

Fielding pulled out the little hardcover and held it up. "It's a book. And there's a letter inside, and—"

"Oh my goodness!" Mrs. Ryan's whole face transformed. Her smile grew, and she put a hand over her mouth. "Come inside, please." She stepped back, making room for them.

Fielding eyed the other two, but they waited for him to go first.

So he did.

❖

"Can I get you something to drink? Or are you hungry? Some cookies?" Mrs. Ryan's voice rang with happiness. Before any of them could really reply, she'd left them in the front entrance while they undid their shoes and stepped through to what appeared to be a bright little kitchen.

"What's happening?" Fielding said, keeping his voice as low as he could.

Logan shrugged.

Joshua, though, was grinning. "Cookies." He raised his voice. "I'd love a cookie, thank you."

Logan rolled his eyes, but then shrugged again. "Yes, please."

Fielding had to laugh. "Thank you. It's very kind of you."

"Come on through," Mrs. Ryan called. "Go grab a seat in there," she said, pointing with one hand. She was arranging homemade cookies on a plate. Fielding followed the other two into the living room, where a long couch dominated a wall opposite a fireplace, and a pair of recliners sat to either side of the window. The whole place was cozy and warm, and the wall with the fireplace was absolutely covered in photographs. Fielding wanted to go look, but it felt a bit too intrusive. He sat on one end of the couch. Logan and Joshua took the rest of the space.

"Help yourselves." Mrs. Ryan followed a second later, putting the plate of cookies on the table and sitting in one of the recliners. Joshua's cookie was half-gone in a blink. Fielding took a smaller bite. It might have been the best chocolate chip cookie he'd ever had. It was so chewy. Was it oatmeal?

"This is really good," Logan said, after taking a bite of his own.

"Family recipe," she said, but she barely glanced at him. Her eyes were on the book Fielding was still holding with his free hand. "Where did you find it?"

"The second-hand shop," Fielding said. "A big tree fell on the highway, and I got stuck here. Me and my friends like to check out second-hand shops, and I had time to kill, so…" He shook his head. "It doesn't matter. But I found the letter in the back of the book." He opened the book and pulled out the envelope. "It says Elinor L. Kelly," he said. "It took us a little while to figure out who that was."

He held it out to her, and Mrs. Ryan took it. To his surprise, it looked like she was on the edge of tears.

Oh crap. Was this a mistake?

She pulled the letter out of the envelope and let out a little sniff that was somewhere between laughter and a sigh. "Code."

"It's a book cipher," Fielding said. Some of the confidence he'd felt at Mrs. Ryan's initial reaction was starting to crumble. "I, uh, translated it if you want to know what it says?"

She looked up at him then, eyes wet, and the little nod she gave him made it clear she was doing her best not to cry.

Fielding bit his lip. Logan gave him the slightest nudge with his elbow, so he took a deep breath and pulled out the diner place mat.

"*I do not wish to be parted*," Fielding said, his voice catching on the last word. He cleared his throat. "*We have no choice. It is not up to us. I wish you to remain here with me. I do not know how I will survive. My love for you is as precious as air.*" He folded the place mat back up, not sure what to do with it. "That's it," he said, forcing himself to meet Mrs. Ryan's gaze.

"Must have been when she moved." She blinked a few times. "She was always a bit melodramatic, but my grandmother always said it was what made her such a good dramatics teacher."

Was. Past tense. Fielding had already assumed it, but it still stung. He'd already known Linda Kelly was dead, but hearing Mrs. Ryan confirm it felt like a second, sharper cut. Still, he couldn't help himself from asking. He needed to know. "Who was she?"

For just a second, Mrs. Ryan hesitated, but then she glanced at Joshua and Logan, and she let out a little snort of breath, as though something funny occurred to her. "Her name was Hope Tremblay, and she was my grandmother's wife for nearly thirty years."

What?

"Her wife?" Fielding stared. It didn't add up. Logan's great-grandmother said Linda Kelly married a man and had kids. Beside him, he felt Logan shift on the couch, and Joshua made a little noise, a cross between "What?" and "Huh?"

Mrs. Ryan held up her hand. "Not legally, of course." She shook her head, then wiped her eyes with her thumb, glancing down at the letter again before smiling back at the boys. "Would you like to see a picture?"

"Yes, please," Fielding said. His head was still spinning, but he very much wanted to see the letter writer—*Hope*, her name was *Hope*—as something other than a crying girl being forced to say goodbye forever.

Except it hadn't been forever.

He had so many questions, but he didn't even know where to

start. And it felt rude to ask when it was obvious Mrs. Ryan was barely clinging to not-crying. He could relate.

Hope was her wife.

Mrs. Ryan had gone to the fireplace and picked up a smaller frame from one end. She brought it back to them, and passed it to Fielding. Logan and Joshua leaned in.

The two women sitting beside each other on a small sofa in the photo were much, much older than the vision of Hope he'd had, but even so… He pointed at the woman on the left. "This is her," he said, absolutely sure. Her eyes were dark, unlike the other woman. And the shape of her chin had the little dent. "This is Hope."

Mrs. Ryan nodded. "That's right. Good guess." She pointed at the other woman. "And that's my grandmother, Linda Landry. This was taken in their home, before Hope passed and my grandmother came to live with us here."

"They lived together?" Joshua said.

"They did. After Linda's husband died—my grandfather. Hope and Linda were childhood friends, though as you know, it wasn't as simple as that. Hope's parents moved away, and they wrote letters to each other for years. Many of them were in code, like this one." She shook her head. "I can't imagine what that must have been like."

"They got to be together," Fielding said, and any pretense he'd had about playing it cool was gone. "She came back. I'm so glad they got to be together." His voice broke on the last word. He cleared his throat.

When he looked up, Mrs. Ryan was looking at the letter again, but now he could see the tears weren't sad at all. She was truly happy to see it.

"Thank you," she said, lifting the paper a fraction.

He nodded, one hundred percent sure his voice wasn't up to words yet.

"They were together for thirty years?" Joshua said. At some point, he'd picked up another cookie, but he held it halfway to his mouth, pausing.

"Almost," Mrs. Ryan said. "After my grandfather died and my father moved out. He was her youngest son. She sold the house she and my grandfather had lived in and moved away, and she went back to teaching. She and Hope lived together, and everyone agreed it was nice for them to have each other for company, what with my grandmother having lost her husband so young. Two teachers, good friends, living together and supporting each other."

"Good friends," Logan said. "Right."

Mrs. Ryan shrugged. "We knew. I mean, my father did, and he told me when he figured I was old enough, just like I told my boys. We didn't doubt she loved my grandfather when she was with him. She was very clear about that."

Joshua grinned. "She was bi?"

"That's what we'd say now. She said her 'heart had a broad capacity for loving.'" Mrs. Ryan wiped her eyes. "I am going to be crying all day."

"Sorry," Fielding said.

"Oh, no." She shook her head. "I'm so glad to have this back. When she moved in with us, there was a mix-up with the books and the coded letters. My grandmother tucked the letters into the books, but the movers got confused as to which books went in which box. By the time we figured it out, some of the books had been sold at the charity shop in their home town." Mrs. Ryan paused again, holding up the letter. "It's amazing to me that this book with the letter made it all the way back here to Hopewell. What are the chances? And then for you to find it?" She shook her head.

"It's Hopewell," Joshua said, as if that explained it all.

Fielding was starting to think it did.

They had another cookie each except for Joshua, who had four, and then Fielding thought they should leave Mrs. Ryan with her thoughts. Also, he'd lost most of the day, and he needed to eat something for dinner before he got on the road. Reluctantly, he thanked Mrs. Ryan one more time, and she walked them all to the front door.

She gave Logan a big hug, then Joshua, then—surprising Fielding—she pulled him in for one as well.

"Thank you," she said, with feeling.

"You're welcome," he said, looking past her shoulder and blinking rapidly at yet another round of sudden-onset sentiment.

His breath caught.

On the porch swing, two old women sat side by side on the chair, sharing a single knitted lap blanket as they smiled and held steaming mugs. Not as old as they'd been in the photo, the closer of the two was leaner and taller, her long, mostly still-blond hair back in a simple ponytail. The other had greyed a little more, was perhaps a little rounder, but there was no missing the dent in her chin or her beautiful dark eyes.

They were laughing silently in the echo, and as he watched, Hope leaned in enough to kiss Linda, shaking her head just the slightest bit.

"Mrs. Ryan, can I ask a favor?" Fielding said, pulling out of the hug and blurting out the words before he could change his mind.

"Of course," she said, not even hesitating. "And call me Rachel."

"Would you be willing to scan the letters for me? And maybe some of the photos? I...I draw. And do digital artwork. I'm going to school in September, and I'd love to put together a portfolio about your grandmother—your *grandmothers*—Linda and Hope. And maybe we could put together a website or something, too? Or even a book. Their story is important. The letters, the way they kept in touch, that they were together." He looked at her, and when he saw the surprise on her face, he held up his hand. "We can change their names if you want. And places. The specifics aren't as important as letting people know they were there. They were happy."

Rachel raised her own hand, and he stopped talking. "Of course I can send them to you. You're right. I've been wondering if I should do something with them for years. And you absolutely must use their names. I insist. No one can hurt them now, and besides...What's the saying? 'Fuck the haters'?"

Joshua laughed out loud.

"Thank you," Fielding said. He glanced at the porch swing. Hope and Linda looked out over the farm, now leaning on each other, arm in arm. "I can give you my email, maybe?"

They exchanged information and then said another round of farewells. The three boys walked back to the Mustang and climbed in.

"Linda and Hope are on the swing," Fielding said, the moment the doors were closed.

"Oh wow." Joshua sounded almost dreamy.

Logan leaned forward. "I wish I could see it."

"Don't worry," Fielding said, putting the Mustang in gear. "You will. I'm going to draw the fuck out of it."

Epilogue

Fielding drove them back to town, and they parked at the diner again. Logan and Joshua both texted their parents to let them know they were eating dinner out, and the three shared a booth while they ate. Fielding had the grilled cheese again and didn't even pretend to mind Joshua's gloating about it.

After they'd eaten, they walked him to the Mustang. There, they faced each other in a little triangle.

"You know that thing I kept saying about never seeing us again?" Logan shoved his hands into the back pockets of his jeans. "To hell with that."

"What he said," Joshua aimed a finger-gun at Logan, but kept his eyes on Fielding. "When are you heading back from the con?"

"It ends on Sunday afternoon. I'm staying overnight with my friends and then setting off first thing Monday." Fielding tilted his head back and forth. "If I time it right, I think I could end up here for a late dinner, maybe."

"You do that. We'll see you there. Text us when you're close. You're our Glimmer now." He pointed at Fielding's shirt.

"I'm the Glimmer?" Fielding said.

"You do magic." Joshua shrugged. "You're the Glimmer."

"I'm guessing you're the Bow in this scenario," Logan said.

"What? No." Joshua flexed one admittedly impressive bicep. "Adora all the way, baby."

"Fair enough," Logan said. "Does that make me the cranky cat-girl?"

"I mean…" Joshua raised his hands, then opened his arms.

"It's a good thing you're hot," Logan said, stepping into them.
Fielding smiled, watching them be cute and totally procrastinating getting back on the road. Was it really just this morning he'd wanted to blow right past this town?

So random.

"I have to go," Fielding said. Saying the words might make him do it.

Joshua pushed Logan right into him and managed to crush Fielding into one huge hug, and Fielding squeezed them back. Logan made a little choking noise, so he stepped back.

He had to clear his throat. Again. He laughed. "I swear to God, this town."

"Stop insulting my town, man," Joshua said.

"See you Monday," Fielding said, getting back in the Mustang before he could come up with another reason to delay. It didn't stop him from watching them walk away, arm in arm, or waving back every time Joshua turned to do the same. Finally, they turned the corner of the loop and vanished out of his view.

He only sniffled a little.

Fielding picked up his phone and sent some of the day's pictures on his group text with Anup and Kristin. He added a quick message.

I'm going to be very late thanks to this fallen tree. On my way now. I'll text when I'm closer, but it's gonna be late late. Like, middle of the night. Sorry.

He hit send and didn't check to see if there was a reply before he pulled his map back up and slid the phone back into its holder, attaching the cord.

He glanced over, and Tate sat there, smiling in his direction.

"Oh sure. *Now* you're back," Fielding said.

Tate turned, looking forward. He pointed at something, and Fielding could imagine his voice, explaining patiently to be careful, to be aware, to act as though no one else on the road had the slightest idea what they were doing.

"We don't know if you're okay," Fielding said. Tate's echo didn't react to his words, of course. It was just a memory, after all. "And I know this isn't you. But for what it's worth, I'm sorry I didn't say goodbye properly before you left."

The echo of Tate settled back in the seat, comfortable and

confident. Everything about his body language made it perfectly clear he wasn't worried in the slightest about Fielding being in control of his most prized possession.

How had Fielding never noticed that before?

"That doesn't mean I'm not mad at you, by the way. I hope…" Fielding paused. "I don't know if you're alive. But I'm going to assume you are."

The echo of Tate turned his head, glancing at something that had been in front of them at some point. He said something, his mouth moving silently.

"When you get back," Fielding said, "I'm going to tell you all about this day, which has honestly been a lot." He turned, facing the echo. "But in the meantime? I'm okay."

Fielding inhaled and reached for Tate with the part of him he didn't quite understand but felt on an instinctual level.

Fielding *pushed*.

"This is not the last of you," Fielding said.

Tate's echo faded, coming apart in wisps that curled inside the Mustang for a heartbeat or two before vanishing. Once the last traces of the echo were gone, Fielding exhaled and glanced at his phone. He had a long trip ahead of him. He tapped at the screen, called up a playlist, and set the music going before he turned the display back to the map.

One shoulder check and two turns later, Fielding Roy pulled his Mustang out onto the road, heading in the right direction.

About the Authors

JEFFREY RICKER is the author of *Detours* (2011) and the YA fantasy *The Unwanted* (2014). His stories and essays have appeared in *Foglifter*, *Phoebe*, *Little Fiction*, *The Citron Review*, *The Saturday Evening Post*, and others. A 2014 Lambda Literary Fellow and recipient of a 2015 Vermont Studio Center residency, he has an MFA in creative writing from the University of British Columbia and teaches creative writing at Webster University.

J. MARSHALL FREEMAN is a writer of novels, short stories, and poetry. He is the author of the young adult fantasy novel *The Dubious Gift of Dragon Blood* (2020) and the upcoming YA adventure *Barnabas Bopwright Saves the City* (May 2022). He is a two-time winner of the Saints+Sinners Fiction Contest (2017 and 2019), and lives in Toronto, Canada, with his husband and dog.

'NATHAN BURGOINE grew up a reader and studied literature in university while making a living as a bookseller. His first novel, *Light*, was a finalist for a Lambda Literary Award. *Triad Blood* and *Triad Soul* are also available from Bold Strokes Books, as is his YA novel *Exit Plans for Teenage Freaks* and his first collection, *Of Echoes Born*. For novella lovers, *In Memoriam*, *Handmade Holidays*, *Faux Ho Ho*, *Village Fool*, and *A Little Village Blend* are shorter queer romances (often with a dash of speculative fiction). A cat lover, 'Nathan managed to fall in love and marry Daniel, who is a confirmed dog person. They live in Ottawa, Canada—with their rescued husky, in case you were wondering how the cat-dog thing turned out.

Books Available From Bold Strokes Books

Three Left Turns to Nowhere by Jeffrey Ricker, J. Marshall Freeman & 'Nathan Burgoine. Three strangers heading to a convention in Toronto are stranded in rural Ontario, where a small town with a subtle kind of magic leads each to discover what he's been searching for. (978-1-63679-050-3)

One Verse Multi by Sander Santiago. Life was good: promotion, friends, falling in love, discovering that the multi-verse is on a fast track to collision—wait, what? Good thing Martin King works for a company that can fix the problem, right...um...right? (978-1-63679-069-5)

Fresh Grave in Grand Canyon by Lee Patton. The age-old Grand Canyon becomes more and more ominous as group of volunteers fight to survive alone in nature and uncover a murderer among them. (978-1-63679-047-3)

Loyalty, Love & Vermouth by Eric Peterson. A comic valentine to a gay man's family of choice, including the ones with cold noses and four paws. (978-1-63555-997-2)

Bury Me in Shadows by Greg Herren. College student Jake Chapman is forced to spend the summer at his dying grandmother's home and soon finds danger from long-buried family secrets. (978-1-63555-993-4)

A Different Man by Andrew L. Huerta. This diverse collection of stories chronicling the challenges of gay life at various ages shines a light on the progress made and the progress still to come. (978-1-63555-977-4)

Busy Ain't the Half of It by Frederick Smith and Chaz Lamar Cruz. Elijah and Justin seek happily-ever-afters in LA, but are they too busy to notice happiness when it's there? (978-1-63555-944-6)

Pursuit: A Victorian Entertainment by Felice Picano. An intelligent, handsome, ruthlessly ambitious young man who rose from the slums to become the right-hand man of the Lord Exchequer of England will stop at nothing as he pursues his Lord's vanished wife across Continental Europe. (978-1-63555-870-8)

Best of the Wrong Reasons by Sander Santiago. For Fin Ness and Orion Starr, it takes a funeral to remind them that love is worth living for. (978-1-63555-867-8)

Coming to Life on South High by Lee Patton. Twenty-one-year-old gay virgin Gabe Rafferty's first adult decade unfolds as an unpredictable journey into sex, love, and livelihood. (978-1-63555-906-4)

Death's Prelude by David S. Pederson. In this prequel to the Detective Heath Barrington Mystery series, Heath discovers that first love changes you forever and drives you to become the person you're destined to be. (978-1-63555-786-2)

His Brother's Viscount by Stephanie Lake. Hector Somerville wants to rekindle his illicit love affair with Viscount Wentworth, but he must overcome one problem: Wentworth still loves Hector's brother. (978-1-63555-805-0)

The Dubious Gift of Dragon Blood by J. Marshall Freeman. One day Crispin is a lonely high school student—the next he is fighting a war in a land ruled by dragons, his otherworldly boyfriend at his side. (978-1-63555-725-1)

Quake City by St John Karp. Can Andre find his best friend Amy before the night devolves into a nightmare of broken hearts, malevolent drag queens, and spontaneous human combustion? Or has it always happened this way, every night, at Aunty Bob's Quake City Club? (978-1-63555-723-7)

Every Summer Day by Lee Patton. Meant to celebrate every summer day, Luke's journal instead chronicles a love affair as fast-moving and possibly as fatal as his brother's brain tumor. (978-1-63555-706-0)

Everyday People by Louis Barr. When film star Diana Danning hires private eye Clint Steele to find her son, Clint turns to his former West Point barracks mate, and ex-buddy with benefits, Mars Hauser to lend his cyber espionage and digital black ops skills to the case. (978-1-63555-698-8)

Royal Street Reveillon by Greg Herren. In this Scotty Bradley mystery, someone is killing the stars of a reality show, and it's up to Scotty Bradley and the boys to find out who. (978-1-63555-545-5)

Accidental Prophet by Bud Gundy. Days after his grandmother dies, Drew Morten learns his true identity and finds himself racing against time to save civilization from the apocalypse. (978-1-63555-452-6)

Counting for Thunder by Phillip Irwin Cooper. A struggling actor returns to the Deep South to manage a family crisis but finds love and ultimately his own voice as his mother is regaining hers for possibly the last time. (978-1-63555-450-2)

Of Echoes Born by 'Nathan Burgoine. A collection of queer fantasy short stories set in Canada from Lambda Literary Award finalist 'Nathan Burgoine. (978-1-63555-096-2)